Shattered

By Leila Kirkconnell

Cover Art: Original charcoal by Kathleen Kirkconnell – Forever in our hearts. Your art will live on.

Edited by: By the Hand Editing

ISBN 9781700533814

Amanda Verchall hesitated for a moment to take in the scenery: the pond in the distance, a water fountain lazily splashing, an array of greenery and flowers surrounding it, and a brick path to the entrance of the facility. Her mom was in the right place.

Brad would be okay, too. He'd be better off without her.

With sure steps, she returned to her car, sat in the driver's seat, and turned on the ignition. She fastened her seatbelt, mocking herself at the irony, but she didn't want to get stopped before she had accomplished her mission.

Slowly, she drove through the parking lot and onto the main highway, aiming for the spot where she was sure it was a point of no return. She had passed by it many times on her way to visit her mother at the previous nursing home.

Those who left the highway never—

Almost two hours to go, and it would be over. No more running, no more shame, no more guilt.

Chapter 1

April 2018

The floorboards creaked when Stephanie Branson and her twin sister, Liz, first stepped inside the house at 282 Magpie Lane. Stephanie, a forty-eight-year-old, and her sister inherited a large sum of money from their grandparents with the stipulation that Mr. Mercer, a financial advisor, oversaw the account; they had chosen him before their death.

The women had their hopes set on a house on the outskirts of town. Though it had seen better days, both fell in love with the property, and though reluctant, Mr. Mercer finally agreed when they promised to do most of the work themselves and only hire help for roofing and structural work. They desired to return this Victorian three-bedroom to its original glory and had no idea they would uncover the secrets that lay within it.

From its appearance, no one had taken care of the property for many years; the shutters were askew, the siding paint was faded and chipped, and the weeds were knee-deep. The inside was worse. The last residents were renters, a father, and a daughter who lived in it for less than two years. Rumor had it the father up and left one day, never to be seen nor heard from ever again. The daughter, perhaps a teenager who had "issues," was whisked away.

The house and its two acres of land also held personal interest for the twins. The property had belonged to their great-grandfather, who built it for his first wife and subsequently abandoned it when she died at the age of forty-one. Eventually, it was sold and changed hands three or four more times before Stephanie and Liz bought it.

Eager to dig into the history of the house and those who had lived in it, the twins had tracked down the names of the owners and kept a scrapbook of what they'd found. The only glitch was the fourth owner. Pouring over the clippings after they closed escrow, Elizabeth said, "Hard to tell if Mr. Balding lived here or not."

Looking up at Stephanie, she continued. "Do you think they rented it out?"

Stephanie shrugged. "Don't know."

The scrapbooks were big and bulky and were the first items to enter the twins' new home. Liz covered them with a plastic sheet she clipped to the table leg. Stephanie ran a protective hand over their project.

A week later, on April 22nd, 2018, Stephanie and Liz started the extensive work of renovating their new home. It wasn't only the plaster and paint that would bring the house back to life. Mice scattered from holes in the walls, and they discovered most of the wires were chewed clean through, forcing them to hire an electrician to rewire the entire place. Mr. Mercer grumbled, but it was too late to rescind the deal.

Wiring done, they proceeded with the rest of the work. Liz and Stephanie stripped the peeling and discolored wallpaper, spackled holes, and filled cracks. Their starting point was the bedroom in the back.

"Urgh, this is really ugly," Liz said. "Who paints a bedroom purple?"

"It'll be gone soon enough," said Stephanie.

It took gallons of the spackling compound to prep the surface, followed by four coats of primer and paint to cover the purple.

Jerry, the contractor, popped his head through the open door, inspecting the work in progress. "Wow."

The twins didn't hear him, their earbuds secured in place. Jerry retreated.

The next day was a big one. Upon close inspection, Jerry found the foundation sagging. He hired a crew to retrofit the supports and reinforce the bricks. The twins felt the workers' presence beneath the bare floors -- the dragging of equipment through the basement door, the calls and responses, and the machinery as it whirred and buzzed. At the abrupt silence an hour and a half later, Liz checked her Fitbit.

"Hey," she called out.

Realizing Stephanie was in a world of her own, plugged into cyber living, she stepped off the ladder and tapped her sister on the arm, motioning for her to pull the earbuds out. Stephanie yanked one out. "What?"

"It's only ten. Why did they stop?" Liz pointed to the floor.

"Don't know." She put her earpiece back in.

Liz pulled hers out. "If they're gonna take a break every hour, we're not going to get done." She flapped her arms around and walked to the window.

Curious, Stephanie followed and stood next to her sister. They peered at the yard. There was no one there.

"No way! Are they taking their break in the basement?" asked Liz.

They shrugged in unison and returned to smoothing the spackle. It wasn't long before Jerry stomped through the house, alerting them to his presence. Both turned to face him. His head rested on his bent arm as he leaned against the door frame.

As if on cue, the twins removed their earbuds, and Stephanie asked, "What's going on?"

Still looking at his scuffed boots, Jerry shook his head before the words tumbled out. "We have a problem. We kicked up bones, and I don't think they are animal."

"What…?" Liz searched for words while trying to make sense of what she heard. "What are you talking about?"

Jerry took off his baseball cap and raked his fingers through his hair. "I'm calling the cops. Just wanted you to know."

He turned to leave, and the twins exchanged confused glances. They let go of the tools in their hands and followed Jerry out of the house, listening to his side of the phone call with the dispatcher.

At the entrance to the basement, the crew gathered, exchanging a muted conversation. All looked up when Jerry and the twins approached. Liz was the first to head to the door. An arm reached out to stop her. She shrugged it off and went in with Stephanie, on her heels. The muffled sound of resumed conversation trailed after them.

Liz's hand flew to her mouth, stifling her shock. It didn't look like an animal skeleton; remnants of tattered clothing clung to its frame.

Stephanie stepped closer, and something caught her eye. She reached for it, looked around, then shoved it behind the overhead beams.

"What are you doing?" Liz asked in a whisper but didn't see the object.

Stephanie put a finger to her lips and motioned for her to go out, but not before someone barked, "Get out! You shouldn't be in there."

Back in the house, the twins' minds whirred with questions. Whose body was it? How did it get there?

Chapter 2

May 3, 2018

The instant messenger box popped open, obscuring the draft Amanda was typing. Annoyed, she clicked it closed, then just as quickly, pressed the message to open it.

"What the hell?" she said aloud.

The passenger waiting for his flight in the seat next to her glared. Amanda did a double take… his eyes. She quickly recovered and mouthed, "Sorry."

Returning her gaze to the laptop, she thought her eyes were playing tricks. It couldn't be!

Sender: *Is that you?*

Amanda: *How'd you find me?*

Sender: *Easy. Googled you.*

Why would he send her a message? It had been over twenty years.

"Damn," she muttered.

The passenger picked up his coat and yanked his rolling suitcase, nearly severing its handle, shaking his head as he strode off.

"Hey, you forgot your coffee," Amanda yelled after him, holding his cup high. He didn't respond, Amanda set the cup next to her, and she returned her gaze to the screen. "Damn. Now what?"

Amanda thought of closing the dialogue box, logging out, and deleting her account, but that wouldn't work. He found her this time; he'd find her again. With a sigh, she typed, "Hi." Lame, she knew that.

Sweat dripped under her arms; this was the day she dreaded. The sender was the only one who knew her secret. The secret she kept buried and pretended wasn't real. The memory made it difficult to breathe at times. Amanda responded, hoping he couldn't see through her words, the worry, the fear.

Sender: *Hello, to you too!*

Cursor blinking, she thought, *What now?* She didn't know what to say.

Sender: *Been a while, hasn't it?*

Amanda: *Yeah. Hey, got to go. Chat later?*

Sender: *Sure. Did I catch you at a bad time?*

Me: *Boss walked in. Got to go.*

Sender: *You're not trying to avoid me, are you?*

Amanda scanned the lounge. There was no way he could be there, watching.

Amanda: *Of course not! Really must go.*

Sender: *Try not to avoid me. It won't work.*

She hit delete and closed the dialogue box, all the while sinking her teeth into her left-hand knuckles. Overhead, the intercom announced departing flights, called passengers to report to airlines, and requested service staff to pick up a wheelchair traveler.

The time at the bottom of the screen announced it was 2:13 pm. With over an hour left before boarding, Amanda hoped to finish the presentation for the five o'clock meeting. But she had clicked closed her focus when she ended the chat box.

Leaning her head against the too-short seatback, Amanda shut her eyes in a feeble attempt to escape what was now inevitable: reuniting with her past. How would Brad take the truth she had kept from him? Would he ever forgive her for what she had done?

Amanda's eyes flew open at something brushing against her leg. She moved the laptop to the side and glanced down, but there was nothing. Her imagination was in overdrive. Heart hammering in her chest, she gathered her belongings, hoping a cup of coffee and watching the planes take off and land would be the distractions she needed.

Just then, her cell vibrated in her pocket. Amanda set what was in her hands on the seat vacated by Mr. Passenger and pulled out her phone, thinking it was Brad. A mixture of relief and disappointment flooded her. She wanted to hear Brad's voice, but he would know from her voice something was wrong.

"Restricted number," the screen indicated.

Pressing the red icon, Amanda declined the call and returned the phone to her right pocket. Once again lifting the laptop, she tucked it in its pouch, secured it to her rolling suitcase, made her way to the coffee kiosk, and queued in line behind two men and a woman.

Amanda's mind traveled to corners of the world it could not afford. Her feet involuntarily shuffled forward, her hands pushing the rolling case. Her eyes shifted from side to side, and once or twice, she turned around, but didn't see anyone watching.

"Ma'am. Can I help you?"

"Miss, are you ready to order?"

"What?" Amanda didn't realize she was already to the counter.

Pointing to the line behind her, then at the menu, Joe -- that was what his badge said -- asked, "Have you decided?"

"Um, yeah. Small coffee and a bagel." As an afterthought, she added, "Please, and thank you." She involuntarily shrugged and winked

"Well, okay then," he said with a wink and a shrug.

That's when Amanda realized he misunderstood her tic. She moved to the far end of the counter, ducked behind a stand of fruits and chips, away from the sign that read "Pick up," and waited for her order.

A girl of about twenty-something snapped a lid on the coffee, called for Amanda, and handed her the cup along with the bagel. Amanda wasn't sure, but she thought she thanked the girl. At least she hoped she did.

Balancing her purchased items and careful not to scald herself with the coffee, Amanda moved to the closest bank of seats facing the tarmac. She stared at the planes taking off and landing. Airports had become her second home. All excitement of flying had vanished long ago. That was what her job demanded, and she willingly answered the call.

After a few sips and a bite, she opened her laptop. She had exactly two hours to finish a report before the five o'clock meeting in San Francisco. Forcing herself not to revisit the unwanted message, Amanda poured herself into crunching numbers and preparing graphs. Success! By the time she was ready to board, she had completed the report and her mind had escaped what she should've dealt with but didn't want to.

"Good afternoon, passengers. This is the pre-boarding announcement for Flight 6005 to San Francisco."

With a satisfying click, Amanda closed the laptop and secured her luggage. A trashcan close by welcomed her half-eaten bagel and unfinished coffee. She pulled her cell from her pocket and flicked to the boarding pass. She had eight minutes before the agent called first class. Even if she was late, her seat was reserved. On impulse, she called Brad.

"Hi," he said after the second ring. "What time is your flight?"

"Should be called in a few minutes."

"Glad you called. Good luck with your presentation. See you on Monday? What time are you coming in?"

"Yeah. Monday. I'll text my flight info later."

"Okay."

Silence. Amanda didn't know what else to say. The reality and magnitude of her past, if uncovered, stifled the air between them.

"Are you still there?" Brad asked.

"Sorry. Yeah." He couldn't possibly know how sorry she was.

"Well, call if you have time."

"Yeah. Sure," came Amanda's weak reply.

"Oh, before I forget, someone by the name of Andy called. He said he was an old friend trying to reconnect. I gave him your cell number and told him you're on Facebook."

Clammy and sweaty, she stuttered.

"What did you say?" asked Brad.

"...boarding First Class..." the overhead system announced.

"Oh, sorry. Nothing. Got to board. See ya."

Amanda ended the call, but her legs didn't support her as she tried to stand. The exit sign loomed large and red at the end of the terminal, tempting her to run, to leave, to vanish.

"...Now boarding row twenty through twenty-six..."

Placing one foot in front of the other, Amanda dragged her case up to the terminal and scanned the barcode on her ticket. When the attendant's eyes briefly met hers, he asked, "Are you all right?"

"Yes. Thank you."

"Let them know on the plane if you need anything."

What she needed could not be had there or anywhere else. What Amanda needed was to erase what happened; that wasn't an option. She had to face her past, what she'd done. The unspeakable act she had committed. But what Amanda said to him was, "Thank you," as she boarded the plane.

Another attendant ushered Amanda to her seat, and a flute of champagne and a plate of fruits and cheese were placed on her tray. She stared at it. She covered it with her napkin and pressed the service bell for the steward to remove the tray; nothing would go down anyway.

Across the aisle sat the disgruntled passenger from the terminal. If he was surprised to see her in First Class, he didn't let on. Instead, he gave Amanda a polite nod and returned his gaze to his tablet. Something in his eyes gave her heart a push; it hammered in her chest, sending electric pulses to her head. She dared another glance, but he was engrossed in reading. His massive frame was barely contained in the extra-wide seat. Something about him was familiar. Perhaps, Amanda had run into him on one of her trips. Most often, she was oblivious to other passengers, focused on the task at hand, but this guy…

Closing her eyelids to half-mast, she angled her body to study him better. He wasn't fat, more like a heavyset athlete, although his gait was anything but athletic. It bordered on a limp, favoring his left leg. Amanda scanned him from his loafers to his thick curly hair painted with wisps of gray. At one point, he shifted in the seat and turned toward her. She closed her eyes all the way, pretending to be asleep.

Panic set in. Amanda's chest constricted, not letting enough air in her lungs. It wasn't the plane descending into San Francisco; they weren't close yet. It wasn't the meeting with the Board members; she was prepared for that. It was Amanda's past clutching at her chest, choking her. She straightened in her seat, gasping for air as she made eye contact with the man across the aisle.

Mr. Passenger gave a sidelong glance and pushed the service button. The steward appeared within seconds. Mr. Passenger pointed in her direction, disinterested.

"Are you all right?"

Amanda grabbed her chest, and she couldn't form words.

A stewardess joined in, handing Amanda a bag, giving instructions.

She wanted to die. She wanted them to leave her alone, but die, she didn't. When her breathing returned to normal and the commotion subsided, someone thrust a cup of tea at her. "Here, sip this."

Amanda's eye twitched, and her shoulder shrugged. The steward's mouth fell open but quickly regrouped, and he lowered himself in the empty chair next to her until he was sure she wasn't going to pass out on his shift. After a few minutes, he left to resume his duties and prepare for the landing.

At four minutes past four, ten minutes ahead of schedule, the pilot taxied to the terminal, thanking the passengers for flying.

"Do you need assistance? Would you like a wheelchair? Is someone meeting you?" came the barrage of questions as Amanda gathered her belongings, ready to leave the plane.

"Thank you. I'll be fine."

On her way out, she noticed the pilot and two staff watching as she exited the plane. They didn't want a lawsuit on their hands, she surmised.

Legs finally steady, insides on the brink of collapse, she made her way through the terminal, aiming for the baggage area sign where a company driver was waiting just past the sliding doors. Stalling, she found the women's bathroom and stared at her reflection in the mirror. The outside looked intact. *I can pull the meeting off,* she decided. There would be time later to deal with the turmoil churning on the inside.

For all these years, Amanda managed to ignore her demons and pretend they belonged to someone else. *What have I done?*

Chapter 3

May 4, 2018

Light seeped in from behind the curtains. Amanda was still awake. There would be no more sleep for her, so she believed.

The previous night, after the meeting, when she had finally made it to her hotel room on the tenth floor, she had seriously considered her options. She had opened the window, imagining rescue workers scraping what was left of her from the sidewalk. The hotel must have anticipated desperation; the pane only opened four inches.

What if I broke the glass? No one to stop me from ending this nightmare. Amanda had banged on the windowpane with her fists, then had used the sweating metal pitcher. Nothing. Besides, she was too chicken to jump.

Still in her hotel room at ten-thirty the next morning, Amanda paced the floor while her cell phone rang and pinged, again and again. She had already missed her eight o'clock meeting but didn't care. It no longer mattered.

The hotel room phone rang. Biting her lip, she reached for it. *If I don't answer, the staff will come in to check on me.* Picking up the receiver, she waited for the caller to speak first.

"Ms. Verchall, this is Fred at the front desk—"

Before he could finish his spiel, Amanda said, "Yes?" She wanted him to end the call and leave her alone.

"We have several messages left for you. Do you wish to have them sent up?"

"No. I'll get them later."

"We have a message marked urgent, Ms.—"

"What is it?" she asked, sure it was the company president.

"Mr. Baker—"

Amanda dropped the phone. Searing hot, burning her hand.

"Ms. Verchall. Amanda. Ms. Verchall…" came the faint voice from the handset as it clattered to the floor.

Silence.

It had begun — the past meeting the present, one incident at a time. Frantic, Amanda gathered her belongings and stuffed them in the rolling bag, but she couldn't locate her laptop. Exasperated, she dropped to her knees, searching under the bed, then crawled across the room, hoisting herself when she reached the dresser. Nothing.

Amanda tore the room, looking for it, but she couldn't find it anywhere. Retracing her steps in her mind, she recalled using it at the meeting, then what? *Did I leave it in the conference room?*

Her phone pinged again. An incoming text message. Hoping it was someone from the corporate office telling her they have her laptop, Amanda clicked on the text icon, which showed the number "7." Seven missed messages. Quickly, she scrolled through them. One was from Brad. She didn't read or answer it. They had an agreement when either was busy that the other would wait to receive a response. Amanda was busy. She still hadn't even thought of what to do about him. Her priority was to find her laptop. She scrolled through the rest of the messages, but none were from Becky, the secretary.

Just then, there was a knock on the door.

"Damn, damn, damn." Amanda glared at the blinking receiver and guessed it was hotel staff.

She yanked the door open, and her jaw fell open. Mr. Passenger stood on the other side of the threshold, her computer case in his hand.

"Ha… How did you get this?" Amanda stammered while she yanked the laptop from his grip.

He let go, raising his hands in a surrender gesture.

Amanda didn't have the presence of mind to question how he found her.

"You could say, 'Thank you.'"

"Yeah. Thanks."

She had a death grip on the laptop and its case, clutching it like a shield against her chest.

"Can I come in?"

She looked around the room. "This isn't a good time."

He peered around her. It wasn't difficult to notice the room she turned upside down in her frantic effort to find the computer. Pointing to the mess, he said, "Oh, that. Don't worry about it."

Her brain twirled and circled, trying to figure out who he was and why he had her laptop. Amanda shook her head. She had to figure out what to do about the past now lurking in every corner, stalking her. Still, at the threshold, Mr. Passenger extended his hand. "I'm Philip Downes."

Once again, she shook her head, except this time in frustration, because she realized Mr. Passenger was the new marketing director for Batwell International, the corporation she worked for.

Amanda shook his hand, still clutching the laptop to her chest with the left one. "I'm… I'm… sorry… damn!"

He lifted one eyebrow, an exclamation that didn't need to be verbalized.

"Damn," she repeated. Then, just as quickly, "Sorry."

"How about I meet you at the restaurant, let's say in thirty minutes?" He pointed somewhere behind him, index finger down, indicating the restaurant in the lobby.

"Thanks. No thanks. I can't."

He turned around, his back to her, and walked toward the elevators as his voice traveled the corridor. "Thirty minutes."

Slamming the door, she let out a frustrated, "DAMN."

Amanda didn't have to meet him. Didn't want to meet him. At that moment, she didn't care if her next promotion hinged on how she handled this Mr. Passenger – Mr. Downes. What she needed was time to figure out what to do.

What if Andrew Baker came for her? What if he…

Frustration and fear coursed through her veins, pumping toward her temples. A pounding headache followed. Merciless. Amanda fell backward on the bed and closed her eyes. A faint hum filtered through the silence, propelling her upward.

Pressing her palms against the sides of her head, she looked toward the sound. The receiver lay on the floor. Letting go of her throbbing head, she bent to retrieve it, pressed the off button, and slammed the phone in its cradle by the digital clock. It winked 11:42 AM. *What time did Mr. Downes leave?*

It didn't take Amanda long to pack her bag. Once she made her exit, she would be lost in the sea of people, but when she looked in the bathroom mirror, it became clear that her messy hair and sunken cheeks would be anything but discreet. She didn't care. It was time. No more putting off what she must do. Escape sounded good. She would vanish, never to be found again. Her other option was what? Tell Brad? So, he'd probably leave her? But that wasn't her worst worry. He wouldn't be the first or the last to walk out on her.

Amanda's life had been a revolving door as far back as she could remember. She didn't feel wanted, and growing up, she was handed over from Auntie to Dad, to Grandma, to foster care. But somehow, she managed to succeed by pretending her past belonged to someone else. At thirty-six, Amanda was a successful program specialist in charge of multi-million-dollar projects because of her intelligence and perseverance to get through grad school by age twenty-three.

She had to admit there was one person who cared, a counselor she encountered in high school.

As she got dressed, her mind wandered to when she entered ninth grade. Her social worker had moved her to a new foster home because of an incident that took place at the previous one. An event that made her stomach turn and her knees wobble. She leaned on the doorframe to steady herself as she relived her past.

The new home was across town, and she no longer attended school with the same kids of her eighth grade, which was good. Ms. Coops, her counselor, was the first person Amanda met upon enrollment. She would become her academic advisor until graduation. Why Ms. Coops took a liking to Amanda, she would never know, but Ms. Coops did. Perhaps, she pitied her.

Ms. Coops knew Amanda was a foster kid; all information in the school district system was accessible to her. The counselor didn't know why, though. She never asked, and Amanda didn't tell. Not that Ms. Coops didn't try to find out in a roundabout way. "I grew up in foster care. I never knew who my mother or dad was," she said to Amanda one day.

Amanda shrugged. "Whatever."

"You know, you can always talk to me. What we talk about is confidential except, of course, if you plan to hurt someone or yourself. I have to report—"

"Yeah, yeah. You're a mandated reporter, blah, blah, blah," Amanda interrupted.

She knew Ms. Coops meant well and cared, but by then, there was no way Amanda was going to let anyone close to her. For one thing, she didn't trust anyone to stay. The second reason, she didn't want anyone to find out what happened, although no one had implicated her in the accident.

Hard as Amanda tried, she didn't get Ms. Coops to forget about her. If anything, the counselor became more insistent. She had over three-hundred students on her caseload, but somehow, managed to find time to call Amanda in at least once every few weeks. This continued throughout her four years in high school.

In her senior year, Ms. Coops insisted Amanda apply for financial aid and to several universities in the area. "You are very smart. I'm not going to stand by and watch you throw away a future that's at your fingertips," she told Amanda one day.

"Okay," Amanda said, but she had no intention of applying. True, she had no clue what she was going to do or where she was heading, but she didn't care.

Ms. Coops didn't let up. She called Amanda in one day, booted up a computer in the counseling office, and watched Amanda complete applications.

To Amanda's shock, she was accepted to all the universities she applied to. Not only that, the financial aid package covered all expenses. Sheepishly, she said, "Thank you, Ms. Coops, for everything."

Ms. Coops beamed as if Amanda handed her the winning lottery ticket.

Graduation from high school and heading to college was the beginning of closing the door to her past. Amanda wanted out, out of the school, and out of the foster care system. She never bonded with the families she lived with, though she was told to be grateful a family wanted her. *Yeah, whatever.*

On graduation day, as the seniors filed toward the field where the school conducted the ceremony, and the band played "Pomp and Circumstance." That had the crowd cheering, whooping, and hollering. Amanda stared straight ahead and didn't look at the stadium. She had no one. Her foster family didn't bother, her mom was still in an institution somewhere, her grandmother too far, and her dad… Amanda bit her lip at that memory.

At the gate to the field, Amanda was startled when she heard her name. Ms. Coops stopped her with a hug and placed an envelope in her hand. She had tears streaming down her cheeks. "I'm proud of you, Amanda. Keep moving forward and upward. You can do it."

It wasn't until later that night, when Amanda was alone in her room, that she opened the envelope to find a gift card for fifty dollars and the sweetest words ever written. She knew she didn't deserve them.

Amanda tucked the gift card in her wallet and ripped the greeting card into tiny pieces. The shredded words made their way to the trash bin in the corner of the room. She closed the lid to the trash and her past, a past she wouldn't tell anyone about, not even Ms. Coops.

The vibration of the phone on the bed jarred Amanda back to her current reality. What *was* her current reality?

The battery on the cell showed "20%." Amanda fumbled for the charger and found it buried beneath the rubble of her belongings, having hastily crammed it into the case earlier. Her clothes lay in a heap on the floor after she emptied the bag in search of the charger.

Gingerly, Amanda stepped over the pile and plugged the cord into the USB port on the lamp base. Once again, she flicked the phone on to read messages while it was charging. Unable to relax, she perched on the edge of the bed, one foot tapping against the side while her fingers hovered over the message icon.

Her eye twitched, and her shoulder shrugged. Stress-exacerbated tics. Amanda ignored both and focused on the messages. She read through Becky's easy enough. Amanda pretty much had predicted their contents anyway. Of course, the company wanted to know where she was, if she was okay, and to "please call right away." Project update and so on. She didn't even bother to read the details.

There were two text messages from Brad. One said to call him when she could. She couldn't. Not yet. Amanda had to re-read the second one: *Hey. Call when you can. I gave Andy your number.*

Brad had sent it on the day before at 2:34 pm. Amanda hadn't told Brad about Andy or any part of her past. Telling him would've opened the door to questions she never wanted to answer.

Worried, she listened to the voicemails. Most were similar to the text messages from work. She deleted them all. There were no voicemail messages from Brad, but that didn't surprise her.

Scattered among the work messages were ones from restricted numbers. No voicemail. They used to come occasionally, and Amanda thought it was telemarketers or someone dialing by mistake. In the past year, she had gotten them with more frequency. *Could these calls have been from Andy all this time?*

At that moment, his words rang in her ears. He had warned her not to ignore him. Deep within, Amanda knew he meant it. Deep within, she knew he was the only one who had witnessed what she did.

Chapter 4

June 3, 1987

Her fifth birthday was special. Amanda's mother, Irene, ordered a clown performer to match the cake she had planned to make. Before the sun came up, Amanda woke to sounds drifting in from the kitchen. She guessed her mother was baking the cake she promised.

Excited, she slipped her feet into her Ernie and Bert slippers and hurriedly descended the stairs, clutching her doll. But, as Amanda approached the midpoint landing, something didn't sound like pots and pans and baking. Tiptoeing down the remaining seven steps, she soundlessly made it to the kitchen door and peered around the corner.

Cabinets stood open, pots, and pans covering every counter. Flour and sugar painted the hardwood floor, leaving clouds in the still air. Her mother sat on the floor cross-legged, wiping away tears, streaking her cheeks with the powdery stuff. Amanda backed away, not sure who that woman was. She looked like her mother, but that wasn't her.

As she pulled back, Irene crawled forward, arms outstretched. Clutching her doll tighter to her chest, Amanda ran out of the kitchen and up the stairs to the safety of her room. Fear tingled her feet, making it hard to move, but she didn't listen. She crawled into the closet and hid behind the boxes and clothes, trembling.

Heavy footfalls approached the bedroom. Amanda imagined her mother dragging the flour and sugar meant for the clown cake, but she didn't care. All she wanted was her mother back. She wanted this woman, Irene's evil twin, gone. This was the third time she'd witnessed her mother's transformation into a stranger.

Making herself even smaller, she covered her head with a jacket that fell, still on the hanger, listening to toys, boxes, and clothes her mother moved.

"Mandy? Amanda! I know you're in here," came her mother's crazed, sing-song voice.

Amanda shrunk further, holding her breath so her mother couldn't hear her. Then, there was silence. Amanda didn't have a watch because she couldn't read one. She didn't know how long she was in the closet, and she needed to pee, but was afraid to leave.

When the doorbell chimed for the third time, Amanda crawled from her hiding spot and peered into the room. No one was there. Still clutching her doll, she ran to the bathroom at the end of the hallway, closing the door behind her. Afraid to make a sound, but unable to hold it in, she finally let out a stream into the toilet. She didn't flush or wash her hands -- she had heard the pipes gurgling whenever her mother used the bathroom.

Opening the bathroom door enough to slip out, she laid on her stomach and crawled to the railing. Auntie Emma was in the hallway. Amanda didn't know who let her in. Sometimes, she just appeared. Maybe she had a key?

The next few minutes or hours were a blur. Amanda didn't remember much except for Auntie Emma, who saw her looking through the railing, ran up the stairs, folded Amanda in a hug, and rocked her. "Are you all right, pumpkin?"

Her tears flowed. Amanda couldn't speak.

"Shh," she cooed. "Everything will be all right."

Amanda wanted to ask about the cake and the clown, but she didn't. Even her five-year-old brain knew not to ask. There wouldn't be a party.

Auntie Emma wasn't a real auntie. She was a neighbor and friend of Irene's since Amanda was a baby. Years later, Amanda found out when her mother was taken away, she gave Auntie Emma a note allowing her to be Amanda's guardian. It was never made official through the courts.

The five years with Auntie Emma passed without anything memorable happening. Amanda went to school, and Emma took good care of her.

She was smart; that's what her teachers told Auntie Emma during parent-teacher conferences.

When Amanda finished fifth grade and had so many awards for reading and math, she got to wondering why she was getting disability checks. *I am normal, aren't I? Well, except for my eye twitching and my right shoulder shrugging even when I don't want them to. Does that make me disabled?*

Amanda remembered bringing the mail in one day and looking through it before taking it to Auntie. Her name was on an envelope, along with her mother's. Curious, she wanted to open it but knew better. Later, Amanda found it along with the rest of the mail in Auntie's office, by the computer. She had to look. So, she tiptoed across the carpet and peered through the stack. The one with her name on it had a check in it. Amanda flipped it forward, and the paper behind it said, "SSI – disability benefits."

One summer day in 1990, after school was out, Auntie was in the kitchen. Amanda approached her, needing to know about her disability. The kids in her school who were disabled went to "special classes" and had "special teachers." She didn't. Some limped. Others were "slow." Amanda was neither.

"Auntie Emma?" Amanda fumbled for a way to ask.

"Yes, sweetheart?"

"Can I ask you something?"

"Sure. As long as I know the answer, you can ask anything."

"What's wrong with me?"

"What do you mean, what's wrong with you? Nothing is wrong with you. Why do you ask?"

Amanda's eye twitched, and her right shoulder shrugged even when she willed them to stop. "I mean, why do I get disability checks?"

"Oh, that," said Auntie, but didn't continue.

"So, why do I get disability checks?"

"I tell you what, you keep up your good grades, and you have nothing to worry about."

After rummaging through pots and pans, making much noise and clatter, she said, "Hey, someone's gonna have a birthday soon. I wonder what that someone wants for their cake this year," said Auntie Emma with a big wink.

"Can I have a chocolate cake with chocolate frosting? Please?" Amanda remembered whining. All talk about disability was forgotten, just like that.

"Sure thing," said Auntie Emma.

Looking back on that day, Amanda was sure Auntie didn't want to talk about what her disability was. Either she didn't know or didn't want to discuss it because it made her uncomfortable. It would be years before Amanda found out it was Tourette's Syndrome.

Though Amanda was told it was a mild case, it nevertheless was a catalyst to her low self-esteem – this, along with trauma she suffered in her childhood. *Do I dare blame it for the unforgivable act I committed? I want to.*

Amanda lived with Auntie Emma until she was ten. Her mother was taken away five years earlier, and she didn't see her until she was fourteen. A few weeks after Amanda's tenth birthday, her dad came to visit. "Time for you to come and live with me," he said.

Her trust in people faded with each encounter. Amanda's mother left, though not by choice. Auntie Emma gave her up, even if not by choice. Her dad didn't care.

Chapter 5

May 4, 2018

Brad checked his phone for the time: Saturday, 7:23 am. He shut it off and lay on his side, hoping for a few more hours of sleep. Thirty minutes later, he rolled over onto his back and stared at the ceiling. The bed next to him empty, Amanda in San Francisco for the third time in a month. He didn't begrudge her the success she'd craved, but there were times it was getting old sleeping alone.

He ran his hand over his unshaven stubble, flung the covers off, and stood for a moment. Stretching, he reached for the blinds and twirled the rod, inviting in the morning light. Brad gazed out the window at the postage stamp of a garden, deciding he'd forego sitting out there for his coffee. He'd head to the local coffee shop instead.

He bent and picked up yesterday's discarded clothes, sniffed, balled them up, and tossed them in the overflowing hamper. The shirt hung limply, reaching for the floor in an attempt to escape. He didn't bother with it. Brad would wait until Amanda returned, and they would do laundry together. This wasn't meant to be an experience for one, he decided.

On his way to the shower, he passed by what served as a dresser. Brad did a double-take at a framed image, their wedding day, twelve years earlier. Realizing their anniversary was approaching in three weeks, he didn't have an inkling what to get his wife. Perhaps, after coffee and breakfast, he'd head to the mall. With that settled in his mind, he walked the few feet to the bathroom.

An hour later, he made it to the local "Brew & Sip." Brad placed an order for an egg croissant and coffee, waited to pick it up, then meandered to the patio area to find a shady spot. A mouthful into his sandwich, he did what most do, especially while alone: flicked his smartphone on. But before he clicked on his messages, the odd phone call he received the day before hovered in his mind. Even stranger was his conversation with Amanda.

Brad replayed the call from someone named Andy. He had been married to Amanda for twelve years, but had never heard her mention the name before. Yet, Andy claimed to be a longtime friend of hers who'd lost touch over the years. Scratching his chin, Brad thought Amanda's reaction when he called her was hurried, but not because of the flight; this wouldn't have been a concern for her since she traveled first class.

Looking up at the sky, he searched the far away clouds for answers. None came. Brad decided he was reading too much into the situation and returned his attention to the food and coffee. He clicked on the email icon and perused messages as he finished his meal and gulped the remainder of the coffee.

He was in no hurry to leave. Amanda wouldn't be back for a couple of days; only if the company didn't ask her to stay on for another "urgent situation." Brad moved his chair to stay in the shade, crossed his ankle over his knee, moving his leg up and down as he continued to stare at his phone. When he was finished with emails and had caught up with Facebook, he gathered his trash and twirled around in his seat to locate the trash bin. The place was notorious for moving it from spot to spot.

Brad emptied his tray into the nearest container, pocketed his phone, and looked around to make sure he didn't leave anything behind. Next on his agenda was the mall.

Crossing the road, a block away, he entered the city-sized mall where his gym was — the equipment called to him as he looked at his reflection in the window. His feet involuntarily took him inside. He would work out, then start his hunt for that perfect anniversary gift. Thoughts of Andy and Amanda's reaction were all but forgotten as he lifted weights, ran five miles on the treadmill, swam fifteen laps, and soaked in the calming water of the jacuzzi.

It wasn't until he entered the first department store that Andy's name flashed back into his mind. Brad ambled, perusing clothes and jewelry, not seeing what he was touching. He wasn't sure he believed the story Andy told him. "I lost touch with her a while back and ran into a mutual friend. She gave me Amanda's new name."

Andy's conversation was short, and Brad couldn't quite make out the caller's last name. He recalled asking, "Who?" but received no answer.

Brad's mind asked too many questions as he walked through the store, realizing he hardly knew anything about Amanda's past.

"Can I help you find something?" a young girl in her early twenties asked, making him realize he was rubbing the fabric of a nightgown between his thumb and forefinger.

He looked up, startled. "Ah, yes, please. How much for this?" he asked as he let go of the material, embarrassed. "It's an anniversary gift for my wife," he stammered.

"Please follow me to the cash register. I'll scan the price unless there's something else you'd like to look at. Hm?"

Brad shook his head and followed Jessica, her name tag said so, to the nearest checkout. Jessica rang the purchase and processed Brad's credit card.

Nightgown carefully wrapped in tissue and placed in a shiny gold and black bag, he left the women's department, clutching onto the handles, distracted. A gift in hand, he walked the half-mile back to his home.

The flag on the mailbox was down, and Brad opened it and retrieved the mail. He set the bag he was carrying between his feet and flipped through the stack of mostly bills and junk mail. One item hand-addressed to "Amanda Verchall, 372 Blue Mist Lane, Longmont, Co. 80501," with no return address, caught his attention. Scratching his jawline with the edge of the envelope, temptation to open it snaked its way to his fingers. He resisted.

He had never doubted Amanda's commitment to their marriage, but that Andy call nibbled on his confidence. Shaking his head to rid himself of unwelcome thoughts, Brad restacked the mail, lifted his keys from his pocket, and picked up the bag. Instead of walking the fifteen or so feet to the front door, he stood, staring at the house.

Brad's mind wandered to the day he and Amanda purchased their two-story house. He recalled how ecstatic both were when they found it. It was their perfect dream home and so close to the mall, gym, and restaurants; all the amenities were less than half a mile from the quiet neighborhood, and it was also close to his work.

An English middle school teacher, Brad biked to work, except for snowy and icy days. Amanda drove the forty miles to Denver, where her company's headquarters were. Since Brad had shorter travel time, he took on the cooking task, which brought his mind back to the present and what to eat for dinner.

Flipping his keys around, he got to the one he needed and unlocked the door, not noticing the tip of a blue envelope protruding from under the doormat.

Once inside, he opened the windows downstairs and propped open the back door. He stood in the warmth of the May Colorado sunshine before grabbing his briefcase from the kitchen counter and heading outside.

He cranked open the umbrella and sat in the shade to correct papers and give his students feedback on their essays. Brad made it through the first three, but his stomach rumbled. He stood and stretched, glanced at the stack of papers, and shook his head. He loved teaching and adored the kids, but the paperwork, not so much.

Opening the refrigerator, Brad scanned the insides, not sure what sounded appealing. He settled on slices of cheese, crackers, and an apple. Grabbing the full plate, he popped a coffee pod in the machine, nibbling on his feast while the coffee brewed. The creamer was in a tray at the back of the counter. As he reached for the container, his arm brushed the mail, then stopped. Setting the plate to the side, he picked up the stack and flipped through it, sorting the junk from what needed to be opened.

Brad carried the junk mail to the trashbin, disposing of it without ceremony, then returned to the other items. One by one, he opened the bills, not many since most came directly as e-bills and automatically paid online. Second to last was the envelope addressed to Amanda. He flapped it against his palm once more, contemplating whether or not to open it.

It wasn't unusual for them to open mail no matter who it was addressed to since most were to both of them. This one was specifically addressed to Amanda. Brad lifted it to the light; that was useless as the envelope was too thick to expose what was inside. Setting it aside, he decided to let it go until his wife came home. He picked up his plate and coffee and walked outside to the stack of essays waiting for him.

Pen poised in his hand, ready to make notations on an essay, Brad took a bite of cheese and apple, washing it down with a sip of his coffee, but instead of reading, he stared ahead. It hit him again; he didn't know much about Amanda's past. He had never questioned it before, never needed to. Now, he was curious. The only things she shared were with no detail: her dad walking out on her, mother institutionalized, and a few years in the foster care system. *Who was Amanda?*

Chapter 6

1992 - 1995

Amanda came home from summer school in July of 1992 and passed an unfamiliar car in the driveway on her way to the front door. She walked the few feet to the entrance, turning after a few steps to eye the car and twisted the handle. She watched the dust dance in the sunlit hallway while muffled voices came from the kitchen. One was a man's. *That is strange. Auntie doesn't have male friends*, she thought.

She tried to be quiet, but her backpack landed with a thud at the bottom of the stairs, and the voices hushed.

"Is that you, Amanda?" Auntie called out.

"Yes," Amanda said as she pushed the kitchen door open.

Two sets of eyes greeted her. Auntie rounded the countertop and placed a protective arm around Amanda's shoulders. "You know who this is?"

She nodded. Amanda recognized her dad from the pictures her mother used to flip through years ago.

There was no hello, how are you, nothing. "I came to get you. Time for you to come and live with me," he said.

When Amanda shook her head vigorously, Auntie Emma sent her to her room. "Your dad and I need to talk."

Obediently, she left. No sooner had Amanda closed the door to her bedroom than the shouting began. Half an hour later, she was told to pack her things. Auntie Emma's eyes glistened when she gave the instruction, and Amanda couldn't read the expression on the man's face.

Her dad, a stranger to Amanda, whisked her away from Rocky Ford, Colorado, driving for hours. Their ultimate destination, the next day, was Longmont. He didn't want Amanda. He wanted the disability check she was getting — she had overheard Auntie Emma say that when she was yelling at him after they sent her to the bedroom. Maybe he did, maybe he didn't, but the bottom line was she had to go with him. She was stuck.

Two days later, Amanda's dad enrolled her in a local school, and the staff didn't care that the address was a cheap motel on the outskirts of town; their first home, a two-month stint. After that, he rented a house when he found a job.

Her heart sank when he pulled in the driveway of that house. Dried weeds were knee-deep, and when he put the key in the door, Amanda sucked in her breath, fearing cobwebs and a deserted place. It wasn't as bad as she imagined. At least there weren't strangers coming in and out of the building all hours of the day and night like at the motel.

The carpet was threadbare, and the kitchen was old. A small oven and refrigerator stood to one side, but no dishwasher. The countertops peeled back at the corners, and a door on one cabinet hung crookedly, with only one hinge holding it up.

The two bedrooms were in slightly better shape. Her dad's room was the larger of the two, and Amanda's had two walls painted purple. She hated the color, but didn't say a word. At least it was quiet in the house.

"Give me a hand, will you?" he asked as he walked back to the front door.

Together they emptied the car and stacked their belongings in the middle of the living room. The house was what they called "furnished." It had one couch, a chair, and a small table with a lamp in the living room. The bedrooms had a larger bed in one, and a twin in Amanda's.

She stood in the middle of the living room and surveyed her new home, choking back tears. Auntie Emma's was an old house, but it was pretty inside and out. The front garden had a birdbath and flower beds, and the backyard had a vegetable garden. Inside, each room was decorated with throw pillows, paintings, and comfortable furniture in grays, whites, and splashes of burgundy.

A huge butcher block table stood in the middle of the kitchen, and granite countertop wrapped the space. Gleaming appliances witnessed the many delicious meals Auntie cooked for them.

Then, Amanda looked back at her new reality.

"What are you waiting for?" he barked, pointing at the cooler and three grocery bags. "Make something to eat and then get the stuff to your room."

Amanda obediently did as was told. The peanut butter sandwich stuck to the roof of her mouth, and she gulped water from a paper cup. It wasn't the last sandwich dinner she would have. It was only the beginning.

The job her dad landed was as a motorcycle mechanic. He didn't tell her that. She overheard a conversation between his buddy, Kevin, and him. Amanda only knew the money he made bought groceries when the check came in, the rest of the month, he spent his paychecks and her SSI money on his two girlfriends: drugs and alcohol.

Eight months after they arrived in Longmont, he added a third girlfriend: a tall, skinny brunette with tattoos that snaked up her arms and legs. Her dad said she was a friend he met at work. Amanda knew friends didn't move in and share her dad's bedroom. He didn't notice Amanda was growing up.

Stacy was her name. She was sort of okay. At least, unlike her dad, she asked, "Have you eaten?" or "Need anything from the store, you know, girl stuff?"

She even bought the items and didn't ask for a reimbursement. Maybe she did, but she didn't do it in front of Amanda, just handed the bags over and retreated to the bedroom or the kitchen.

A year later, Stacy left one day and never came back. Her dad said, "Kids bother her."

She believed him. *Everyone else didn't care and left because of me, so why shouldn't Stacy?*

Once Stacy was gone, Amanda was back to waiting for her dad's paydays to get food and personal necessities. He didn't care if she went without. At least the school offered two meals, and the nurse supplied her with hygiene items.

Amanda remembered begging the nurse not to say anything to anyone. Even a dad who didn't care was better than living with strangers; the alternative was foster care. Amanda didn't want that. She knew enough kids who lived in the "system" and hated it. So, she did the best she could to get by and not complain. It wouldn't have mattered; no one noticed or cared.

At twelve, two years after they arrived in Longmont, Colorado, her dad said, "Mandy, we need to talk."

Surprisingly, he didn't appear to be drunk or high. Her stomach clenched. She had not seen him sober before. With dread, Amanda followed him to the kitchen. The smell of cooking wafted through the hallway before she got to the door. She wrapped her arms around herself, bracing for what was to come. The unknown unnerved her. He was too nice and had cooked a meal; he'd never done that before.

"I made spaghetti. Hope you're hungry."

Amanda said nothing. *Was he going to tell me he decided to sober up? Found someone to marry?*

Her dad piled noodles and sauce on her plate. Her heart sank; he didn't even know she was allergic to tomato sauce. Amanda twirled the noodles, shaking off the sauce. Her dad didn't notice. He sat opposite her and shoveled in mouthfuls of food. Halfway through the plate, with his eyes still gazing at his dish, he said, "I need to go away."

"Okay," she said quietly.

He looked at her, sandy-brown eyebrows forming two question marks above his ink-blue eyes. Amanda realized she looked nothing like him. Her curly black locks to his straight golden ones, her plain face to his high cheekbones and dimpled chin. She stared.

"Okay," she repeated, but he didn't make a move to leave.

"Okay?" he asked.

"Yeah. If you want to leave, it's okay. I'll clean up the dishes."

He shook his head, hair bouncing. Amanda noticed his hair was long, past his shoulders. *Shouldn't he be getting it cut?*

"You don't understand. I have to leave."

"Leave?" she repeated dumbly.

"Yeah. I've already packed. I'll be leaving tomorrow."

"I don't understand. Where are you going?"

Scraping the last of his food and shoving it in his mouth, he spoke around the sauce and noodles. "Your grandma will pick you up tomorrow at ten. Be ready to go."

Confused, Amanda was unable to stop the tears. Silently, they rolled down her cheeks onto the uneaten spaghetti. He didn't notice. He didn't care. No one did.

She had only seen her maternal grandmother, Bee, a handful of times since her dad moved her out of Auntie Emma's house. He had sent Amanda for a two-week visit when she was eleven, and her grandmother drove to Longmont three times, but didn't stay with them.

"But… but…" was her feeble attempt at protesting.

"The decision is made. Be ready by ten. She's already in town, staying at a motel. So, don't make her wait."

"Where are you going?" Amanda asked, not believing what was happening.

"I'll get in touch with you when I get there. Nothing to worry your pretty little head about."

His fork clattered to the plate as he dropped it and reached in his pocket. "Oh, before I forget, Kevin and Steven will be by to pick up the bike around seven in the morning," her dad said, tossing the keys on the counter.

Once again, Amanda faltered, "But…but—"

"But nothing. Take care of yourself. Do what your grandmother says. Just so you know, this ain't your fault. I wasn't cut out to be a dad."

On his way out of the kitchen, he said, "I'm going to Arkansas. I'll let you know when I get there."

She never heard from him again.

Reluctantly, Amanda cleared the table and filled the sink with hot water. Tears mixed with the dish soap as Amanda faced another reality she had to live with. Her eye twitched, and shoulder shrugged, her tics intensifying with the stress.

Not gonna let this happen again! Amanda's inner voice screamed.

She opened the cabinet under the sink and took out a bottle. There was no internal debate. She knew exactly what she must do. "No. Not gonna let it happen," she whispered to a brewed pot of coffee sitting on the side of the sink, ready for her dad.

That night, Amanda curled up with her nightmares after cleaning the kitchen. In the distance, she heard her mother's disjointed words, Auntie Emma turning her back to her as she drowned, and her father on a motorcycle, a ghost blending with the horizon. Startled when the fingers of fear shook her awake, Amanda ran out of her room into the silent hallway and to the kitchen. The clock above the oven let her know it was 4 am on May 29, 1994. What was the noise that woke her up?

She ran to her dad's room empty. Aimlessly, she wandered the deserted house that never was home — her heart hammering in her chest. Amanda returned to the kitchen and looked around. The coffee thermos wasn't there. The key to the bike was gone, too. When did Kevin or Steven come? Was that the noise she heard?

Amanda peered out the kitchen window. Darkness shrouded the yard, and she couldn't see too well. She ran to the living room and looked out. The only things in the circle of light from the driveway lamp were moths, fluttering.

She bit her nails. She only meant to put a little bit of the stuff in the coffee, enough to stop him from going. So, where was he?

Chapter 7

May 4, 2018

Hair still wet, Amanda slung the laptop case and a duffle bag on her shoulders, checked her wallet for credit cards and money, and glanced at her carry-on, debating whether she should take it. She needed the clothes but didn't need the burden of lugging it around.

When she opened the door and peered into the hallway, it was silent and deserted except for a housekeeper's cart at one end; she appeared focused on sorting through linen for what she needed to ready the room. Amanda hung her head low, scooted past the maid to the bank of elevators, and pushed the down button.

Reconsidering her move, she took the stairs. If she landed in the lobby, Mr. Downes might have been there. The last thing Amanda needed was to deal with him. Surely missing the meeting had already sealed her fate with the company, especially after not showing up to work earlier. She shrugged at the thought. It truly didn't matter at that point.

By the sixth floor, Amanda was glad she left her carry-on case in the room. She leaned over the banister at the landing and looked down; it was a vortex, an illusion. One step at a time, she descended, armed with a plan.

Amanda skipped the lobby and took the next flight down to the underground parking. As she pushed the door open, a gust of cold air assaulted but didn't deter her. She followed the exit signs.

The attendant waved at her. "Ma'am, no pedestrians through here."

She ignored him and ducked under the arm with a big sign that read, "Wait for attendant to open the gate."

The man yelled, this time louder, "Ma'am—"

Amanda ran. She didn't hear what else he had to say. By then, her lungs were on fire and her legs were cramped. She made it to the street where cars, buses, and trucks whizzed by. To her left was a coffee shop. She ducked into it and, after ordering coffee and a sandwich, pulled out her laptop and phone to charge.

The first thing she did was contact Brad, knowing he would call and report her missing if he didn't hear from her within a reasonable amount of time; her silence had gone on for more than twelve hours. She was sure by then that the company would have called him, looking for her.

Turning her phone on to text, it buzzed incessantly – missed calls and messages. Amanda glanced at the charge. Nineteen percent, enough to send a message.

She had her words planned: *Hi, I'm heading home later today. The flight will get in after 10:00 — no need to wait up. I have my car at the airport. See you in the morning.*

A text promptly arrived: *Okay. Safe travels.*

Not even a minute later, a second text arrived: *Oh, I have a surprise for you.*

No, she thought, *I'm the one with the surprise.*

Next, Amanda booted her laptop. Since she hadn't used it much, it was almost fully charged. While she waited for the background screen to appear along with her apps, she took a sip of coffee and a bite of her sandwich. She wasn't hungry but needed to keep up her strength to carry out her plan.

She had deleted Andy's chat. Amanda clicked on the Messenger icon and typed his name. A new chat box opened, and she typed, *I have a few minutes to chat before my next flight.*

She waited and waited, but no response.

Nervously tapping her foot and absently sipping and eating, she stared at the open window on her laptop. *Where is he?* her mind screamed.

He was so anxious to get hold of me and now, silent? He has to answer me. She wanted to find out what he was after, and the sooner she did, the sooner she might be able to divert a disaster.

An hour went by. Her phone almost fully charged, she gathered her belongings, dumped her trash, and left the coffee shop. Now that Messenger was open on her phone, Amanda turned up the volume to hear a notification should any come through. With her free hand, she pressed the taxi app.

"Three minutes for Dahl to arrive in black Nissan, license…"

Forty-five minutes later, Amanda arrived at the airport, a ticket and boarding pass ready – the advantage of having a driver and technology. She glanced at her phone as she exited the car — still, no message from Andy.

Amanda had exactly thirty minutes to make it through security and to the gate. She ran, mumbling apologies as she pushed and shoved her way through. Out of breath, hair now in full frizz mode, she arrived at the gate, no one in line.

The agent looked at her, "Can I help you?"

Amanda showed him her boarding pass.

"We already closed the gates."

"Please?" she begged.

He wasn't listening. Amanda waited while he spoke on the phone to an unknown entity, all the while looking at her. A few seconds later, he said, "You'd better hurry."

He scanned her boarding pass and opened the door to the long jetway to the plane. Once again, she ran.

Nestled in her first-class seat, Amanda looked at her phone one last time before she had to switch to airplane mode. Nothing from Andy and a ton of other messages still waited for her to read. Once in the air and connected to the Wi-Fi, she would deal with them.

Amanda leaned her head back, closed her eyes, and considered her options again if she didn't get hold of Andy.

What did he mean that a blue envelope waited for me? At that thought, she jolted upright, her eyes darting around the small cabin.

Fifteen minutes into the flight, an announcement let her know was okay to use electronic devices. Quickly, Amanda switched on her phone and plugged it into the USB port in the armrest. She didn't have a backup charger and needed to be sure her cell remained accessible. One by one, she read the messages and deleted each, including Brad's. Then, the message from a private number which read: *I'll find you when I'm ready to talk. Do not. I repeat. Do not contact me.*

With a few minutes left before landing in Los Angeles, Amanda sent an email to her boss, apologizing for her no-show and promising to fill him in on her emergency as soon as she could. In closing, Amanda typed, "I would understand if you ask me to resign."

Amanda had enough money saved that Brad didn't know about. Enough for her to... but she let go of that thought; she wasn't at that stage yet. She clicked send and closed her laptop. Her phone was still connected to the Internet, and she opened Facebook, debating whether she wanted to delete her account. On a whim, she clicked on the search bar and typed "Andy Baker."

She stared at the long list of Andy Bakers, but none looked to be the one. Andy had to be in his mid-forties – she didn't get a chance to finish her search. The Internet disconnected, and the plane started its descent into LAX. Luckily, Amanda didn't have to change planes and only had fifty-five minutes before taking off again to Denver.

Once on the ground, she connected to her cell service, and after a few minutes, found Andy Baker. Passengers disembarked, and a new crop came on board, bumping luggage along.

Amanda clicked on his profile and expected to have no access to personal information, but he had to have had a public setting because there he was, with every minute piece of personal information ready for her to read. She clicked "About." Andy had listed his hometown as Colorado Springs. When she checked his marital status, there was no information. Amanda clicked on "Friends," hoping to find what? She had only seen Andy a handful of times at the Baker's home. It was during holidays and when he had a few days off from college, and her mind raced. Was he home when...? He couldn't have been. Was he? Her heart jackhammered in her chest. Why else would he contact her? Why would Andy care?

Amanda brought her knuckles to her mouth, stifling a "damn" that wanted to escape.

Chapter 8

1995

Amanda's grandmother, Bee, came by at 9:50 am and found Amanda sitting on the front steps, staring at her feet. "Got all your stuff?"

"Yeah." Amanda nodded grabbed her few belongings, and walked to the car.

She opened the back door and tossed her items on the seat. She had gathered her meager possessions and gone through all the rooms, looking for things she might have forgotten. She found a lunch sack filled with papers tucked beneath the towels in the hallway cabinet. She peered inside, then removed the contents and shoved them in her box of treasures.

When she closed the car door, she looked back to where her grandmother was standing, but she was no longer there. She waited, but rather than coming through the front door, Bee came around the side of the house. "What the heck happened here?" she said.

"What do you mean?" Amanda asked, struggling to keep the panic from her voice.

"There's glass everywhere back there"—she gestured somewhere behind her—"and fresh tire marks dug in the mud."

"I don't know what you're talking about. I didn't hear anything," Amanda said, walking to the back of the house.

The basement door was wide open, mud streaks across the wood. She crept forward and peered through the opening, but it was too dark to see inside. She backtracked to where her grandmother waited.

"We'd best be going," Bee said.

"How long will it take to get to California?"

"Oh, honey, no. I moved here a while ago. My place is less than twenty minutes away."

Amanda kept looking behind her as she returned to the car. Part of her was tempted to check out the basement, but she dismissed the urge; there was nothing there. Though it was dark, she was sure she would've seen if anything or anyone was in that gaping hole.

She had spent the morning searching for her dad, but there was no sign of him. The coffee thermos was gone. Her hope was for him to drink some when he woke up. He must not have, or perhaps what she put in wasn't much, not enough to affect him. She wanted to dismiss thoughts of him, but couldn't as her life fell into a companionable routine with Bee.

A few days into her stay with Bee, she asked her grandmother to take her back to the old house under the pretext that she forgot something she "really, really, needed." Bee obliged and stayed in the car while her granddaughter fumbled with the lock. What Amanda hoped was to find her dad still there, or that he had come back.

She unlocked the door and stepped over the threshold to be assaulted by an awful smell that wasn't there a few days earlier. Amanda covered her mouth and nose with her hand and quickly retreated to the fresh air outside. She locked the door and descended the four steps, aiming for the car when something protruding from the mailbox caught her attention. She lifted the flap and extracted the mail that had piled up, flipping through it as she made it to the car and strapped on her seatbelt. The stack was mostly bills and advertisements. Before setting them on the floor by her feet, she flipped through the mail one more time.

One by one, she looked at the front and back of each item, making two piles: ones she'd toss in the trash and the other she'd open later. A plain envelope tucked in a throwaway grocery ad caught her eye. Curious, she picked it up, ran her finger under the sealed flap, and ripped it open. In it was a single sheet of lined paper. Amanda unfolded the letter. "I know what you did…"

Her grandmother oblivious, Amanda's mouth went dry, and her heart raced. The realization she'd killed her dad struck her in the ribs, and she couldn't breathe. Someone knew what she did, and Amanda was sure the police would be after her in no time. And for the next long months, she lived in fear of being discovered. But, the police never came, and Amanda eventually let go of all thoughts of her dad.

Once again, Amanda was uprooted, this time, to a stranger's home. At Bee's, Amanda had a room of her own. A once upon a time sewing and craft room that Bee converted into a bedroom for Amanda. Because the house was small, Amanda shared the space with the sewing machine Bee no longer used, but wouldn't get rid of. She didn't mind. The home was clean and comfortable, and there was nothing she needed or wanted.

Unlike when she lived with her dad, Amanda and her grandmother spent weekends and holidays sightseeing and visiting craft fairs. Bee also made sure all of Amanda's needs were met, that included refilling medication on time and having Amanda see a doctor regularly. However, her grandmother didn't have a full understanding of Amanda's disability because aside from the tics, Amanda seemed "normal." But, her medical care was many steps above what her dad offered, which at the time was nothing.

Amanda's life with her grandmother didn't last long. In November of 1995, Bee had a heart attack and could no longer look after Amanda. Her grandmother's friend of many years, Margaret, contacted social services for assistance. The assistance they offered was to remove Amanda, now thirteen-and-a-half, from her grandmother's home and place her in foster care.

So, midway through eighth grade, Amanda was yanked from her grandmother's home and deposited into the Baker's. Since then, the years leading to graduation at eighteen were anything but stable. She was placed in six homes, shuffled from family to family.

46

During her short stay with the Baker family, soon after she turned fourteen, Social Services located her mother, who had moved from a full care facility to assisted care in a city south of Denver. In an attempt at reunification, the social worker scheduled a visit. Their hope was once Irene was released to independent living, Amanda would be shuffled to her care and out of the system.

The image Amanda carried with her during the nine-year absence was of a crazed woman who vacillated between cuddling and loving and outright hysteria. The trepidation in meeting her was justified, though deep within, there was the magical hope of finding the loving mother again.

On a Tuesday afternoon in July of 1996, Amanda's social worker drove them to meet with Irene. Sweaty palms, pulse drumming in her ears, she entered the gated facility after a staff member buzzed them in.

Irene sat in the garden under a canopy of climbing vines, hands folded in her lap, waiting. When she saw Amanda, she opened her arms, inviting a hug. Starved for her mother's love, Amanda quickly closed the short distance and fell into the embrace, leaning her head on Irene's shoulder, both bathed in tears. When Irene finally let go, Amanda backed away and sat opposite her, the only seat available.

Irene's eyes scanned Amanda from head to toe. "You've grown so much," she said.

"I turned fourteen last month."

"Tell me about you. I want to know everything."

Amanda knew Bee had kept Irene informed. She frequently sent letters and pictures.

"I live with a foster family in Colorado Springs," Amanda offered, hoping her mother would tell her she'd soon take Amanda home with her.

Irene nodded and stared at her hands.

Silence.

Hoping for more, Amanda asked, "How are you doing?"

Eyes still gazing at her hands, Irene nodded, and an almost inaudible, "Fine," tripped over her lips.

Silence.

The social worker approached, breaking the awkwardness. "Time to say good-bye."

"Will you come back to visit?" asked Irene, opening her arms for another hug.

This time, Amanda bent and gave her mother a peck on the cheek but didn't hug her back. She couldn't. Irene was a stranger. The realization that this woman would never be a mom to her, not now, not ever, hit her soul. Fighting tears, all she could say was, "See you."

"Come back and visit." Irene's voice followed Amanda across the brick pathway.

Nothing was said on the drive back until Amanda asked, "Will she ever be okay?"

The social worker replied, "Perhaps one day."

Amanda knew it was a lie, but her mind asked for the lie, anyway.

The Bakers had three kids of their own and cared for five foster children ranging in age from three to sixteen. The biological children were Mags, age two, and Matt, seventeen, a junior in high school. They also had an older son, in his early twenties attending college somewhere in Arizona.

Amanda took a liking to Matt and flirted with him every chance she had. But, Matt had his eye on a sixteen-year-old foster girl, Ashley. Amanda felt she was prettier and decided to make Matt like her. She went out of her way to give him special attention, from leaving origami hearts by his dinner plate to doing his laundry.

"It's nice of you, Amanda," said Mrs. Baker one morning, "but *he* needs to do his laundry."

Semi-embarrassed, Amanda stopped washing Matt's clothes. Instead, she wore skimpy skirts and shorts and off-the-shoulder tops that barely covered her. None brought Matt closer. She watched him slip further and further away, avoiding being home alone with her, changing directions when he entered the narrow hallway and saw Amanda in it. He even took to locking his bedroom door at night. Yeah, she used to open it and peek in to stealthily watch him.

The rejection made Amanda angry. The tics increased in frequency. And, Ashley became her target. She took to taunting, harassing, and telling lies about her. Nothing brought more pleasure than seeing Mrs. Baker rip into Ashley. The infractions Amanda reported to Mrs. Baker escalated until one day, leaning against the closed door, she heard the foster mother's raised voice, "If you keep this up, I'll send you away."

Oh, the butterflies of excitement fluttered in Amanda's mind at the prospect of getting rid of Ashley once and for all, carrying with them a new plan. Matt would finally be hers.

Amanda's plan was simple; it was to make sure Ashley was moved out of the home and, hopefully, as far away from Matt as possible. Smiling to herself, she marveled at her brilliant mind and how easy it would be. Her eye twitched and her shoulder shrugged in agreement.

To divert attention from herself, she lay low for a while and didn't report on Ashley. But, with the plan in place, Amanda set out to accomplish phase one. It was simple, knowing Mrs. Baker would flip out if she saw Matt and Ashley hugging and kissing. Next time Amanda witnessed their despicable act, she would send one of the little kids to tell on them.

What Amanda accomplished instead wasn't what she planned. Though it haunted her for many years, there was no guilt, only the fear of being discovered. When no one pointed the finger at her, she was able to bury the incident in the recesses of her mind… until the message popped up on the laptop in the airport, twenty-two years later.

Now, I have to face the consequence of my actions.

Chapter 9

May 4, 2018

Although Brad was glad Amanda planned to cut her business trip short, he felt unsettled at the same time. The envelope on the counter called him more often than he wanted. Each time Brad picked it up, he was tempted to rip it open. Perhaps, he wouldn't have bothered with it had he not received Andy's call earlier. What was Amanda hiding?

From halfway across the kitchen, he tossed the envelope for the last time. He missed his target, and it landed with a soft whoosh in the sink. He ran to rescue it from the wet surface. Too late; the ink blended and smeared, though he could still see Amanda's name. Frustrated, he set it aside and reached for his phone. 4:30 pm, the digital readout told him.

On a whim, he pressed "call back" next to Andy's message. On the third ring, Brad chickened and was about to end the call when he heard, "Hello?"

"Oh, hey. This is Brad. You called me earlier. I'm just curious. Who did you say you are?"

"Ask your wife. She should be on her way home."

"Wait! What did you say?"

"You heard me."

Brad scratched his chin with his left hand and pressed the phone tighter with his right. "Wait. Wait. Who the hell are you?"

A dead line was the resounding answer Brad received. He tapped his foot and stared at the envelope. "Oh, the hell with it," he said to the empty kitchen and grabbed it.

With one swift motion, and before he changed his mind, he ripped it open, parts of it soggy in his hand. Brad carefully extracted the contents, one sheet of cream color paper now discolored by the bleeding ink. One word in jerky handwriting: "Murderer."

Brad let go of the letter as if fire scorched his fingers, and he watched it flutter to the floor. It didn't make sense. No way would Amanda kill anyone. What kind of game was this?

The fancy gift bag caught his attention as he strode out of the kitchen. He grabbed it and tossed it in the hallway closet. Until he figured out what this insanity was, the anniversary would have to wait.

He glanced at his phone again. 4:38 pm. Brad paced the hallway, climbed the stairs, went back down and through the kitchen. Amanda wouldn't be in until late, and he couldn't wait to get to the bottom of this madness.

With doubt creeping into his core, he once more ascended the stairs and stood at the threshold of their bedroom. The bed was unmade; he hadn't bothered earlier. Laundry overflowing, he didn't care. And their wedding picture stared back at him from where he left it, teetering at the edge of the dresser.

As he approached the dresser, Brad ran his fingers through his hair until it spiked. He picked up the photo, turned it upside down, and placed it on the dusty surface. Once more, he lifted it and set it facing him and the room.

Hesitantly, one by one, he pulled the drawers open and felt through and under Amanda's clothing. He then moved to the closet and removed all items from the top shelf, rummaging through boxes. There was nothing but shoes on the floor. He slammed shut the sliding mirrored door, almost shattering it. What was it he hoped to find?

Not caring what the room looked like, he quickly made his way to her office. Though Amanda never locked the door, Brad had only been in there a handful of times over the years. As far as he was concerned, it was her space where she worked on her projects while at home. He didn't have his own space; anywhere he wanted to work or be alone, he worked undisturbed.

Vacillating between guilt and the need to know what was happening propelled him forward. His misgivings would have to wait. Brad twisted the handle and pushed the door open. The office was silent, the remnants of the daylight glistening on the surface of the glass desk where a computer silently sat. He flicked on the light.

To the right of the desk stood a four-drawer, black filing cabinet, and on the opposite end was a chair and a closet not in use to his knowledge. Brad pulled the first drawer open. He wasn't sure what he was looking for but hoped to find something that would shed light on the bizarre events and the past he didn't know about.

As he peered through the files and found nothing of interest, his gaze multi-tasked searching the corners and under the manila folders. The next drawer contained the same, work files, and no evil lurked within the contents. The third and fourth drawers netted a goose egg as well. Leaning on one knee, he hoisted himself up and circled a few times, thinking and rubbing his chin.

It was approaching 6:45 pm. Brad ignored his hunger and moved to the closet, sliding the door open. To his surprise, it wasn't empty; he had not been in the room for years and thought storage items were on the rafters in the garage. Plastic and cardboard boxes, three deep, lined the narrow carpeted floor; each container was labeled with year and contents. All appeared to be tax-related, work-related, and other miscellaneous items: holiday decoration, picture albums, and the like. Brad slid the door shut.

Then, he opened it again, reaching for the box with the albums. It only took a few minutes to determine there was nothing there of interest, only baby pictures and a handful of others throughout Amanda's growing up years. He had seen them before. One caught his attention as he flipped through the book. A picture of a man who looked nothing like Amanda stared back at him. His right arm was draped over a pre-teen girl's shoulder. Brad didn't remember this picture, but it had to have been there all along. He pried it from its spot and turned it to read what was on the back, "KODAK 1994" printed in light gray ink. There was writing, but Brad couldn't decipher it. He'd ask Amanda about it, but not now. Carefully, he placed it back in its holders, closed the album, and returned it to the box he toed in place.

A small table with a lamp stood next to the reclining chair a few feet away from the closet. He bent and popped the door open. A stack of magazines and newspapers filled the cavity. Brad reached for the door to close it, but something gold and shiny caught his eye.

He grabbed handfuls of papers and set them beside him on the floor. There, beneath the stacks was a wooden box with brass corner trim. He lifted it and was surprised by its heft. Brad turned it around to face him but quickly realized it had a lock. He rummaged further in the small space, hoping to find a key, but there was none. He would have to wait to find the key, or when he confronted Amanda, he would ask.

He poked at the lock with a small key on his keyring, tried to pry the lid with his fingers. All efforts were unsuccessful. Reluctantly, he returned all the scattered items and covered the box as he found it, all the while, curiosity ate away at him.

A few minutes later, his head swimming with a barrage of unwanted thoughts, he descended the stairs and returned to the kitchen. There, the letter lay, glaring at him. He picked it up and shredded it to small pieces. He had to be wrong. Amanda wasn't hiding anything from him, and whoever wrote that vile letter had to be mistaken. Wouldn't Amanda be in jail by now if she hurt anyone?

"Ridiculous!" he admonished himself. He opened the refrigerator, scouting for something he could make for dinner, and settled on a salad with cheese, hard-boiled egg, and pear slices.

Brad carried his plate into the living room and flicked the television on, but his mind wouldn't quit racing. He reached for his phone as he popped a mouthful of food and slowly chewed while, with his other hand, he sent a text message to Amanda. *Hopefully, you have Wi-Fi and can get this. I'll be up waiting for you. Looks like we need to talk.*

On the last leg of the flight from LAX to Denver, Amanda stared at the message. There was no "xoxo," nothing. What did Brad want to talk about? Then, a thought hit her. Was Andy's threat real? What did Andy say to Brad when he called?

The time on her phone was 8:05 pm. Her plane was scheduled to land at 9:48 pm. Suddenly, going home and telling Brad the truth didn't seem like a good plan. Amanda's chest tightened, and she struggled to breathe. It was the same feeling she had on that dreadful day, back in August of 1996.

Chapter 10

March 6th, 1996

Although Amanda's tics were subtle, they were still noticeable. She wasn't aware she had them until she started school. Kindergarten kids asked, "Why do you wink?" or "What's wrong with your shoulder?"

The kids didn't know any better. They were curious, but Amanda responded with anger. She lashed out and tried to hide the tics by looking down, but it wasn't something she controlled. It just happened. So, Amanda withdrew. She sat by herself at school, had lunch by herself, and found solo games to play. She became a loner. Perhaps that's what made her gravitate toward working on projects which didn't require teamwork. Little did she know, the career she chose would pitch her in front of audiences to lead presentations.

At fourteen, when other kids had boyfriends and enjoyed social activities, Amanda longed to be cured of what she perceived to be a disease. The medication she took since she was young stopped when she moved in with her dad. He didn't care enough to refill prescriptions. "You don't need this stuff," he had said to Amanda one day.

No one had ever bothered to explain what the nature of her disability was. Amanda craved to know the truth. Maybe there was a cure for it. The only thing she knew, it was Tourette's syn--something or another, one of her social workers told her.

She wanted to look up her disease, but there was only one computer at home, and priority was given for the older kids to type their papers for school. However, there were computers at school, a computer lab their teacher took them to, to learn how to research and do other things during that period. There were also two computers in the library, but most of the time, they were reserved for those who signed up to use them.

One day, first thing in the morning, Amanda went to the library and checked the list. There were five names ahead of hers, but all were for after school. Before she changed her mind, Amanda printed her name on the sign-up sheet. She wanted to know but also, was afraid of what she would find out about her disability.

Amanda watched the second hand drag across the face of the clock, refusing to hurry up. When fourth-period bell signaled lunch, she already had her belongings packed and was out of the door ahead of most students. Usually, Amanda was one of the last to leave.

"What's your hurry?"

"Got a hot date?"

Sneers and jeers raced with her shadow across the icy walkway. She ignored them, although hot tears threatened to escape. When she got to the library, someone was already on one of the computers, but thankfully, the other stood empty of an occupant. Quickly, she made it to the desk, signed in next to her name with date and time, and raced to the empty computer. When she pressed the button to boot it up, nothing happened. Her reflection stared back on the dark screen. She tried once more. Nothing. Amanda crossed her arms on the desk and put her head down, letting the tears roll and drip on her shoes.

A gentle voice came from her left, asking her if she was all right. Without looking up, she shook her head. The librarian must've figured out the source of her distress and, her distorted voice coming from beneath the desk, said, "All fixed. Someone unplugged it."

Relief flooded Amanda, and she lifted her face to the bright screen.

"Let me know if you need help. Okay?" said the librarian, then turned around and walked back to the circulation desk where a queue was forming.

Amanda glanced at the clock and realized she only had twenty-three minutes left of her lunchtime.

Looking around the library, she noticed no one was close by to watch her screen. The kid seated in the next corral was feverishly typing what looked like a report. Bringing her attention back to the monitor, Amanda launched the search engine and typed "Tourette," misspelling it multiple times before it finally appeared as "Tourette's Syndrome." She had no idea what either meant.

The only sites that came up were medical sites, and Amanda couldn't access the information. They required a login by "staff." Frustrated after spending time typing in different words, she logged out and held back the tears that were pushing to clamber over her lashes and spill onto her cheeks.

Her stomach rumbled, and, using her hunger as an excuse to keep her head down, she fumbled through her backpack for a granola bar that was at the bottom, wiping the tears with her other hand.

By the time she reached the exit sign that read "No food and no drink," Amanda had found the precious treat and quickly unwrapped it as the bell signaled it was the end of lunch. Big bites filled her mouth, making it hard to chew as she quickly walked across the quad and to her fifth-period class.

Throughout the fifth period, her thoughts whirred. There had to be someone who knew what Tourette's was. Her mind scrolled through the list of people she knew: Her foster parents, her teachers, her doctor, but she trusted none. Her doctor would know, but she was never alone at her appointments.

Just then, a thought occurred to Amanda as she looked at Beth across the aisle from her. Beth walked with a limp, and her left arm dangled uselessly by her side. Aside from this, she was smart. Beth always had the answers to questions the teacher sprung on the class. She readily smiled at Amanda and gave her a pencil when she didn't have one.

As she stared at Beth, Amanda recalled the few times Beth wanted to sit with her at lunch, but Amanda made excuses to avoid her. It was bad enough other kids thought she was a freak; to hang out with Beth would seal her fate as the freakish kid. But Beth might be the only one who could help, albeit not intentionally.

In class, Amanda averted her gaze when Beth looked her way and pretended to be engrossed in writing, although, she had lost track of what the teacher said to do.

Beth didn't share Amanda's period six class. Amanda saw her walking across campus to the Special Education building. Amanda didn't have time after school. The Bakers picked another kid and her up from school each day, and Amanda didn't dare be one minute late. So, she resigned herself to catch up with Beth the next day. It killed her to wait because she really, really wanted to know what her disease was and how to cure it, and she believed Beth to be the access to that information.

It wasn't difficult to find Beth the next morning. As soon as the foster family dropped Amanda off, she went straight to the building she saw Beth aim for the day before. She had to skip the free breakfast for this precious extra time, but what she wanted couldn't wait. Sure enough, Beth was outside one of the rooms.

Amanda retrieved the two brand new pencils from her backpack, and when she got to where Beth stood, she extended her arm, the two bright red pencils leading the way. "I…" Amanda stammered. "I want you to have these. You know, for the pencils you gave me."

A moment hesitation, then her eyes became bright, and the tips of the curve of her smile reached them. "Thank you!"

"Well, okay. See you later." Amanda turned to walk away.

"Wait," Beth said. "Um, where's your first-period class?"

"M-5."

"Mind if I walk with you?" Beth asked.

Amanda looked around, not wanting other kids to see her with Beth, but decided it didn't matter anyway. None of them gave a damn what happened to her, and they made fun of her no matter whether she was alone, or with Beth, or someone else. "Sure. Where's your first period?"

"Oh, I have to do some testing with the school psychologist."

Amanda's ears perked up. *School psychologist.* She used to see a psychologist when she lived with Auntie Emma, but it was so long ago, she didn't remember why she saw Dr. Redd.

They walked in silence across campus until they reached a small office no bigger than a closet, with a plaque that read "Ms. Lamb." Before Beth could knock, the door opened, and a thin, silver-haired woman took a step out, not realizing the girls stood there. "Oh, hi, Beth. I need to go to the restroom. I'll be right back. Mind if you wait here?"

Beth nodded.

"Who do you have with you?" Ms. Lamb pointed toward Amanda.

"Oh, this is Amanda."

It had to happen. It just had to. Amanda winked at Ms. Lamb and shrugged her shoulder before her mouth engaged, and a weak, "Hi," emerged.

Surprisingly, Ms. Lamb didn't miss a beat, wasn't shocked by Amanda's tics, and said, "Glad to meet you. Would love to get to know Beth's friends. How about I call you in for a chat?"

Amanda stared blankly at Ms. Lamb; this was too easy. It was exactly what she aimed for: a private conversation with a psychologist. *Surely, she would know about Tourette's syndrome.* "Yeah. Okay."

As Amanda walked to her class, she felt a giggle form and bubble within, but she stifled it. Finally, she was going to get her answer and wouldn't need to chummy up to Beth after all. *Well, I'd better be nice to her. I may need her at some point.*

Ms. Lamb didn't call that day or in the next two weeks. Amanda purposely passed by the office, waving and smiling when Ms. Lamb's door was open. Just when Amanda thought that this door, too, was closing against her quest, a call slip came to her third-period class a few days later. She practically flew out of the classroom and to Ms. Lamb's office.

"Thank you for coming," Ms. Lamb said.

"Oh, it's okay." Butterflies fluttered in Amanda's stomach.

"Would you mind answering a few questions about your friendship with Beth?"

Amanda arched her eyebrows in puzzlement.

"Oh, nothing too difficult or personal. Just general questions," Ms. Lamb assured.

"Ah, why? I mean, sure, but why?"

"Beth said she told you about her upcoming meeting…" Ms. Lamb didn't finish.

"Yeah, but I have no idea what that is. Anyway, I don't know much about Beth, except she's smart and kind. She gave me pencils when I didn't have any." Amanda added, "Well, we're not friends. I mean, we don't hang out."

Ms. Lamb looked into Amanda's eyes when she winked and shrugged. Her nerves made it happen again. When Amanda became anxious, the annoying tics happened in threes. Without hesitating, Ms. Lamb asked, "Do these tics happen often? How long have you had them?"

Amanda opened her mouth and closed it.

The silence stretched like a rubber band between them, wanting to snap back into the conversation.

"I don't want to make you uncomfortable, but just so you know, I work with kids who have tics," Ms. Lamb said.

Amanda knew Ms. Lamb wanted to say, "And other disabilities," but didn't. She cast her eyes downward. This wasn't as easy as Amanda thought it would be.

Noticing her discomfort, Ms. Lamb asked, "Okay then. What makes you think Beth is so smart?" she asked with a broad and beaming smile.

Amanda tapped her foot and forged ahead. If she didn't ask then, the chance might be lost. She bit her lip and looked sheepishly at the psychologist. "Since I was five or younger. I don't remember."

Ms. Lamb said nothing. Her gentle gaze traveled between Amanda's eyes and the top of her head. Amanda wondered what the psychologist was thinking but plowed on. "My auntie said it was Tourette's. I used to take medication, but hadn't in three years, until I moved in with the Bakers."

"Ah-ha" was Ms. Lamb's response.

"The kids always made fun of me, but I don't care."

Another "Ah-ha."

"Do you know what Tourette's is? I tried to look it up on the Internet but didn't find anything." Amanda cleared her throat, though there was nothing there to dislodge.

"Well, let me see if I can give you something to help you understand it."

Ms. Lamb bent toward a stack of papers on a cabinet beside her desk and rummaged through it. *She sure is messy. I'd be punished until eternity if my side of the room looked like this.*

Ms. Lamb's voice brought Amanda back to the closet-office as she placed an article between them. She pointed to the words she read and periodically looked at Amanda. *Perhaps to see if I understand.* After reading half the page, she asked, "Any questions?"

Amanda nodded and said, "I don't get it."

"Let me see if I can explain. Tourette's syndrome is a tic disorder, which you already know." She stopped when Amanda opened her mouth and gestured for Amanda to speak.

"I want to know if it will go away. If my di… if I didn't stop taking my meds, would it have gone away?"

"Most research to date says there isn't a cure for Tourette's, but, for most people, it gets less and less as they grow older."

Disheartened, Amanda let a tear escape and didn't bother to wipe it dry. When her eye twitched and her shoulder went up, then down, she grabbed her backpack and ran out of the office.

Chapter 11

May 4ᵗʰ, 2018

Stephanie and Liz had made good progress. They had breathed life into the old house. The two bedrooms were completed, fresh paint, new molding, bright new lights, and ah, yes, electric outlets in every wall – no more single hanging light bulbs and nowhere to plug a phone charger!

Standing in the kitchen surrounded by peeling and broken countertops, scuffed and cracked flooring, the twins ignored Jerry, who had unfolded the plans for the remodeling. Liz took a sip and motioned to the far wall with one finger, the rest wrapped around her latte. "I think the six-burner stove should go over there. What do you think?"

"Let's leave everything as planned," said Stephanie. "But we should consider putting glass doors on the corner cabinet. We have so many antique glass pieces—"

"Hm. Maybe. What about an extra shelf over there?" Liz pointed to the area above where the refrigerator would be.

"Good idea. And, I think a butcherblock table in the middle will be perfect with—"

"You need to finalize your plans. We'll be gutting the kitchen in the next day or two," interrupted Jerry.

Finger still pointing, she swiveled to face Jerry. "What day will the crew start tearing it down? Steph and I will go over the plans one last time. Oh, just leave the paperwork on the counter. We'll get it back to you."

Jerry nodded, rolled up the kitchen layout, and put it on the counter, away from the sink. Liz and Steph sipped their coffee before tackling the next project, the hallway.

"Jerry, appliances confirmed? Cabinets ordered?"

"I'll check again, but I did get a confirmation email this morning. I forwarded it to you."

With that, Jerry left the kitchen and aimed for the back door. Stephanie's voice caught up with him before he turned the doorknob. "Heard anything about our downstairs neighbor?"

Liz stopped mid-step and turned around to face Stephanie and Jerry. She wasn't as keen as her twin to find out about the remains and would just as soon forget it. Stephanie, curious, arched her eyebrows and set her coffee down. Jerry shook his head.

"I wonder if they'll let us know who that was and how he died?" asked Stephanie.

"They might. Maybe when the autopsy is done. Don't be surprised if the police visit you to ask more questions," Jerry said, turning the knob.

Liz, anxious to end the conversation, said, "Let's let Jerry get back to work. We can talk about this later."

"Do you have the detective's card on you?" Stephanie asked Jerry.

He fumbled for his wallet and extracted the already battered card. "Here you go."

Liz shifted from one foot to the other while Stephanie pulled out her phone and took a picture of the card with the case number. "I'll give Detective Miller a call in a bit."

Jerry twisted the door handle and left.

Liz wrapped her arms around herself. "This whole thing creeps me out."

The twins plugged in their earbuds, and with the same gait, curly ponytails bouncing, they walked to the hallway. Liz climbed the two-step ladder armed with a putty knife, a tub of mud, and a screwdriver while Stephanie gathered her supplies and reached for the taller ladder.

About half an hour into the work, Stephanie descended and aimed for the kitchen to retrieve the coffee she left behind. On her way, she pulled her phone from her back pocket and pressed *gallery*. She didn't have to think long. Her fingers decided for her. The call went to voicemail, the recording letting her know that Detective Miller would return the call as soon as possible.

Absently, she picked up her cup and took a sip, her mind wandering through the maze of possibilities of what might have happened to the man or woman in the basement. How long had the body been there? Why hadn't anyone looked for them?

When she walked through the hallway, Liz looked down at her sister and pulled out her earpieces. "Everything okay?"

Stephanie nodded.

The twins had a fine-tuned emotional connection; nothing got past either. "What's wrong?" repeated Liz.

"The idea of having a dead body in this house without knowing the whole story drives me bonkers. I wish Miller would call."

"Personally, now that the basement is finished and you can't tell anything was ever there, I'd rather we just leave it to the police—"

"But, doesn't it bother you not knowing?" Suddenly, a thought occurred to Stephanie. "What if… what if whoever killed him comes back for—"

"Stop! You're freaking me out. If they haven't come back by now, they're not going to. Besides, the police are handling it. Come on. Let's get back to work." With that, Liz returned her earbuds to their spot and climbed the two steps. Vigorously, she scraped and opened cracks, hoping the movement and the sound drowned her fears.

Stephanie hesitated for a few minutes before returning to her task. Each time she lifted her wrist, her Fitbit let her know it had only been ten minutes since she last checked – no calls from Detective Miller.

It wasn't until a day later when her phone vibrated, indicating an incoming call. Stephanie pulled it out of her pocket and glanced at the screen. There was no name, but she recognized the number. With one swift motion, she turned the music off and pressed the green button to accept the call. "Hello."

"Ms. Branson?"

"Yes, this is she."

"This is Detective Miller returning your call."

"Oh. Yeah. Glad you called. Have you found out anything about... you know... the body?"

Liz was soon by Stephanie's side, gesturing for her to put it on speakerphone.

"Just a sec, Detective. Can I put you on speakerphone? My sister wants to hear what you have to say."

"Sure, but there isn't anything to say. The investigation is still underway."

Stephanie indicated to Liz there was no news and returned her attention to the call. "But, you will let us know, right?"

"Ms. Branson, once we have an official word on who the person is and the cause of death, it will be on the Coroner's website." Miller paused for breath, then said, "It is complicated. There's next of kin to take into consideration, procedure—"

Stephanie cut him off in mid-sentence. "Yeah. Yeah. I understand, but they found the body in *my* house. I should be able to find out what happened!" Then, feeling bad for being rude, she said, "Look, I'm sorry, but this whole thing had us rattled. You do understand?"

"I'll be in touch if and when I can discuss the case with you."

With that, the line went dead. Stephanie smacked the phone against her leg.

Liz chewed on the side of her thumb. "Come on, Steph. Let's leave it be for now. Okay?"

Stephanie had no choice but to let it go.

The pair scraped, puttied, and prepped the hallway walls until the muscles in their arms ached. Stephanie was the first to get off the ladder. She tapped her sister on the leg and mouthed, "Wrap it up."

On her way to the living room where the table with the stack of scrapbooks stood, she peered into the kitchen. Through the open window, she heard the chatter of the workers along with hammering and machinery. She took the few steps to the back door and opened it.

"Jerry."

He looked up.

"How late are you guys planning to work?"

"We still have daylight. Maybe four-thirty or five. Need anything?"

"Stop in before you leave. Let's figure out the kitchen and finalize ideas."

"Yeah. I think the glass doors will look nice and the shelf…" interjected Liz, who materialized at Stephanie's side.

"Okay," Jerry said as he returned his attention to the crew.

Liz walked into the house, Stephanie following her. "I'm starved," she said, looking over her shoulder.

"Me, too," Stephanie agreed and grabbed her purse.

The house was not yet livable, although the twins spent most of their waking hours there. So, they glanced at their progress in the hallway, both twisting their heads to look at the same time, returned their gaze forward and, in step, walked out of the house and to the car.

"I'm…" both said at the same time.

"You…" both said.

Stephanie signaled to Liz with her hand to go ahead, while with the other, she turned on the ignition.

"I was just going to say. I'm tired of take-out and fast food."

"You read my mind," said Stephanie and put the car in reverse.

Later that evening, Liz pulled out their laptops.

"Let's scan all this mess when we're settled in," said Stephanie, sorting through the loose papers and scraps still needed to be placed in the books.

"I wish we could do that now. Sure beats papers and crap! Okay. I booted your computer, too. Where do we start?" Liz asked, handing a laptop to her sister.

Stephanie moved her head from side to side, loosening the kinks before responding. "I really want to know who that guy is… was." She left the room.

Liz asked, "Where are you going? I thought we're going to continue researching the property?"

"Hang on. I'll be right back."

She returned a few minutes later with a weathered, fake-leather, black bag and carefully placed it on the worktable. Dust emanated from it, and both sneezed.

"What the—"

"Shh."

"Where did you get that from? What is it?"

"As you can see, it is an old bag," said Stephanie, unclasping the lid ever so carefully. Then, suddenly, she said, "Wait!"

She moved to the only window in the room and pulled down the shade, making sure she locked the door next. Stephanie returned to the table and pulled the chair forward and sat. Her fingers ran over the outside of the bag, and she closed her eyes, feeling the cracked leather.

"What the hell are you doing?" Liz's voice snapped Stephanie back to the room. "Do you mind telling me what this is all about?"

"You won't believe it. Do you remember the day the crew found the body?"

"As if I can forget."

"Well, while everyone was outside waiting for the cops, I snuck in the basement to… well… take a look. I've never seen a real-life skeleton before." She took a deep breath, reliving the moment.

"Yeah, and?"

"The body was on the far side, underneath the kitchen, and I was too afraid to get closer—"

"Will you just spit it out?"

"It was kind of dark down there, and I tripped on something. Thinking it was debris, I made my way around it and walked toward the body, but chickened out."

When Stephanie stopped to take a breath, Liz said, "You know? You're getting on my last nerve. If you didn't see the body, then why all this mystery? You know I don't like word games."

Ignoring her sister, Stephanie went on. "I retraced my steps and thought I'd better leave before the police or the crew came back down. On my way out, I saw this." She pointed to the bag.

"You didn't. Oh, no, you didn't."

"I sure did, I picked it up, and when I made it to the door, I saw a uniformed officer walking toward the basement with Jerry. So, I shoved it behind a post and covered it with dirt."

"When did you get it out? You never said anything to me."

"I waited until the day after. When the crew left, I brought it up and hid it in the closet behind the storage boxes."

"You're going to get us in trouble. What if this belonged to, you know… you know… him?"

"Yep, I'm hoping it belongs to Mr. Mystery."

Liz's eyes sparkled. She was no longer worried about getting caught with the bag. She was no different than her twin. Curiosity ruled the day. "Well, come on. Open it."

Stephanie worked the belted straps as carefully as she could. The first one came undone. The second detached and came away in her hand. She set it aside and opened the bag. Item by item, she removed the contents. The musty smell permeated the room, irritating their eyes and the back of their throats.

Liz stood on tiptoes, leaning over the table, eyes wide in anticipation. It wasn't long before bound papers, a leather pouch, a wallet, and a few other items were free from their trap.

"Okay, Liz. You start with this stack, and I'll go through this one. Just be very careful; most of these papers have almost disintegrated."

Picking up a stack each, they gingerly and methodically unbound the papers and read through them. "Nothing here. How about you?" asked Stephanie.

"I'm not sure what we're looking for," said Liz.

"Anything with a name on it. Anything with personal information that may lead us to who this guy was."

"As exciting as this is," said Liz, "somewhere deep inside me, there's a voice that says we should turn this over to the police."

"We will, but not just yet."

Liz flipped through her stack again in case she missed or overlooked a piece of information. She stopped at one, shook her head, and set it aside. "The names on these bills have been crossed out. I wonder why? Maybe they have nothing to do with Mr. Mystery."

"Nothing here, either. I'm not sure what these papers are for and why anyone would keep them," said Stephanie.

"Hey, did you see what's on the back of the one in your hand?"

Stephanie flipped it over and silently read the words written in cursive.

Interrupting her, Liz asked, "What does it say?"

Stephanie raised her index finger for Liz to give her a minute and continued to read. A few moments later, she said, "Wow," and handed the paper to her sister. "Here, you read it for yourself."

Liz took it and brought it closer to the light.

Stephanie leaned back in her chair while her twin read the letter. Curious, she pushed herself upright and picked up the stack she had fumbled through, flipping each paper to look at the back. Only one other had a handwritten letter. "When you get done, go through your stack in case they have letters."

Liz nodded and continued to read the last paragraph. "What do you make of this?" she asked and read it aloud. "'So, last week, I didn't feel well. My friend teased and said I may be pregnant. What do you think of that? You know it's your kid if I am, don't you? Anyway, let's hope A. doesn't find out.'"

"I don't know. Until we know who wrote it and why, it doesn't make sense." She shook her head. "Weird, these papers have dates and names crossed out."

"Yeah. Some do, most are from the early eighties and late seventies," Liz said as she picked up her stack once more to look at the dates. She hoped she could read through the lines.

The twins looked up, and their eyes met. "The strange part is there are no names on this letter. How about the other one?"

Stephanie shook her head. "Nope. No name."

"What else is in the bag?" asked Liz.

Stephanie brought out the last two items, one wrapped in a moth-eaten rag, and laid them on the table between them. With the tips of her fingers, she pulled the remaining strands of material to reveal a small box. Liz reached to grab the box, and Stephanie swatted her hand away. "Don't get in a hurry. Let's not wreck it!"

Liz backed off and sat in her chair, watching Stephanie finish unwrapping the box. When she was through, Liz reached for a small button on the side and pressed it. The lid popped open, and Stephanie turned the box so that Liz could see. The first item she pulled out was a plain gold ring. She squinted to read the inscription on the inside of it. "Forever, 1979."

"Huh." Stephanie handed the ring to Liz.

"Huh," Liz said and set the ring next to the box.

The next item was a folded, discolored paper. "Here, you work on this," said Stephanie while she pulled out another folded paper and carefully, so as not to rip it, flattened it on the table. "Looks like a birth certificate. What's yours about?"

"This one looks like a birth certificate, too. Can you read the name on yours? Mine is so faded it is hard to read."

"I'm dying to find out, but I tell you, my eyes are getting tired, and I'm pretty worn out. How about we tackle this tomorrow?"

Liz nodded, all too eager to get home, take a shower, and lie in her cozy bed.

They gathered odds and ends, returned them to the bag, and Stephanie took it back to its hiding spot.

Chapter 12

May 4, 2018

The pilot started the descent into Denver Airport. With each increment, Amanda's stomach lurched further in her throat, and it had nothing to do with the shift in altitude. When the wheels finally thumped along the runway, she sucked in a breath.

Two gentlemen occupied the seats across the aisle from her. Amanda didn't make eye contact for fear they would misconstrue her winking. She had taken to keeping her eyes averted to the ground or straight ahead when in public. She was no longer embarrassed by her disability but hated to have to explain it.

Amanda's seat was at the rear of the plane. She hadn't used her company-purchased, first-class return ticket. She closed her eyes and waited for the passengers to leave. She was not in a hurry. All the plans and lies Amanda prepared and rehearsed, vanished with Brad's text: *I'll be up waiting for you. Looks like we may need to talk.*

We need to talk. We need to talk, reverberated through her aching head.

"Miss."

She opened her eyes. Only a handful of passengers were in the front, ready to exit. Grabbing her purse and laptop case, she stumbled, disoriented, to join the last of the queue ready to disembark.

Her haggard look must have attracted attention. Pantsuit wrinkled, hair unruly, she looked nothing like the successful businesswoman who boarded a flight the day before. *Yesterday?*

Making her way through the terminal was like traveling through a fog. She remembered walking into the bathroom and staring at the reflection in the mirror, a stranger gazing back at her. She didn't care, didn't try to improve her appearance. Amanda left and walked out into the cool night toward her car.

The drive home, too, was relegated to mental fog — forty minutes of staring into the night until she turned onto Main Street from C119. As Amanda approached the mall, half a mile from her house, she couldn't stop her eye from twitching or her shoulder from shrugging their rhythmic three-count sequence, making it difficult to focus on the road ahead. *I can't do it. I can't face Brad.*

The mall parking lot was practically empty at that late hour. Amanda pulled in and reached for her pills, realizing she had missed her earlier dose. A few mouthfuls of stale water helped to wash the two little pills down, and she sat and waited.

A third ping sounded in the quiet car. Amanda had ignored the previous two and didn't bother to let Brad know she had landed and was on her way, but to where?

The message was from Brad. Amanda looked at the blackness that surrounded her, her car a silent coffin. Her fingers drumming on the steering wheel, she had to decide: return to the airport and catch the next flight out to a place unknown, or drive the few blocks to the two-story blue house with white trim?

Driving across the empty stalls, diagonally, she aimed for the far exit, leading to a street one block away from her house. Brad's car, which he rarely used, gleamed under the streetlight as she passed it, turning into the driveway. She twisted the key in the ignition, and the car fell silent. She removed the key, placing her hand in her lap, not wanting to unfasten the security of the seatbelt and face the unknown.

The house was dark except for the living room. The television hues of blues and reds danced on the walls and reached Amanda through the window, muted by the sheer curtain drawn closed. She shivered, hot and cold at the same time. A shadow moved across the television glow. Brad.

Before she could gather her wits, the front door swung open and Brad stood at the top step, staring at her. Hesitantly, she unfastened the seatbelt, reached for the door handle, and when she looked up, Brad was right outside her door, arms folded across his chest.

Amanda pushed the door and stepped out. There were no hugs, kisses nor hellos.

"I… I…" she stuttered but didn't finish.

Brad said nothing.

She ran her fingers through her hair. The tangle of curls was too far gone to tame. Dropping her hand to her side, she pushed the door shut.

When she didn't make a move, Brad motioned to the car. "Do you need help with your stuff?"

Amanda shook her head. "I'll get it later."

"Let's get out of the cold." He turned and walked up the two steps in the dark.

He hadn't turned on the outside light; the motion sensor would take care of the lights. She took a step, then turned toward the car to retrieve her laptop. When she clicked the unlock on the key fob, Brad stood in the doorway. The light came on briefly and went out when he turned his back and walked into the house.

Amanda ducked into the passenger side and picked up the case. She hadn't figured out yet how to explain the absence of the luggage she left at the hotel; it was the least of her worries. There were much graver issues to deal with, far worse than lost or forgotten or left behind bags.

Once again, she locked the car and walked the few steps to the front door. Her movement triggered the motion sensor, and the lights flooded the space, illuminating the walkway to the short fence and beyond to the street. Amanda was on stage, wondering if she would be able to pull off another rehearsed performance.

Distracted, Amanda tripped on the doormat and grabbed the doorframe to steady herself, but when she did, she let go of the laptop. It crash-landed on her toe. "Damn. Damn. Damn." Her words shattered the silence of the night and brought Brad back to the hallway.

Straightening, she picked up the laptop case and slung it on her shoulder, this time careful when she took a step across, and then went into the house. Brad backed up, allowing her to pass. The railing was the closest, so that's where the computer bag landed, hanging off-kilter.

Afraid she wouldn't be able to get up from the steps because of sheer exhaustion, Amanda bent and pulled one short boot off, then the other, leaning with one hand on the wall for balance. She kicked at them with her bare feet. One boot landed upright and the other on its side by the hallway table. She didn't care.

"Want something to eat or drink? I saved a salad and pasta for you." Brad's monotone voice was anything but inviting.

"No, thanks. Not hungry." Amanda didn't mean to sound ungrateful, but his coldness wasn't helping her attitude.

She unwound her scarf and shrugged off her coat, tossing them on a chair by the stairs. As she left them behind and walked past the hall mirror, she had to backtrack. She looked worse than imagined. Her reflection screamed, "Get away from me."

As if Brad heard her thoughts, in the bright light of the kitchen where she finally made it, he looked her up and down, then up again, but didn't meet her eyes. His gaze rested just above Amanda's left temple, his words soft, yet biting. "You look terrible."

Amanda shrugged and winked. He didn't react. He was used to her tics. As he stared just beyond her, she moved the high stool enough to climb on it, awkwardly sitting sideways as if a guest in her own home. Without giving her bubbling words any thought, Amanda slammed her hand on the counter. "You know what? I'm tired. I don't want to talk."

With that, she hopped off the stool and made her way upstairs, all the while imagining Brad's expression: mouth agape, eyes rounded in surprise. His usual. He had to have mastered it while teaching. Perhaps it was effective with kids. Amanda wasn't one of them.

The shower on hot, blasting her aching muscles, she leaned against the wall and let the water take away her thoughts; they swirled with the soap down the drain, and she watched. When she felt a chill as the stream cooled, she twisted the handles shut and reached for her towel.

Her nightgown and robe hung limply on the back of the door. She grabbed it and slipped it on. Bunching her hair in a ponytail, she swiped at the steamed-up mirror and looked deep into the eyes that stared back at her. They were empty, void. *Good,* she thought, *I feel nothing.*

There was a part of her curious about what Brad had to say, but the other part rebelled in denial. Whatever it was, it would have to wait until the next day. Amanda still had to figure out what she wanted to do about work, but that, too, would have to wait. With that, she entered their bedroom for the first time since she left two days earlier. *Was it only two days?*

Regretting she didn't turn on the light in the bedroom, Amanda stumbled across the floor, dodging what felt like discarded clothes. Of course, Brad wouldn't have taken care of the laundry on his own. Her eyes quickly adjusted to the dark, and the glass of the lamp reflected a sliver of a moonbeam, enough for her to find the bed and flop down on it. She scooped the bedding to the side as she lifted her legs and slipped them under the covers. She closed her eyes and willed her brain to shut down.

Amanda didn't expect the mattress to shift, but it did with Brad's weight as he sat on his side about forty-five minutes later.

"Who are you, Amanda?" he asked through the darkness.

She sucked in her breath. Pretended to be asleep. Lay motionless.

"Who are you?" he whispered.

Chapter 13

August 12, 1996

Her plan to get rid of Ashley was simple. Except it didn't go according to the blueprint. After lying low for a few weeks, Amanda decided it was time. Ashley not only took Matt away from her; she relentlessly tormented Amanda. Everyone saw her as sweet and innocent; she was anything but.

Early on, when Amanda first arrived at this foster home, the kids didn't bother with her. She was just another misfit, reject, that no family wanted. Ashley was different. From day one, she noticed Amanda's tics and would wink at her when she stood close to Matt. Though they weren't allowed to touch or kiss, Ashley would rub Matt's arm, back, or smooth hair away from his face when Ms. Baker wasn't looking. And when she saw Amanda looking her direction, she'd shrug a shoulder, mimicking Amanda's tic. Maybe that was why Amanda became more interested in Matt and determined to rid them of Ashley.

The time was drawing near for Amanda to put her plan into action. The summer holiday wasn't free time. They had to wake up early, eat breakfast, and each had chores to complete. The Bakers arranged for outings to the park, the library, and such after the kids read and worked on math for at least an hour a day.

Sunday the twelfth was no exception, but unlike the rest of the week, the kids spent Sundays at home. The Bakers went to church, but didn't force the foster kids to go along. Amanda lounged in the room she shared with Ashley and waited for her to leave. At about eleven, she gathered her laundry and placed it in a basket. She left the room, winking and shrugging her shoulder at Amanda, who pretended to be engrossed in the book she was reading.

When she heard the last footfalls on the stairs and then the kitchen door open and close, Amanda thought of moving forward with her plan, but chickened out. She was still determined to have

Ashley kicked out of the home but looking for and destroying journals and personal belongings would only get Amanda kicked out, too. She'd bide her time and wait. It wouldn't be long before she had the opportunity; Ashley was good at breaking the rules when no one was looking.

It didn't take long for Ashley to return. She pushed the door open and glared at Amanda, who sat innocently on her bed reading and didn't meet Ashley's stare. Sneaking glances, she saw Ashley promptly go to her dresser drawers and open each one. Then, she looked in the closet and under the bed where she had stored some of her items in small boxes. At that moment, Amanda was glad she didn't touch Ashley's things. Still, Ashley kept up the search.

"Okay, pissy brat, where is it?"

Amanda winked and twitched. "What're you talking about?"

"You know damn well what I'm talking about. Where is it?" she hissed.

Amanda returned her gaze to the book that she wasn't reading. Suddenly, Ashley, with two long strides, crossed the room and yanked the book from Amanda's hand. Gritting her teeth, she spat, "I said, where is it?"

Cowering, Amanda raised her hands to protect herself from what she thought was coming, but Ashley ripped open Amanda's dresser, then the closet, and threw open the bed covers. Amanda curled in the corner, arms still raised high, protecting her face and head.

Somewhere from the house, she became aware of footsteps and laughter. The Bakers were back, but Ashley didn't seem to hear them through her anger. Amanda opened her mouth to scream.

One of Ashley's hand grabbed her hair and yanked while the other covered her open mouth. "Don't you fucking make a sound."

Amanda didn't.

"Ashley?" Matt called from the hallway.

With her hand still clasping Amanda's mouth, her eyes round and red with rage, she shot Amanda a look of warning. Amanda blinked and tried to nod. Ashley let go, composed herself, and sweetly said, "I'll be right out."

Amanda kicked as hard as she could, her foot landing squarely in Ashley's stomach. Ashley doubled over, but only for a moment, then she hauled off and slapped Amanda hard across the face. "You bitch! I'll get you."

"Ashley? We need to get going," Matt insisted.

Ashley straightened, clutching her stomach where Amanda's foot made contact. "Can you give me a minute?" she asked Matt.

"Sure, I'll wait for you on the porch. Andy will be here any second."

Slowly, Amanda sat up taller, defiant. She won. Her cheek stung, and tears pooled at the corners of her mouth. Pathetic. She whispered, "I'm gonna tell."

"What did you say?" Ashley once more approached, but the voices in the hallway halted her. She stuck her tongue out, winked and shrugged her shoulder before she left the room, slamming the door behind her.

Amanda sat for a while, staring at the floor, contemplating her next move. Whatever misgivings she had vanished with Ashley's venomous attack. Curious as to what Ashley thought Amanda had of hers, she stood and was about to rummage through Ashley's belongings when something purple peaked from under the decorative pillow on the bed. Before she walked the few steps, the door opened, and there was Ashley.

"What do you think you're doing?" she barked, eyeing Amanda, who stood dumbly in the middle of the room.

"Nothing," Amanda said, and threw back her shoulders, daring Ashley to do something while the door was open, and someone could pass by.

Amanda backed up and sat on her bed, hugging her knees tightly as she watched Ashley open the drawer and take out a pair of underwear and an outfit. Then, her eyes traveled to a red streak on Ashley's pants. *Good,* she thought. *She had her period and wasn't prepared. Huh, I bet Matt and Andy saw this… Hope she was embarrassed.*

Ashley took her items, and Amanda heard the water running in the bathroom. A few minutes later, she returned, paler than she had been. Ashley sat at the edge of her bed and rummaged for a small medicine container, popped the lid open, and swallowed two tablets whole.

Amanda backed into the corner of her bed.

"What're you looking at?"

"So, no sex tonight? Your period, huh?" Amanda dared for the words to escape. "Ms. Baker will be happy to know what you and Matt do behind her back."

Amanda wasn't as brave as she let on, so with these words, she bolted off the bed and ran out of the room and into the hallway. *She wouldn't dare touch me out here where she could be seen.*

From the hallway by the railing, Amanda watched Ashley jump off her bed, but soon, landed back down, holding her stomach with both hands. A few minutes later, she stood. She walked out of the room and got within a few inches from Amanda. "I'll kill you if you so much as breathe a word to anyone. I'm not playing."

Amanda shoved Ashely away from her. Ashley shoved back. One more hard push and Ashley doubled over as Amanda ran back to the bedroom. She closed the door and leaned against it, listening. As if time stood still and sped up all at once, she heard a thud and a scream.

She opened the door to find Matt screaming, and Andy stood frozen, staring at Ashley at the foot of the stairs. She looked lifeless. Amanda stared. Then chaos ensued, crying and shouting – an ambulance – and social services whisked Amanda away.

Chapter 14

May 4, 2018

Who am I? Brad had asked the winning question. *I'll tell you who I am. I am a victim of her fate, of her lies. But, a better question would be, why is he asking?*

It didn't take long for the answer to the second question to arrive. In the still of the night, her eyes slit. She watched Brad, who stood by the bed. Amanda felt his gaze boring into her, trying to read what was on the inside. With one swoop, he gathered his pillow and a throw from the back of the chair and walked toward the open door. She lay still, waiting for him to make his way to the living room, where she assumed, he would spend the night. This was the first time they'd ever slept apart when both were at home.

Her eyes fluttered open enough to watch him. At the doorway, he leaned against the door frame, head on his forearm for what seemed to be an eternity. Before walking out, he turned around one last time and whispered, "Did you kill someone? I feel like I no longer know you."

Amanda gasped and hoped it wasn't audible. Her heart carried its drumbeat into her ears. She couldn't hear what else he said if he said anything at all.

Sleep didn't come that night. After tossing and turning for hours, she got out of bed and tiptoed to the kitchen, passing the living room where Brad slept on the couch, just as she expected he would. Grabbing a glass and filling it from the fridge dispenser, Amanda headed for her office. At the landing, she turned around and looked through the darkness at Brad's sleeping form.

Talking herself out of the doubt creeping in, she twisted the handle to her office, flicked the light on, and quietly closed the door. In her chair, she cradled her head in her hands. There was no way anyone would have known what happened that day. There was no way, Amanda reasoned, that Ashley came to, especially after seeing her lifeless form at the bottom of the stairs. Besides, it would be Amanda's word against Ashley's.

Just then, a thought occurred to her. Was it possible Ashley didn't die? She shook that thought away, but as she physically shook her head, another thought crept in. "No!"

She sat straighter. Could Andy have been…? Was it possible this Andy was not Andy Baker but the other Andy?"

She booted her computer, clicked on the Internet browser, and typed Ashley Carr. The Internet gave her hundreds of results. It wasn't what she expected. Amanda narrowed her search to Ashley Carr 8/12/1996… nothing. Another attempt using obituaries for that month and year. Nothing.

Her hands were sweaty; she dried them on her nightgown. Her mouth was parched, and she reached for the glass of water, but it almost slipped from her hand. Amanda rubbed her hand on her nightgown and took a sip, all the while, her other hand scrolled down pages and pages of Internet results. Once again, nothing.

Social media was next, but tons of Ashley Carrs popped up there, too. One by one, Amanda clicked on each and read the bio on the ones closest to the age she thought her to be.

Amanda moved between social media sites and didn't land on any that may have been her target. What if she were still alive? If Ashley must not have said anything – they would've come after Amanda years ago. But then, the other reality reared. The one she most dreaded, but she was sure, there was no way, no way, anyone would've known about it. Her fingers rapidly typed, Andrew Bairn death 1994, and her heart stopped.

An article dated 5/31/1994 read, "A hiker who wishes to remain anonymous found an abandoned car with someone who appeared to be sleeping. When the hiker looked closer through the driver's window, it was apparent to him the man was dead. He promptly retraced his steps, found a payphone, and called 911.

"'…had been dead for a few days,' said an officer on the scene. 'Cause of death to be determined by an autopsy.'"

Amanda's fingers flew over the keyboard as she looked for a follow-up article but found none. She accessed the coroner's site, but there was no further update as the case was too old and before law enforcement made them available online.

She leaned back in her chair and swiveled from side to side, then propped her feet on the edge of the desk, considering the possibilities. Wouldn't the police have contacted her by now, or her grandmother when he was found? Where was her father?

Something fluttered in her peripheral. Amanda turned her head to find the source. A corner of paper stuck out from the filing cabinet. She was sure she didn't leave it that way. She was meticulous. She wouldn't have left anything out of order; she always needed to control her environment and maintain order.

Slowly, she lowered her bare feet to the carpet and opened the drawer. She was puzzled because she had not needed nor pulled anything out of that particular file – doubt and dread flooded her. Had Brad been looking through her stuff?

Her eyes darted across the room in search of anything amiss. The closet door was a fraction of an inch ajar. Panicked, Amanda dashed across the room and got on her hands and knees, wrestling with the papers and magazines in the end table, under the lamp, but she didn't see her box. She pulled everything out and tossed it next to her. Relief flooded her when her hands grabbed the box. She turned it over and from side to side and checked the lock. It was still secure. Amanda clutched it to her chest, protectively.

When she realized the possibility Brad may have invaded her private space and gone through her things, she leaned into the tiny cabinet and fumbled in the back upper corner. A loud sigh escaped her lips when her fingers touched the tape and outline of the key. There was no way he looked in her box of secrets. Amanda returned the box to its hiding spot and buried it within the magazines and papers.

87

The closet still bothered her. Amanda leaned on one knee to pull herself to standing and rounded the table and chair, sliding the closet door open. Nothing was amiss. The boxes were stacked as she had left them, but still, she wanted to be sure.

She walked back to the office door and locked it, then returned to the stack of boxes. One by one, she moved them out of the way. She reached underneath the last one in the corner, pulled the carpet back, and peered under the flap. Her other box of treasures lay undisturbed where she had left it. Carefully, she pulled it out and popped open the lid.

Her fingers stroked the memory book. It'd been a while since she looked inside. Gingerly, she opened the cover and read the first page written so long ago:

6-2-1992

Today, it was hot. Auntie and I worked in the vegetable garden. Auntie is so patient. She showed me how to pull the carrots from the ground. They were huge and orange!!!

She flipped forward to a day in 1994, but she quickly slammed the journal closed — no time for traveling back in time. The past was moving forward too quickly to meet her present and decide her future.

It took only a few minutes to return things to order and go back to her desk.

Not finding anything online bugged her. Amanda returned to her Internet sites, obsessed with finding an article, a memorial, anything, no matter how minute. Hours passed, she found nothing.

Her eyes gritty, her head pounding, morning would soon be approaching and with it, Brad's questions. She trekked to her bedroom, glancing at her husband's form on the couch as she crossed the landing.

Chapter 15

August 1996

"Who are you?" Matt hissed as Amanda passed him, standing outside while the paramedics hovered over Ashley's still form —and Andy's drawn face peering at the scene.

She shrugged and turned her head so he wouldn't see the wink. She stared ahead and took another step forward. The social worker asked Amanda to wait in the car while she took care of something with the Bakers. Amanda took another hesitant step forward but almost tumbled when a rough grasp jerked her backward.

"Who are you?" This time, a growl.

Amanda thought Matt was going to hit her. She raised her hand to block the smack that was coming, but it didn't. Instead, a maniacal roar of laughter. "You bitch!"

She heard his deep inhale, then, "You'd better be looking over your shoulder. You're gonna pay for this."

Matt's feet pounded the ground hard, running up the stairs to the house. Mesmerized, Amanda stared after him. "You are wrong. I didn't do anything," she whispered.

Andy was in the doorway, glowering at her. He hesitated, clenching and unclenching his fists, slowly turning to face Amanda, and spat. He walked in and slammed the door shut. Amanda made her way to the car, shrunk in the seat, just as she used to in the closet when Mama was not her mama and cried until murmurs accompanied by approaching footsteps, dragged her to the present.

Ms. Skeep, the social worker, got in the car, fastened her seatbelt, and lowered her window. "I'll be in touch, Ms. Baker."

Mr. Baker waved and retreated. Abruptly, she turned around. "Ms. Skeep, wait."

"Yes?"

Mrs. Baker came to Amanda's side of the car, rolling her finger in a circular motion. Amanda obediently lowered her window halfway, turned her head toward Mrs. Baker, let her curls cover her face, and waited.

"Take care of yourself." Mrs. Baker didn't wait for a response. None was coming.

Ms. Baker wrapped her arms protectively around herself. With her head down, she turned and walked up the path toward the house. That was the last time Amanda saw her.

The social worker put the car in reverse, backed up, then pulled into the street. Amanda wanted to ask where she was taking her, but what difference would it have made? Another foster home. It wouldn't be her mom or her dad.

There were times Amanda wondered why they didn't return her to Auntie Emma. She asked one of her workers one time, but all he said was, "I don't know. Is she related to you?"

"No. I lived with her for five years. Why can't I go back to her home?"

"Let me look in your file. I'll let you know."

He didn't. Another worker took over the case, and by then, it didn't matter. No one wanted her, and Amanda learned to live with that reality.

They arrived at the new foster home forty-five minutes later. Ms. Ellie, the new foster mom, had a deep and kind voice. She showed Amanda to her room she shared with two other girls. She showed her the dresser she could use and pointed to one of the girls. "Look after her. I'll be back in a bit."

The taller girl, Michelle, crossed the room and took Amanda's one small suitcase. Without a word, she opened it, hung the blouses, and refolded the pants and underwear. "Here, you put these away, and I'll hang up the rest."

Dumbfounded, Amanda nodded, although her instinct was to grab her clothes from Michelle's hands and tell her off. Amanda didn't and did as she was told, looking over her shoulder every few seconds. Ashley visited her nerves, making her anxious.

When the task was done, Michelle grabbed the other girl's hand. "Her name is Becky. She's shy." Then, she gestured toward Amanda. "What's your name?"

"Amanda."

Silence.

Amanda knew the questions would come later. "Why are you here?" "Where's your mom?" – Funny, they never asked about her dad. Amanda stood in the middle of the room, and the two girls held hands on one of the beds and stared at her.

"Which…" Amanda motioned vaguely.

"Oh, this is your bed," Michelle said, pointing to one of the beds.

Amanda kicked her sandals off and instantly regretted it. The carpet in the middle of the room was rough and scratched her soles. The two girls giggled at her reaction. She glanced at their feet. They were not bare. Amanda's feet found their way back in the comfort of her worn-out sandals, and she moved toward the bed.

Hers was the closest to the door. Each bed was against one of the walls. The fourth wall had a built-in closet, and nothing obstructed it. Amanda sat at the edge and looked at her feet, letting enough time pass for her tics to do their thing and hoping the two girls didn't notice. Notice, they did. Their gaze never left her from the minute she stepped foot in the room. What was weird, neither said anything and neither laughed, but Amanda saw the curiosity and questions in their eyes and ignored it.

Half an hour later, Ms. Ellie returned. "Are you settled in? Need anything?"

Amanda wasn't sure how to tell Ms. Ellie she forgot her toothbrush and personal items. They were left in the Baker's bathroom on the side of the long counter by the sink.

Michelle spoke up. "Ms. Ellie, we put everything away. Amanda's suitcase is in the closet with ours." After a moment of hesitation, "Ms. Ellie"—she sheepishly looked at Amanda— "I didn't see no brush, no nothing."

Amanda cringed and let her curls cover her face.

"No worries. I think we have extras," Ms. Ellie said. "Now, go wash up and get ready for supper. Becky, you set the table. Michelle put the rolls in the oven. Amanda, you do the dishes after supper."

She finally looked up to watch Ms. Ellie's slim, tall figure, weave its way out of the room. Ms. Ellie stopped and held the doorframe with one hand turning her face to look at Amanda. "Ms. Skeep will be by later when the police get here."

Ms. Ellie didn't see the dread in Amanda's eyes when she turned and left the room. The two girls looked at Amanda questioningly, as though to ask, "What have you done? Why does the police want to talk to you?"

Amanda rose from her bed and left the room, the two girls at her heels, whispering. She turned once, but they didn't see her. Their heads bent into each other.

"What?" Amanda snapped.

Neither responded and by that time, they were in the kitchen where Ms. Ellie had busied herself with flipping burgers and frying potatoes.

Amanda stood in the doorway, and the two girls skirted her and went straight to their chores. Without missing a beat, Ms. Ellie said, "Don't just stand there. Make yourself useful."

It was neither command nor was it said meanly, but Amanda's insides iced up.

"On second thought, Becky, show Amanda where the extra hygiene items are. Make sure she gets everything she needs." Turning to Amanda, she asked, "Do you have a towel?"

Amanda shook her head, and her tics made their attack. Ms. Ellie's hand holding the peeler hovered a few inches above the potato she held in her other hand, and her mouth hung open. The tics became worse, and Amanda ran out of the kitchen, hearing the peeler clatter to the countertop, followed by a thud that had to have been the potato.

She reached the bathroom and locked herself in. Not only did she leave her toothbrush, but she also left behind her medication. Amanda slid to the floor and wrapped her arms around her knees.

The banging on the door was relentless.

"Amanda, I know you're in there. Open up," came her mother's crazed voice.

She curled into a tighter ball, her hair creating a veil of curls so no one could see her.

"Amanda, please open the door. I have a key but would much rather have you open it."

It wasn't her mother. It didn't sound like her. Her eye twitched so much she couldn't see. Even when Amanda tightened her grip on her legs, the jerking didn't stop.

"Amanda, I'm coming in."

The keys jingled, and Amanda scooted between the tub and the toilet. She heard the door open, hinges creaking, and dared a look between the strands.

Ms. Ellie's feet, clad in black sneakers with fluorescent lime-green stripes, came closer. Amanda shrunk farther away from her, fearful. But the feet didn't get to her. Ms. Ellie closed the lid to the commode and lowered herself on it.

"What's wrong with you, child?" she asked.

Amanda didn't respond. She couldn't.

"What's all that jerking and twitching about? Your social worker said nothing about you having issues. You nervous about something? Is it about what happened before you got here?"

Amanda trembled. *I have issues? What did Ms. Ellie know about what happened?*

"Well, she'll be here in a bit. We'll get to the bottom of this."

Bottom of what? Her head reeled.

"Come on now; everyone's waiting on supper. Wash up and get to the kitchen," her command was firm but gentle.

She stood to leave, then said as if she remembered something, "Before you leave, look in the cabinet by the shower. All the stuff you need will be in there. Take only what you need. Others…" Without finishing, Amanda watched the lime-trimmed sneakers walk to the door.

"Now, get up and do as you're told."

Amanda waited until Ms. Ellie left. The twitching was less, and she hoped she wouldn't have any more for a while. Her face blotchy from crying, curls wild, she stood and looked around. She was alone. The door was closed; she hadn't heard Ms. Ellie shut it.

After scrubbing at her face and raking her fingers through her hair, Amanda opened the doors to the supply cabinet. She picked a green toothbrush and looked through the assortment of combs and brushes. None would work on her hair. Farther toward the back of the next shelf, she found one that would work, then looked through the rest of the items and picked what she needed, set them on the counter next to the others' belongings, and left for the kitchen.

All eyes were on her when she entered, but no one said a word. Ms. Ellie served supper, and they ate in silence. Amanda wondered where Ms. Ellie's husband was. She figured she would find out eventually.

After they finished the meal, Becky, Michelle, and Ms. Ellie cleared the table and stacked the dishes by the sink.

"Just rinse them and put them in the dishwasher. The only thing you need to wash by hand, are these." She pointed to two pans on the stove.

While Amanda attended to the dishes, Ms. Ellie wiped the table and the stove and brought the two pans to the sink. Amanda heard the television and laughter from the family room and imagined Michelle and Becky curled up on the couch, watching a comedy show.

Before she got to the two pans, the doorbell rang, and Amanda stiffened. Ms. Ellie walked out of the kitchen. It had to be the police. She grabbed one pan and scrubbed it hard, working through her anxiety. In the hallway, Amanda heard Ms. Skeep's voice and two others she didn't recognize.

Must be the police. She scrubbed harder.

"Amanda," Ms. Ellie called out.

Amanda ignored her, pretending not to hear.

Ms. Ellie's voice got closer. "Amanda, set the pans aside and come into my office."

"Your office?"

Ms. Ellie must've realized Amanda had no idea where that was. She motioned for Amanda to dry her hands and follow her. Amanda did.

When they entered the office, Ms. Skeep was by the window, and two officers sat in the wingback chairs. Amanda clasped her hands and stood by the desk.

"I'm Officer Brown, and this is Officer Mattice. We'd like to talk to you about what happened this evening."

Amanda stared at both officers, defiant.

"Have a seat, Amanda. This shouldn't take long," Officer Brown instructed, then looked at Ms. Ellie, who stood in the doorway. "If you'd excuse us, please."

Ms. Ellie backed out of the room, and Ms. Skeep walked across the room to close the door. On her way back, she guided Amanda to a sofa opposite the officers. She sat motionless until her eye twitched, and her shoulder made a wave of shrugs. Ms. Skeep looked at Amanda. "Did you take your medication?"

Amanda shook her head.

"Why not?"

"I—"

Ms. Skeep interrupted, "Darn, I knew we forgot something. I'll go back to the Baker's when we're done and get them for you.

Amanda shrugged. Partly Tourette's and partly, well, her.

The officers exchanged a look, but neither said anything in response to the conversation.

"So, Amanda, tell us what happened tonight." This time, it was Officer Mattice who spoke.

It wasn't hard; the lie readily arrived at her lips. "I don't know. I was in my room reading when I heard a scream. I went to the landing and saw Ashley lying at the bottom of the stairs."

Amanda sat straighter and ignored the twitching.

Chapter 16

May 5th, 2018

Brad heard Amanda walking around upstairs and kept his eyes shut. He was torn. How could he doubt his wife, the woman he loved? What if the letter was a hoax and she was innocent?

When the bedroom door closed, he rolled on his back and stared at the ceiling. If she was guilty of anything… of killing someone, wouldn't she be in jail? Had she served a sentence and was released?

He felt foolish and wished he didn't destroy the letter. He should've saved it and confronted her with it. Most probably, he thought, she had a good explanation, or perhaps this was nothing but a hoax. Was he willing to destroy his marriage on suspicion?

"No," he whispered into the cover.

But, there was that niggling feeling eating away at him — first, Andy's call, then the letter. Deep in his gut, he didn't believe it to be a coincidence. There had to be something Amanda was hiding from him. She never lied to him, not outright, but wasn't withholding information about her past the same as lying?

Brad pressed his palms against the sides of his head, willing the thoughts to disappear, to recede into the crevices of oblivion. He shut his eyes tight, but just as quickly opened them, watching the dawn dance on the ceiling and around the room. The sheer curtains were no match for the morning sun that would soon stream through the window. He rolled over and knew sleep wasn't an option. He reached for his cell phone to check the time. 4:38 am.

The dawn crept over the mountains and spilled into the living room, and the house grew more silent. He waited for what seemed like an eternity, but there was no longer movement upstairs and no footfalls on the steps. He sat, folded the throw he had covered himself with, and set it on the arm of the couch. Now what? Wait for Amanda to come down so he could have it out with her, or slip out to the gym? He didn't want to sit and wait. But he was the one who insisted on talking, he reasoned.

Brad had to hold her accountable. It was too late to pretend the call didn't bother him and the letter didn't arrive. He knew if he didn't deal with it, it would gnaw on his insides.

Within what appeared to be an instant, the sun flooded the room. He stretched to release the kinks from his back that had settled in from lying on the couch and from later sitting for two hours hunched over his phone, absently flipping from site to site. He had already checked Amanda's Facebook page, her friends list on there, and Googled her name. His doubt led him to second guess who she was. Even her maiden name became a doubtful issue.

During these hours, he reflected on what he knew about her. He recalled she had told him she lived in foster care for most of her life, and her mother was ill. When Brad had asked her about her father, she shrugged and didn't offer any information. He remembered asking her questions about her life, her family, where she lived, but now, twelve years later, he realized, she never told him. Why did he not pursue answers?

In twelve years, she had not once asked him to visit her mother, even on holidays when he had suggested it. He didn't even know what the illness was nor where Ellen lived. No, Ivy? Brad scratched his chin. What was her name?

Pacing the living room, thinking, he flipped through their wedding album, slammed it shut, and raked his fingers through his hair. It bugged him. What was Amanda's mother's name? Why couldn't he remember? Then he decided, what difference did it make? He wouldn't know where to find her anyway.

Brad absently circled the room, then abruptly stopped and stared up. Would he dare chance going in Amanda's office to rummage some more? He took tentative steps toward the stairs, put one foot on the first step, then a movement, a faint sound from their bedroom had him retreat to the living room where he straightened the pillows, refolded the blanket, and left for the kitchen to make coffee.

He filled the water container, popped in a pod, and waited for the brew light. The school papers he started reading and correcting remained untouched on one of the far counters where he left them the day before. He could tackle them while he waited for Amanda to wake up, but he wasn't sure he could concentrate.

The stubble on his jaw itched. He needed a shower and a shave, but that had to wait. His clothes were in the bedroom. He didn't want to go in there, not yet. Brad felt like a stranger in his own home. He had to bring this charade to an end. Whatever Amanda was hiding, she had to tell him. She had to answer his questions. He needed to know who he married. Skirting this was not something he could live with.

Coffee in hand, he sat to read the essay on top. He had to read it again, but still couldn't focus on the words. He looked at his phone. 7:06 am. Brad took a sip of his coffee, eyes gritty from lack of sleep, nerves jangled.

He flipped through his messages. If Amanda's lack of response to his texts the night before didn't bother him then, it rattled him now. Then, the doubt flipped to the other side. Had he misjudged her and jumped to the wrong conclusion? What if he was wrong, and she didn't respond because of his attitude. "Wake up already and get down here!" his mind screamed. *Maybe I'm wrong. Maybe, I should wait until I hear what she has to say.*

The discarded, torn, and smeared letter had him teeter-totter emotionally on the brink of falling and shattering to pieces.

Chapter 17

May 5th, 2018

The sun was out, but the room lay in shadows, the blinds obliterating most of the light. If Amanda slept, it was a few minutes at a time. She glanced at the phone. 7:32 am.

She had two things to deal with: her job and Brad. How much longer would she be able to put this off? She rehearsed her story throughout the night and was confident she could field any question Brad threw her direction.

"Who's Andy?" he would ask.

Simple. Amanda would tell him the truth. The older son of one of the foster parents. Of course, it wouldn't be the entire truth she would tell because she had already woven the story for why he called so many years later.

Next question? This would be tricky to answer. "Did you really kill anyone?" or "Who did you kill?"

Amanda thought long and hard about this one. She had been thinking of the answer for over twenty years. *You've got this, Amanda,* her inner voice reassured her.

The pill container by her side of the bed rolled off the nightstand as Amanda turned, knocking it down with her hip. Perhaps a reminder to take her medication. Her head spun when she bent to pick up the bottle. She hadn't eaten since… when? Clutching the edge of the bed, she retrieved the pills and swallowed two, dry, before she left the bedroom to face the day.

On her way out, she changed her mind and reversed direction toward the bathroom. She showered and changed out of her nightgown, bunching her hair in a loose ponytail; her appearance was the least of her worries. Amanda tossed her dirty clothes on top of the already full hamper, and scooped up the loose items, shoving them in with the rest. Laundry wasn't at the top of her list, either.

With trepidation, she opened the door, wondering if Brad was waiting for her downstairs or if he'd gone to the gym. She hoped he was working out as she descended the stairs one step at a time, slowly. In the hallway, Amanda wrapped her arms around her waist, took a deep breath, and entered the kitchen. Brad's stare was already focused on her entrance; he had to have heard her footsteps.

She averted her eyes, but then determinedly, lifted them to his in defiance.

"Coffee?" he asked.

"That's okay. I'll make my own."

"Suit yourself," he said, but Amanda saw regret and guilt in his eyes.

This gave her the boost of confidence she needed. "So, what do you want to talk about?" she asked, her back turned to him, busying her hands with the coffee maker.

"I'll wait till you finish and sit down."

"I can listen and make coffee at the same time." She couldn't suppress the snarkiness.

In her periphery, Amanda detected a movement. Brad was looking up at the ceiling, summoning patience. He did that when exasperated, probably a teacher thing.

"Have it your way. Who's Andy?"

Amanda laughed aloud, her attempt at deflection. "You're not jealous, are you?"

"Who's Andy?" he repeated solemnly.

"Well, if you must know, he was the eldest son of one of my foster parents—"

"That was a long time ago, I'm sure. Why is he calling now?"

Well, Brad, you're not the only one who wants an answer to this question. Though, which Andy was it? Aloud and without skipping a beat, she said, "He wanted to tell me his dad passed away."

"Oh," was the only word Brad uttered.

Amanda couldn't read whether there was doubt behind it or if he believed her. She had no idea what the phone call was about but continued her bluff. "So, is that the important stuff you wanted to talk about?" she pushed.

She was sure Brad didn't know she heard his questions in the dark. She turned away from the sink and carried her freshly brewed cup to the counter and sat opposite Brad, who stared at the rising steam from her cup, absently rotating his cup round and round, catching the handle in his left hand and then his right.

"Okay, maybe…" he didn't finish his thought.

"Maybe what?" Amanda nudged him to a fight. She no longer cared. She wanted this nightmare to end.

Reflecting on the empty cup he rotated, he said, "There's one more thing. No, there's more than one thing."

He looked up, and she met his gaze, waiting for the question to assault her.

"Who are you, Amanda? I mean, who are you? I know nothing about your history, family, background. Nothing. Why is that?"

"I told you, I grew up in foster care—"

"Yeah. You also said your mother is ill. You realize, we've been married twelve years, and I don't even know her name or where she's at?"

Amanda bit her lower lip to stop the trembling. "I told you, she's ill." Sucking in a breath and letting it out, she continued. "Why, all of a sudden, do you want to know about my mother?" She got up and walked to the sink, dumped the coffee, and watched it swirl into the drain.

"Well, I told you everything about my family. I thought—"

"You thought wrong. I never asked you about yours. Why can't you respect I don't want to talk about mine?"

Amanda watched him shake his head. He wasn't about to let go of the subject. She waited for him to approach it from a different angle.

Sure enough, after he cleared his throat, he said, "You're right. I didn't ask because I didn't want to push you, but don't you think we've been married long enough to talk about our families openly? You see, it's called trust. How can we continue to share a life when it's built on secrets?"

She looked out the window at the patch of lawn they called a yard. A bird fluttered in the birdbath water, and droplets glistened in the morning sun. Amanda wished to share its freedom, unburdened by the past or the present.

Amanda rinsed the cup and placed it in the dishwasher, all the while wondering why he didn't ask the question she anticipated – the question he asked in the dark.

She pushed off the sink and crossed her arms. She turned around to face him, leaning her back at the edge, feeling the water seep into her blouse, but not caring. "You will never understand," she said, eyes downcast.

"Try me."

She shook her head.

"What do you want from this marriage?"

The question took Amanda by surprise. She looked up. "What do you mean?"

"Honestly, Amanda, this is no marriage. You're gone most of the time, and when you're home… well—"

"Wait a minute. You knew what my job was like before you married me. Don't you dare bring it up now." Her voice raised a few decibels, indignant as if she had the right to be, but she was on a roll.

Just then, as if on cue, her phone vibrated with an incoming text. Amanda flicked the screen and pressed her thumb to unlock it. The message was from an unknown number. She debated whether to read it or ignore it.

Brad's voice interrupted her thoughts. "I don't want to throw our marriage away, but I can't go on like this. Maybe, if we can sit down and talk, we can work through whatever it is that's happened or is going on. What do you say?"

Well, if all Brad wanted to talk about was her family, it sure would beat having him revisit last night's question. "Okay, but—"

"I'll fix us breakfast, and then we can go out for a walk and talk. Deal?"

Her stomach rumbled in agreement. "I'm going up to my office. Call me when it's ready?"

"Yeah. Sure."

Amanda walked out to her car to retrieve her purse. Her laptop was where she left it hanging the night before. Unlocking the car, she reached for her bag in the footwell on the passenger side. Amanda figured she had enough time to make it upstairs before Brad realized there was no luggage. She slung the strap over her shoulder and closed the car door.

As she walked back to the house, she rummaged in her purse for her business phone, knowing there would be a ton of messages waiting for her. Not paying attention to where she was going, she stubbed her toe against a short rise in the middle of the walkway leading to the front steps. Before her favorite word escaped her lips, something drew her attention away from the pain. She hobbled forward and neared the entrance. A blue-colored paper peeked from beneath the doormat.

Her heart hammered, and her vision blurred. Amanda steadied herself and bent to pull it out. It was an unsealed envelope with no name. *The blue envelope. Andy.*

With shaky hands, she opened the flap and extracted the paper. Amanda unfolded it and stared at the bold letters. "MURDERER!"

Realizing Brad could've found it, she fumbled to put the letter back in the envelope, but it fell from her hands. Once again, Amanda bent to pick it up, and when she straightened, Brad stood in the hallway by the kitchen with a spatula in his hand. Her mouth fell open, "I... I..." but the words didn't arrive.

"Breakfast is ready," was all he said and returned to the kitchen, leaving her standing, isolated on the island that said, "Welcome," but Amanda knew she wasn't.

She tucked the envelope in her purse and walked to the stairs hiding her bag under the laptop. How long was Brad standing there? What did he see?

Chapter 18

January 1997

The officers appeared one more time at Ms. Ellie's, and the interview, just like the one before it, saw a performance by Amanda worth an award. They played good cop, bad cop, threatened, promised, and tried several tactics. Amanda stuck to her story – confident no one saw what happened. Amanda plowed forward with her rehearsed speech.

When there was a lull in the conversation, she asked, "Is Ashley okay?"

"We cannot discuss her case with you," both Ms. Skeep and the officer told her.

Mustering tears, she pleaded. "But she looked so bad…"

After a while, there was nothing more to do, and they had to leave her be. She was then sure no one had seen the incident; no witnesses to her crime. If Ashley lived, it would be her word against Amanda's. In her mind, this was over. She would tuck it away in the same box of memories as her dad's.

No one spoke, and Amanda didn't get an answer. Though it bugged her, she had to let it go as she followed the adults out of the room.

Ms. Ellie let the officers out, closing the door behind them. She motioned for Ms. Skeep to stay. "Do you mind? I need to speak with you."

"Sure. I have a few minutes," Ms. Skeep said as she followed Ms. Ellie back to the office and closed the door.

Amanda tiptoed and put her ear to the door, but the wood was too thick for her to hear the conversation. Only muffled sounds reached her. She retreated to her room, the wheels in her brain turning, and the thoughts slamming into each other. But, she silenced them as she'd done before.

September 3rd was her first year in high school, a ninth grader. There, she blended with the crowds; the high school was too big for anyone to stand out. Amanda kept to herself, and the only person who interfered in her life was Ms. Coops, her counselor. Amanda didn't want such scrutiny and resented the intrusion.

She didn't altogether let go of the need to find out what happened to Ashley but had no connection to anyone who knew her. What she didn't know, and wouldn't know yet, was that Social Services moved Michelle to a home in the Bakers' area, to the high school near their home.

One day, determined to find out whether Ashley had survived, she ditched school and rode the bus across town to where Ashley's school was. She concocted a story to gain access to the school but knew better; there was no way they would let a teenager on campus who didn't attend the school.

She waited across the street. At 11:47 am, the bell rang, and students filed out, some leaving campus for lunch. Amanda scanned the crowd for Ashley or someone she knew. All were strangers. She followed a small group at a distance and hid behind a tree outside a fast-food restaurant.

The group left the shop with their bags of food. Amanda's stomach rumbled. She ignored it. As they passed by where she was, she followed them. None noticed. All were too engrossed in their conversation while taking bites from their sandwiches. At the gate, she looked around her. No adults. Amanda followed the group inside. No one questioned her presence.

When lunch was over and the students disbursed to their classrooms, one security guard and two other adults stood at the top step of the administration building, monitoring the kids. One noticed her. "Young lady, get to class."

Realizing he was addressing her, Amanda waited until he looked the other way, took off running out of the gate, and leaned against the block wall.

Not only didn't the trip net nothing, but that evening, she was also punished by Ms. Ellie for ditching. "You know the rules," Ms. Ellie admonished. "Why would you break them?"

Amanda had no response. At least none she would say aloud. She accepted her punishment and used the isolation time to rethink what she needed to do. Being relegated to her room while others watched television or engaged in their favorite activity was no punishment for her. She rarely joined their activities anyway and relished her time alone.

She decided she would give visiting the school another try, but in the end, Amanda didn't go through with it. It was too much of a risk to be seen anywhere near Ashley's school, especially because Matt attended the same one

Time had gone by, and when no one came for her, Amanda believed the incident was behind her and she had nothing to worry about. Neither Ms. Ellie nor Ms. Skeep brought it up after the last visit from the police, though her foster mom did try in a roundabout way to find out what had happened. "Done with the police?" she once asked.

Amanda shrugged.

"You let me know if you want to talk about it."

This, too, earned a shrug.

"I'd just have to trust that none of what happened is going to trouble us now, I guess, right?"

Amanda continued her silence and looked out of the kitchen window where she and Ms. Ellie were setting the table for dinner. That was the last time the subject came up.

Chapter 19

May 5th, 2018

Brad had his back to Amanda when she entered the kitchen, steam rising from two plates on the counter. The frying pan sizzled when the cold water hit it. She watched him add a few drops of soap, stir it, then returned it to the stove to soak. Slowly, he turned around and crossed the tiled floor.

He pulled himself up on the barstool; he didn't have to lift far. Brad was at least foot taller than Amanda. She stepped on the footrest and hoisted herself up onto the stool next to him. After a moment, Amanda picked up her fork and waited for him to reach for his before she began to eat. Though hungry, she was in no hurry to start. She wasn't sure she could swallow. Her nerves were a tangled mess, and the butterflies fluttering in her stomach had no intention of settling down.

Silently, they picked at their food.

Twenty minutes later, pointing with his fork, he said, "I thought you liked your eggs over easy."

"I do. Thank you."

"Look, you don't have to eat it. I don't know what's going on, but I don't think a walk is going to fix it. If you have something to tell me, just do it now, and let's be done with it."

He must've realized he was tapping the air with his fork as he spoke because he put it down. It slipped off the edge of the plate to the granite countertop with a ping.

Amanda lifted her gaze to meet his. "Okay, you want to know? I'll tell you," she said as she set her fork on the plate with a clatter.

Brad stared at her. Amanda could see in his eyes that he was conflicted. Throughout their years together, he wasn't one to deal with discourse well, nor with emotions. He could not compartmentalize. She was sure, in the end, he would walk out of their marriage if he knew the truth.

"What do you want to know?" she asked

"Everything."

"That's not possible…" she said, then quickly added, "in one sitting."

"Then, start with who's Andy?"

"I already told you who he is."

"Look, if you're going to play games, forget it." Brad rose to leave, gathering plates and cups.

"Okay. Okay." Amanda had no choice. She repeated what she'd said about Andy, the eldest son of foster parents… his dad died…

Brad raised an eyebrow. "Really. I don't know what happened to you and why you feel it is necessary to play games. I'm going to say one last time, either you tell me what happened in your past, who's Ashley, why someone would say you kill—"

"I said, okay!" Amanda interrupted him, slamming her palm on the counter. Suddenly, her mouth fell open, and her eyes widened. "What did you just say?"

Brad set the dishes in the sink and returned to his seat. "I tore it up."

"You tore what up?"

"A letter came, and I opened it…"

When Brad didn't finish his sentence, Amanda asked, "A letter from who? To who? You?"

Sheepishly, Brad looked away.

"I asked you a question!"

"The letter was addressed to you. I didn't see any harm in opening it."

"Who was it from? What did it say?" Amanda spat the words at him.

"There was no return address. It only had one word… 'Murderer.'" Brad choked as he said the last word. "What does that mean, Amanda?" He was almost in tears.

Amanda took a deep breath and told Brad the truth, her version of the truth. All the truth except the part where she struggled with Ashley before the fall. But, she didn't tell him about the other Andy.

Brad shook his head.

"That's it. That's what happened. I'm here, aren't I? I was never arrested."

"I don't get it, Amanda. If that was all there is to it, why didn't you tell me before now?"

"I didn't think it was important," Amanda huffed. "A long time ago. I was only fourteen."

Brad paced before returning to his seat. Leaning over the counter that separated them, he said, "Okay. Let's set Ashley and Andy aside." After a momentary hesitation, he added, "For now."

"For now?" she asked with indignation. "No. If there's anything else, spit it out."

Brad's eyebrows lifted, and his eyes widened, clearly taken aback by Amanda's attitude.

Not wanting to create more doubt in his mind, she said, "Look, if there's anything else we need to talk about, let's be done with it now. I told you who Andy was and what happened with Ashley. Well, at least what I think happened. I haven't heard from them until now and am just as confused as you are as to why he'd contact me."

"How do I know you're telling the truth now? I want to believe you. Don't you think it odd you'd get a letter saying murderer? Maybe you should call Andy and see what he wants."

"I told you I called him. His father died."

Silence.

Sheepishly, Amanda lowered her gaze. "I lied. I didn't call him. I've only seen him three or four times, and that was a long time ago. So, no, and I don't know why he called or what he wants."

More silence as Brad shook his head.

"What I didn't lie about is what Ashley did to me. What I didn't lie about is I got tired of being attacked."

There was a fleeting hesitation, a softness in Brad's eyes.

Amanda took advantage of it and plowed ahead. "I told you, you wouldn't understand. You had your mom and dad, your sisters, aunts, and uncles. I had no one. I was shuffled from place to place like discarded and second-hand clothes."

That did it. Brad's flash of hesitation was what Amanda needed to gain his sympathy, and it must've worked. He rounded the counter and stood behind her, hands gently kneading her tense shoulders. She leaned into him, and no more was said.

Chapter 20

2004

November descended with a thud of snow and ice. Amanda stared mesmerized out of the fogged window of her apartment at the flurries. Grabbing the edge of her sleeve, she swiped at the glass for a better view, then wrapped her arms around her middle. She was alone. Truly alone.

It was her senior year in college, and the only person who may have celebrated her success so far died a week earlier. The funeral put together by Bee's friend was simple, no frills. A handful of friends from the nursing home sat solemnly, probably wondering if their send-off would be the same.

Right before her death, when Amanda visited her grandmother, Bee rambled on, incoherently mentioning names Amanda never heard of. She tried to prod her grandmother into clarity, but that didn't happen. At one point, Bee pointed to an object on a shelf. Amanda stood to retrieve it, thinking Bee wanted it, but as her hand touched the box, Bee went into hysterics, making Amanda retract her arm back to her side.

Margaret, Bee's friend, had gathered Bee's meager belongings, and after the service, handed the small trash bag to Amanda.

The ticking of the heater brought Amanda back to her room, and she turned to face the chair, which held her grandmother's items.

The colorful glass urn containing her ashes stood on the mantlepiece above the decorative fireplace. Amanda crossed the room and ran her fingertips over the curves, wondering what would happen to her remains once she died. She had no friends, and the only living relative was her sick mother. Her dad...? She wouldn't allow her mind to travel down that road for now. Instead, she walked to the bag and undid the twist tie, not sure what she would find in its dark depths.

One by one, Amanda pulled out the items; a blue-green cardigan, the only piece of clothing, was the first. Amanda scrunched it, sniffing the scent, an unfamiliar detergent, probably the commercial ones they used at the nursing home. She set it aside, opening the mouth of the bag wider to see inside better.

She flipped the floor lamp switch on and returned her attention to the contents. From what she could see, there were papers, what appeared to be a shoebox, and another object at the bottom. Amanda pulled out the papers and fanned them. Bills and letters. She set them aside; she'd read them later. The shoe box was next. Amanda moved the bag to the floor and sat on the chair. Someone had taped the lid. She ran her fingers beneath it to pry it up. Inside were photos and a handful of letters.

One by one, Amanda stared at the faces, then flipped them over for names and dates. She only recognized a few: her grandmother, her mother, and of course, herself when she was very young. None of the images were of her father. Setting the box aside, she got up and picked up the only album she possessed that contained her history in photos, which wasn't much. At the back, six empty pages waited for the new additions.

Amanda couldn't help but flip through the album, starting with the first page. None of the pictures from her grandmother were the same as what she had. She dismissed this, flipped to the rear of the book, and slipped in the new images. Once done, she returned to the bag, pulled out the rest of the letters, and added them to the stack she extracted, another project for later.

The last object was wrapped in a frayed towel. Amanda carefully pulled it out and removed the material. It was a beautifully carved wooden box. Amanda recognized it instantly; it was the box her grandmother pointed to when she last visited her at the *home*. She flipped it around, looking for the latch. On the fourth side, there was a small hole, and when she held it up to the light, it was a lock. Curious about its contents, she turned the box round and round, hoping for a key to be attached somewhere, but there was none. She looked in the bag in case it had fallen, but it wasn't there. She set it aside. It had to wait until the next day when she would take it to a locksmith, and if that didn't work, she would pry the lid open. So, Amanda placed it on the mantle.

She had homework to complete. Amanda could no longer be distracted by Bee's items. She grabbed her backpack and retrieved her textbooks and notes, moved the floor lamp closer to the couch, and got comfortable. No sooner had she opened to the chapter than her eyes traveled to the little box. What could be in it?

Her legs involuntarily moved to the kitchen, where she rummaged in a drawer and found a screwdriver she brought back to the other room. She carried the wooden box to the couch and sat cross-legged, cradling it in her lap. Not wanting to ruin the finish, she slowly inserted the tip of the screwdriver in the gap between the lid and the body, wiggling it, but the lid didn't budge. She tried again, and this time left a scratch. Not wanting to do more damage, she set the box aside, resigned to waiting until the next day.

Not far from her reach was the stack of mail and letters. She reached for a handful and opened the first, an invoice from the nursing home. Her eyes widened at the total amount. "Damn!" she said before reading the bottom of the invoice. "For your records – not a bill."

She had never seen medical bills before. Medicaid paid hers as she had no insurance nor income, and her mother's she'd never had to deal with. Amanda fingered the paper, her thoughts drifting to her grandmother, who was instrumental in getting her the help and medication she needed.

Her tics were there, but their presence no longer dominated her life. Now that she was at college and away from immature kids, she found the students to be more accepting of those with disabilities, though she segregated herself from that title for the most part. She wondered why her dad didn't want her to have medication. Was it his negligence, or did it go beyond that? Embarrassed to have a kid with a disability.

She blinked and grabbed her book, the need to complete the task, the importance of graduating and getting her degree propelling her to flip open the pages. Finishing college would be her ticket for a life away from her past, but she couldn't focus, the words dancing on the page. Digging through her grandmother's items opened a door Amanda had shut. It had been ten years – ten long years since she last saw her father. He wasn't supposed to leave her. She only meant to make him a little sick or sleepy – just enough to make him stay, but he left anyway. He, too, walked out on her and never looked back.

Amanda was sure if he were alive, there was no way for him to figure out what she'd done. She only put a few drops in his coffee, not enough to hurt or kill him. Maybe he didn't drink it. Otherwise, he wouldn't have been able to leave. Unless... he waited until he was on the road. "Oh, no!" escaped her lips.

What if he got sick while driving? What if he crashed? Hurt someone or killed them or himself? Wouldn't the police have come for me by now? She shuddered. Amanda would not allow herself to think about it anymore. All of this was in the past, and there, it would remain.

The next day, Amanda put the box in her backpack, determined to get it opened and find out its contents. After classes, she walked downtown to a locksmith store. The older man behind the counter looked up when the bell above the door jingled as she walked in. "Good afternoon, young lady. Can I help you?

After her tics subsided, triggered by nervousness, she pulled out the box and set it on the counter between them. "Can you open it?"

"Who does it belong to?" Bruce asked. Amanda figured this had to have been his name. There was no one else working in there, and the sign outside said, "Bruce's Lock and Key."

"My grandmother. This was with her things. She died and I... I..."

117

His bushy eyebrows raised questioningly when she looked up. She said, "You can check it out. She died at the *home*. Her name is Bee—"

"Never mind," he interrupted. "So, why don't you have the key? Do you know what's in it?"

"Da…" Catching herself, she said, "No, I don't. That's why I brought it here. I don't want to damage it with a screwdriver."

Bruce's fingers were busy. "Looks like it's too late for that," he said, pointing at the scratches and shaking his head.

Amanda said nothing as Bruce fumbled with a tool he inserted in the lock. Less than a minute later, he made eye contact with her. "Here you go," he said as he flipped open the lid, but before he could see what was inside, Amanda yanked it from him, quickly closing the lid.

"Thank you. How much do I owe you?" she asked.

With knitted eyebrows, he said, "Nothing. On the house."

"But I want to pay you, for your trouble."

"That's okay. No trouble."

Clutching the box to her chest, she inched her way back toward the door, turned around, and bolted out, leaving Bruce scratching his head. She had no idea what was in the box, but given her dysfunctional family life, there was no telling, and she didn't want a stranger to see her items.

Amanda practically ran home. Once inside her apartment, she didn't wait to sit. She opened the lid and peered inside. It was a collection of trinkets, jewelry, and papers. She moved toward the couch and folded one leg beneath her to sit, then one by one, she removed the items.

A pearl earring with a note: "For Amanda." Amanda clutched the pearl to her chest. These were a gift from her mother. She had lost one or misplaced when she lived with her dad. She'd thought they were safely tucked away with her treasured possessions. Next, she lifted out a pearl ring. "Damn!" It was another item she'd left behind. She slipped it on her finger, but it was too small.

She looked at each trinket. Some were meaningless to her. Amanda set those aside. She then unfolded the pieces of paper. The first handful were incoherent scribbles. These, too, meant nothing to her, but she set them aside instead of tossing them in the bin next to the couch. At last, she came upon a series of numbers. Amanda flipped the paper; the only thing written on the back was "For you."

Who was "you?" *Me? Someone else? Who else? My mother?* But that didn't make sense. Surely, not her mother, who was out of it and wouldn't have received this box. Then a thought: a bank account?

Thinking back, she'd gone with her grandmother to the bank many times. She knew exactly where it was. Amanda grabbed her purse, made sure she had bus fare, and headed to the bank on the other end of town, hoping for money left for her, no matter how small the amount was.

She arrived to disappointment. There was no bank account there with that number. Disheartened, she crumpled the paper and tossed it in her coat pocket. Months later, she found it and stashed it in her box of treasures.

Chapter 21

May 6, 2018

Amanda woke up early, too early; her tired body and mind told her so. Brad's side of the bed was undisturbed. Amanda wasn't sure how she felt about her husband's absence, but it wouldn't be anything she'd pursue.

The phone beckoned her. Amanda lifted it and looked at the time. 8:46 am. She rolled on her back and scrolled through her messages. Realizing it was Sunday, she would send a message to her boss; he wouldn't get it until the next day as it was his policy to not read company emails during what he called "family time."

Slowly, she extricated herself from the tangles of bedding and reached for her morning pill. She put it under her tongue and walked to the bathroom, where she cupped her hand under the stream of cold water and drank. Returning to the bedroom, she stripped the bed and grabbed fresh clothes before she made her way to the shower.

Twenty minutes later, Amanda was dressed and ready to face whatever the day brought, determined to deal with any adversity that came her way. Perhaps it was time to face the past, deal with it, and move on into the future no matter what it held. She could no longer shoulder the burden of her secrets.

Carrying the laundry basket and kicking at the bundle of bedding, she made it to the top of the stairs and peered into the living room, but Brad wasn't there. *Good,* she thought.

Usually, Amanda and Brad tackled the laundry together, but today, she didn't care if he helped. She made her way down the stairs, kicking the bundle ahead of her, and set the basket on the floor. The house was quiet.

"Brad?" she called out tentatively.

No answer.

Amanda took the basket and emptied it on the floor of the laundry room to sort and load into the washer, then returned for the sheets, towels, and pillowcases. Laundry started, she made her way to the kitchen and popped a pod into the coffee maker. While the coffee brewed, she rummaged through the refrigerator, looking for something to eat, though she had no appetite.

A slice of bread and strip of cheese along with the coffee would do. Steam rose from the cup in the cool breeze that snuck in from the partially opened window. Amanda reached to close it when movement outside caught her attention. Realizing it was the paperboy delivering the news to her elderly neighbors, she closed the window all the way and sipped her coffee before grabbing her food and walking toward her office.

One step at a time, she ascended the stairs. The only noise breaking the silence was the sound of the washer. She didn't wonder where Brad was. She knew he was at the gym and most likely would stop by the local coffee shop afterward, his routine on Sundays. Why would it change today?

In the office, Amanda curled one leg under her and sat. She pushed the chair closer to the desk with her other foot while booting her computer. While she opened emails and perused one at a time, she nibbled on her bread and cheese and sipped her coffee. She could no longer ignore the neglected company emails. She set her cup to the side and clicked on *compose*.

As her teeth bit on her bottom lip, she quickly typed an email to her boss. She had opted for honesty. Dealing with issues head-on would be how she handled matters from this point on, and she would start with her boss. The email was short and to the point. In it, Amanda apologized for shirking her responsibilities and threw herself at the mercy of her boss. She didn't go into detail. She would wait until she received a response to decide if and how much she would share.

The rest of the emails held no interest, and she clicked on the little red X by each. Amanda ignored the emails from the secretary and others from various people in her company but didn't delete them. *For now,* she told herself.

That done and out of the way, Amanda looked at her watch. She had about an hour before Brad got home. Earlier, she noticed his briefcase on the far counter in the kitchen and was sure he would be buried in correcting papers for at least three hours when he got back. She figured she had enough time to pull out the box and papers she had hidden. It was time to deal with the contents and, maybe, destroy them afterward.

The washer bell sang its tune, and Amanda left her office to switch the load to the dryer and the stack on the floor into the washer. Methodically, she took care of the task and returned to her office.

Just as soon as she crouched on the floor and opened the small cabinet, she heard a car door slam shut. She looked at her watch; it was too early for Brad to be done and home. She returned to the cabinet, pulled out the stack of magazines, and flipped through them before she set them next to her on the floor. Amanda fumbled for the taped key and pulled it loose. The box now exposed, she brought it closer to her heart.

Startled by the front door opening and closing, Amanda was sure the car couldn't have been Brad. It was several minutes between the time she heard the car and the front door. If it was Brad, he was as predictable as a clock; he would've been in the house at least five or more minutes sooner.

Frantically, she pocketed the key and returned the papers, quietly closing the cabinet door. Her footsteps muffled by the carpet, she headed for her chair and sat gazing at the screen.

"Amanda?"

"In the office," she responded.

"I'll be in the backyard. Got to finish grading."

122

"Sure," she said.

She would wait until he was out in the yard, busy with essays, before returning to what she wanted to do. In the meantime, it was Facebook and the Internet, where she would spend the next half hour until Brad was securely engrossed in his task.

No sooner did she open her browser than she heard Brad's footsteps thumping up the stairs. "Damn." Amanda watched him cross the landing and lean against the door frame.

"Hi," he said.

"Hi. I started the laundry."

"Yeah, I heard the dryer."

An awkward silence followed. Amanda noticed Brad averted his eyes, tapped a rolled paper against his leg, and looked at his feet. Puzzled at the rolled newspaper since they didn't subscribe to any, she pointed and asked, "What's that?"

"It was weird—"

"What was?"

"Mrs. Krupp came up to me with this…" Brad extended the paper toward Amanda.

She didn't reach to get it or say anything. Her eyebrows arched upward, forming an unasked question, to which Brad said, "Take a look."

He moved forward, and Amanda lifted herself from the chair, reaching for the paper. She unrolled it and laid it flat on the desk, Brad hovering close by. She let out an audible gasp as her eyes scanned the headline, then the short article.

"I told you, weird," said Brad. "She's such a strange creature. Why she needed to give me the paper is beyond me."

Recovering from her shock, Amanda waved her hand in dismissal. "You know, she's in her eighties, and anything happening in this town is a big thing to her. Not the first time she's done this."

"I suppose," said Brad.

Amanda folded the paper as if she didn't care and said, "I know you have papers to grade, and I still have work to do. Maybe we can go out to dinner tonight? I don't think we have anything here to fix."

Brad nodded and turned to leave, but before he reached the top step, Amanda said, "Mind if you hang the clothes? They should be dry by now."

"Sure," he said as he descended the stairs.

Amanda treaded carefully around Brad. Neither wanted to upset the fragile truce. For sure, she didn't want Brad to question her anymore. At least, for now, she was in a safe place, her past tucked away from Brad's prying eyes.

Amanda inhaled sharply, and when she heard the laundry room door open and close, she quickly unfolded the paper. It wasn't the headline that made her gasp. Though not common, finding a body in a house wasn't exactly shocking. It was where they found the body that had Amanda clutch at her chest and fight for air.

She read and re-read the article. The police didn't know how long the body had been in the basement of the house she and her dad rented years ago, but from the appearance of the remains, it had been in there a while. "Skeletal remains," the article said.

What did that mean? Could it be her father's? It if was, would they be able to tell how he died and connect his death to her?

Chapter 22

May 6, 2018

Brad didn't miss Amanda's reaction to the news in the paper. He carefully watched her face when she read it. Her outward nonchalant response at the body found in the old house, and her subsequent dismissal of the event didn't hide what Brad saw in her eyes. Was it fear? For a moment, he saw her brows furrow and her eyes widen. In recognition?

The Amanda that was with him was nothing like the one who left on Thursday, only a handful of days ago. It was as if she had traveled through a time warp and had taken everything familiar with her.

He shook his head and tried to let go of the craziness that rattled around in there. Brad wondered if he was becoming paranoid, but the reality was, he did get the letter, and he did watch Amanda transform into someone he no longer knew. None of this was an active imagination.

One by one, he pulled out shirts, blouses, and pants and put them on hangers, straightening them as he hung them from a wire rack. Surprised not to find more of Amanda's clothes in the bunch, he turned around, pushed the door open, and stepped into the hallway. "Hey, did you leave your suitcase in the car?"

"No, why?"

"It seems there should be more of your clothes in here."

"I don't know what you're talking about. There's another load in the washer."

Brad returned to the laundry room, stopped the washer, and looked inside. Only towels and sheets filled the tub. He stared at the wet pile and scratched his chin, closed the lid, and pressed the start button. Puzzled, he looked through the rest of the laundry on the floor; it was mostly his clothes. He chided himself for being silly. There had to be a logical explanation – he was making too much of this.

When he finished, the washer stopped. He transferred the wet clothes to the dryer, tossed the remaining load in the washer, started it, and decided he'd better get to grading papers before the day ran away from him.

Brad grabbed the stack of papers and sat at the kitchen counter with the first essay in front of him. The house too quiet, he pulled out his phone and plugged in his earbuds. He clicked on one of his playlists and read the first paper, making notations as he went along. By the third essay, several messages had come through. He heard the dings and opted to ignore them, but now, he was ready for a break.

Brad stood, stretched, and with one hand, flicked through his phone. The messages were from friends. He quickly responded to each. The notifications were next: National headlines, then local ones. He scrolled through, deleting each as he moved from one to the next until one caught his attention. It was the same one his neighbor had pointed out, except this one had an update as it was digital.

"Interesting," thought Brad, his eyes scanning the update.

It wasn't long before he returned his attention to the essays. There was no escaping this part of teaching. He had promised his students he'd have the grades and feedback done by Monday, the next day. So, he immersed himself in reading and jotting notes for two more hours until the early evening light covered the kitchen in shadows. He toyed between turning on the light and continuing and going out to dinner early. His stomach decided for him.

He straightened the stack of papers, left it on the counter, and headed for the stairs. Looking up from the lower landing, he saw the light like a halo around Amanda's door. "Do you want to take a break for dinner?" he yelled.

No answer.

Once again, he yelled, "Amanda… How about we go out to dinner soon?"

Still, no answer. Thinking she didn't hear him, he took the steps two at a time and pushed the door open. As soon as he appeared in the doorway, he watched her stretch her arms protectively over items on the desk.

Brad approached, and Amanda swept the items in a small box closing the lid. Pointing, he asked, "What's all that?"

Amanda stumbled on her words. "Um, nothing. Just stuff I've had for a long time."

Waiting for Amanda to say more, Brad stood arms folded. She didn't.

"So, stuff from your childhood?" he asked.

"Yeah. Just nothing, stuff." Amanda's response was too quick and dismissive while she secured the lid on the box and set it on her lap.

It was clear to Brad that his wife wasn't going to share the contents with him. "Well, I came up to see if you are about ready to go to dinner."

"Yeah. Sure. I'll be right down."

"Here," he picked a paper from the floor by her desk and reached out to hand it to her, but not before he saw the title, "Birth Certificate."

Amanda snatched it from Brad, startling him.

"Whoa," he said, turned around, and left the office still shaking his head in disbelief.

Why was she making a big deal about a birth certificate? his thoughts probed.

The little voice in Brad's head reminded him there were too many unanswered questions. *Whatever happened since Amanda left,* the little guy poked, *it had to do with her past, who she is or was, and what secrets she is hiding.* Brad could no longer ignore the voice that rattled him from the inside. He had to know. He had to find out what his wife was hiding but had no clue how to go about it. He did not like confrontation and was uncomfortable engaging in a verbal volley.

While waiting for her, he finished the rest of the laundry, his mind traveling to dark corners. By the time she appeared in the doorway, he was done and ready to leave for dinner.

Brad exited first and walked to his car. Amanda followed. Just as he fastened his seatbelt, waiting for Amanda to do the same, Mrs. Krupp tapped on the passenger window. He could tell Amanda didn't want to roll the glass down, but he didn't want to be rude, so he pushed the button. The window hissed as it went down.

"Yes, Ms. Krupp?" Brad said.

"Did you hear anything more about the body? You know…" she pointed vaguely behind her.

Brad noticed Amanda busied herself with looking for something at the bottom of her bag. He lifted his eyes to Ms. Krupp.

Amanda pushed the window button, effectively putting a barrier between herself and Ms. Krupp and said, "Sorry, we need to get going. We have a dinner appointment," as she did so.

Startled by his wife's rudeness, he lowered his window and said, "Maybe I'll stop by later, and we can talk."

"Why would you do that?" Amanda asked while he backed out of the driveway.

"Don't you think you were a bit rude to her?"

"She's obsessed with something that doesn't concern her."

"But you didn't have to be rude to her. She meant no harm."

"Whatever."

They drove in silence for a few minutes. Brad couldn't stand Amanda's attitude and didn't understand how their relationship had taken a downturn in such a short time. If he wasn't hungry and the refrigerator wasn't empty, he wouldn't have been trapped in this car with her, not today. "How about Frank's Deli?" he asked.

"Okay. Fine," she responded, now scrolling through her phone. "They have good sandwiches and soup."

A few minutes later, they arrived at Frank's Deli. The place was mobbed and loud. Brad didn't care. He needed the distraction. He needed to be away from the home that had become a morgue.

When he saw Amanda hesitate, he almost asked if she'd rather go elsewhere, but he didn't. *The hell with it,* he thought. *I'm tired of pussyfooting around her.*

Without waiting, he made it inside and gave his name to the receptionist.

"It'll be fifteen minutes," the girl said.

"Sure, no problem."

By then, Amanda made it in and scanned the crowd. "How long of a wait?" she asked.

The hostess didn't wait for Brad to respond. She said, "Fifteen minutes."

Brad scanned the waiting area, and he moved toward one of the benches with enough room for them. Two women joined a few minutes later after a party of three vacated their seats when the hostess called their name.

The four crowded on the bench, waiting for an available table. Amanda buried her nose in her phone, and Brad did the same, interrupted only by the hushed whispers of the two women. Although they tried to be discreet, it wasn't hard for Brad to overhear part of their conversation.

"What do you make of this?" the blonde one asked, pointing to an aged paper.

"Honestly, I couldn't say," the dark-haired one said.

More hushed whispers, then, "Liz, why do you suppose they won't tell us how the guy died and who he is?"

Liz shrugged, and Brad's ears perked up. He looked at Amanda, but he couldn't tell if she, too, overheard the partial conversation, although, he would have been surprised if she didn't.

"Steph, what else was there?" Liz asked.

"Not sure, a container of sorts. Looked like a box. I saw Detective Miller put it in a bag with his gloved hands."

Amanda fanned herself and swayed.

"Are you all right?"

"Yeah. I need to eat."

"Brad, table for two. Brad, table for two."

Chapter 23

May 6, 2018

Frank's Deli was a gathering place most locals frequented, though it was anything but a deli. They offered gourmet meat platters to sprout sandwiches and everything in between.

A popular diner, Frank's eatery wasn't an intimate place. The din of conversation permeated the premises, and all too often, one had to shout at their table to be heard over the hubbub.

Liz and Steph were seated one table over from Brad and Amanda. Stephanie waved to them as they took their seats and spread their napkins on their laps. From behind her menu, Liz asked, "Do you think she's okay?" She pointed with her head and eyebrows to Amanda.

"Who knows? You don't suppose she's a reporter and overheard what we said, do you?" Panic etched Liz's face.

"Nooo. If she was, don't you think she would've approached us by now?" asked Stephanie dismissively.

"You're right."

"I think I'll have the meatloaf with mashed potatoes."

"Sounds good, but I haven't decided." After consideration, Liz made up her mind. She lifted her gaze to her sister's and said, "So, tell me about the container you found."

Stephanie glanced around. "Later," she said when "Paul" (that's what his name tag said) approached to take their orders.

"What can I get for you?" Paul's chipper voice intruded.

Liz ordered the meatloaf, and Stephanie opted for the fish and chips. "Oh, and two coffees, please," said Liz.

After Paul left, Liz insisted, "So, tell me about the container."

Stephanie bent over the table and whispered, "I think it was a thermos. Oh, remember the case I found and put away?"

Liz nodded.

"Well, the thermos was next to it. One of those camping ones with a glass liner."

Liz gasped. "Do you suppose it belonged to the dead man?"

But, before Stephanie responded, Liz said, "Wait, we don't have it, right? You gave it to Detective Miller, right?" When Stephanie didn't say anything, Liz said, "You're crazy, you know. You're going to land us in jail. Why didn't you tell Detective Miller about what you found? Isn't it bad enough you—"

Stephanie wanted to clamp Liz's mouth shut, but that would invite stares. So, she pinched her sister hard, and Liz sucked in a sharp breath. "You need to lower your voice, Liz. The last thing we need is to draw more attention to the matter!"

Liz rubbed her wrist. "Honestly, you didn't have to do that."

"Here's the thing, Liz. One, we don't know who that guy was or what he was doing in our basement. Two, we don't know how he died. Three…" She ticked off on her fingers. "Three, the damned cops aren't telling us anything, and it is *our* house."

"You're right."

"Let's eat, and we'll discuss this when we get home."

Something made Stephanie and Liz turn their heads to the right at the same time. The couple who shared the bench with them seemed to be into a heated argument. It couldn't have been a friendly discussion; both had scowls on their faces, and they watched as the woman snapped her napkin on the table. Her husband or boyfriend jerked back in his seat.

"Don't you wish you were a fly on the table?" asked Liz.

"Wonder what has her worked up," said Stephanie. She got up.

"Where are you going?" asked Liz.

"Where do you think?"

Liz watched her twin weave between the tables to the back of the restaurant. On her way back, she hovered by Brad and Amanda's table. They were no longer arguing. The man had the local paper spread out on the table, and the woman reached to fold it and get it out of the way.

Stephanie stood motionless, pretending to wait for the busboy to clear the way, while she stared at the couple and what was on the table.

"I don't get why you are reacting as if they found the dead man in your house, Amanda?"

She watched the woman's fingers flutter to her mouth, looking around her as if searching for an escape route.

"I… I…don't get why you're obsessed with something that isn't your business," Amanda said.

Stephanie could no longer keep quiet. "Excuse me. I'm Stephanie Branson, and over there, is my twin, Liz."

Amanda gaped, and Brad extended his hand to shake Stephanie's. "Yeah, you two sat next to us while we…" Brad trailed realizing, the name she offered him was the one glaring at him from the pages of the newspaper. "I, um, glad to meet you." Brad fumbled for what to say. Turning to Amanda, he said, "Is this a fantastic coincidence? We were just talking about what you, I mean, the papers are saying."

Brad stood to shake Stephanie's hand. Amanda remained seated and reached for her glass of water.

"I couldn't help but overhear your conversation… well, as you can see, I was stuck in this spot, and I didn't mean to eavesdrop." Stephanie gestured to the busboy and the blocked path.

"Oh, no worries. Would you like to sit with us?" asked Brad.

133

"That would be lovely, but our meal should be arriving soon. Are you all right?" Stephanie asked Amanda.

"Yes. Yes. Fine," Amanda responded, gulping big sips of water.

"Oh, I'm Brad, and this is my wife, Amanda."

"Nice to meet you, Amanda, Brad."

Stephanie checked her path. A waitress now blocked the way to her table. She shook her head and pointed to the obstacle. Brad nodded in acknowledgment.

"So, anything new from the police? Did they identify the dead man?" asked Brad, ignoring Amanda's coughing fit.

"Not really. They won't tell us anything until they locate the next of kin and make the proper notification."

"I see. This is stranger than fiction," said Brad.

"You can say that again. We bought the house a few months ago. It belonged to my great grandfather way back when, and we wanted to restore it. The last thing we imagined was finding a body in the basement."

"I'm sure you can track down who lived there before you bought it through assessor records."

"Easier said than done. The house was a rental, and a kid and her dad were the last to live there. We have the owner's name, but I can't find him. I am still looking. He may be dead by now. Who knows—"

A thud interrupted Stephanie. Amanda had fainted and fallen off the chair. Waiters, waitresses, and patrons rushed to assist. Someone barked, "Clear the area, please."

An off-duty paramedic, Stephanie recognized, knelt next to Amanda, checking her pulse and flashing lights in her eyes. Brad stood gawking, his hand involuntarily massaging his chin.

Stephanie, watching Amanda, touched Brad's shoulder. "Hope she's okay. I wrote my number on the paper. Let me know how she is." She made her way back to the table where Liz was picking at her salad.

"That was weird," she said as she sat and placed her napkin in her lap.

"What was all that about?" Liz asked around a mouthful of food.

"Hell, if I know. But I can tell you this: the guy is obsessed with our house. Makes me wonder."

Liz nodded, and both tackled their meal in silence.

Chapter 24

May 6, 2018

Disoriented, Amanda came to. She scrambled up but immediately leaned against the chair. The room spun, and the faces around her doubled.

"Hey, hey, miss. Take it easy," said the man hovering above her. "We have an ambulance on the way."

Brad, dumbfounded, nodded. Amanda stared blankly at him, then tried to stand. He quickly reached for her, but she swatted his arm away. "I'm fine. I don't want an ambulance."

Amanda heard a woman at a nearby table tell the manager, "She toppled over, but didn't hit her head on anything that I could see."

The manager looked concerned and insisted on having Amanda properly checked at the hospital.

"No, I don't want to go to the hospital. Just take me home," she said to Brad.

After fumbling for words, the manager pointed to a waiter, and the young man quickly packed Amanda's and Brad's food in to-go containers, following them out to Brad's car. "No charge. Hope you feel better," he said when Brad reached for his wallet.

Amanda walked on shaky legs, determined not to be taken to the hospital. Brad hovered near her, opened the car door, and waited for her to be seated before closing it gently.

"I think we should have you checked," he said when he made it to the driver's seat and closed his door.

"I said, I'm fine. I'll eat something when we get home. I'll be just fine."

They drove the short distance in silence. Amanda felt Brad's stare boring into the side of her head every few minutes. When they arrived home, she pushed her door open and fished in her purse for her keys. She had to take her medication and eat something. She'd never fainted like that, but deep down, she knew what had gotten her. It wasn't the medication. It wasn't not eating. Her past was now with her.

"Wait."

Amanda didn't. She unlocked the door and went in, straight to the kitchen, leaning on walls. A minute later, she heard the front door closing with a soft thud, and Brad's footsteps on the tiled hallway floor before he appeared in the kitchen.

"You should eat something."

Amanda wrapped her arms around herself, protectively waiting for the barrage of questions. They didn't come. Instead, Brad unpacked the bags. "Do you want to eat out of the containers or a plate?" he asked.

"Doesn't matter."

"Do you have your pills with you?"

Amanda's shoulder shrugged, and her eye twitched three times. "No."

"Are they on the nightstand?"

Amanda nodded, and Brad left. While he was gone, she opened one of the containers and wrinkled her nose. Though her stomach was rumbling from hunger, her appetite wasn't available to greet the food, but she took a bite anyway.

When Brad returned, he handed her the medication and filled a glass with water, bringing it to her.

"Thanks."

"If you don't feel better after you eat, I'm taking you in whether or not you like it."

137

"Why do you care?"

Amanda watched Brad's face contort with pain at her harshness. The only words from his lips were, "You'd better eat."

She took her pills, chasing them with water, and ate one-fourth of her meal. Her stomach was tied in knots, rebelling.

"Done already?" asked Brad when she closed the container and pushed it aside.

"Yeah."

"How do you feel?"

"Fine. Thanks."

"You sure we shouldn't go in to have you checked?"

"Yeah. I'm already feeling better."

"Well, I'd better get back to grading papers. The last load of wash is in the dryer. I'll take care of it. Let me know if you need anything."

"Sure." *What I need is for this nightmare to end. I want it over. Either come and jail me or let me be.*

Amanda watched Brad clear the counter and put the leftover food in the refrigerator. She eyed the newspaper still on the corner and hoped he wouldn't take it. She had every intention of tossing it in the bin after he left the kitchen. But, after three strides toward the hallway, he turned around, picked it up, and looked at it before rolling it and walking off once again.

Slowly, hanging onto the railing, she made her way up the stairs. Holding her throbbing head in her hands, she entered the office and shut and locked the door. She needed time to think and plan her next move. Amanda heard the shuffling of papers in the living room. She would be undisturbed for at least a few hours.

Chapter 25

May 6, 2018

"I'm stuffed." Liz patted her stomach.

"Me, too," said Stephanie, taking off her coat and tossing it on a chair in the living room. "Still early. Want to tackle…" whispering and pointing behind her, she mouthed, "the case?"

Liz nodded. "Why are you whispering? No one is here."

Stephanie retrieved the old briefcase and placed it on the table between them. Liz reached for the light and turned it on. The first item Steph pulled out was one of the birth certificates. "Wait…" she said, lifting one finger.

She bent and picked up her purse. Fishing through it, she retrieved a magnifying glass.

"What's that for?" asked Liz.

"Remember, we couldn't read what was on the birth certificate?"

Liz carefully unfolded one and laid it between them, under the table lamp. Steph lifted the magnifying glass, then lowered it, and after several attempts, she steadied her hand. "I can only make out some of the writing."

"Let me look." Liz tried to grab the glass from her twin's hand.

"Stop! I finally have it in focus."

"What does it say?"

"Do you have paper and a pen? Or your laptop would be better. I'll dictate it. Okay?"

It only took Liz a few moments to pull out the laptop, plug it in, and boot it up. "Okay, ready."

"Says at the top, 'Colorado Certified Abstract of Birth.' Wonder what 'abstract' means."

Liz shrugged. "Don't know."

Stephanie returned her attention to the paper. Peering at the faded pinkish and blue-edged paper, she said, "There's a long state number. Last digits that I can make out are 1902."

"Okay."

"There's a date on the right. Looks like September 13, 1984."

"Is that the birth date?"

"Yeah. Wait. Hold on." Stephanie squinted and adjusted the magnifying glass once more. "Don't think so. I can barely make out the words, but I see 'iled.' Oh, I bet that's date filed. That's it. Date filed."

"Not the birth date?"

"No. I see another date. I bet that's the one. Let's tackle this one line at a time."

"Yeah. Sure."

Looking at her sister, Stephanie asked, "What are you doing?"

"Looking up the difference between abstract and birth certificate while you figure out what's on that paper."

"Soooo?"

"About the same. You can use either."

Stephanie returned her attention to the pink and blue paper. "I can't make out the name, but I think it has NDA—"

"First or last?"

"First, Liz, first!"

"Don't get huffy!"

Ignoring Liz, she said, "Last name looks like Muncher, Mulcher, or maybe Macken?"

Liz, puzzled, said, "I'll type all of them with a question mark."

Stephanie didn't answer, but said, "Next... ALE. Must be sex, and I can't make it out. Looks like someone spilled bleach or something on this paper. The center is all but wiped!"

"Anything else you can see?"

"Hang on for a sec. Wait, let me hand you this. Maybe you will have better luck. My eyes are dancing all over the letters."

Stephanie exchanged the birth certificate for the laptop, then rubbed her neck. "Okay, let's see what you get."

Liz lifted the paper to the light. "You're right, the middle is all but wiped out, but I can make out what's on the edges, I think. Ready?"

"What do you have?"

"Date of Birth, June something, two at the end. Can't make out the rest. Wait a minute. Why would they file in 1984 when the birth was... do you think 1982? Could it be back in 1972?"

Liz squinted again and adjusted the magnifying glass to read the next line.

"Just a sec," said Stephanie.

Liz continued peering at the birth certificate while Stephanie went online in search of a sample 1972 birth certificate. Then a 1962 one. "Hate to tell you; the 70s don't look much different than the 80s. The 60s well, there is a slight difference. So, I'll just type 1982 or 1972 with a question mark."

"Fair enough. Next... Boulder."

"You can see it?"

"No. I can see the Bo on one side and the der on the other. Has to be Boulder."

Neither Stephanie nor Liz were able to extract the parents' names and ages, nor the signature and issue date. Setting this aside, they pulled out the other paper, the typing at the top clear: County of Los Angeles, California Birth Certificate, but like the other, difficult to read. What the twins were able to read was a partial name: Brown or Bowen, year of birth: 1961, sex: Male, but that was about it.

"Do you suppose this is the father and daughter who rented this place?" puzzled Liz.

"Could be. Let me Google the name and see what comes up."

"Okay," Liz said as she reached for a stack of bills, letters, and what looked to be newspaper clippings. "I'll start on this."

Half an hour later, Stephanie said, "Pfft. Too many Browns and Bowens. The closest I can get to the name is an article about a dead guy, but that isn't the same name. Not even close."

"I just finished sorting this pile. I'll start looking through the bills first."

"Okay, but it's getting late. I need a hot bath and my comfy bed."

"Can we just get through these? I really want to be done and give this mess to the police. We shouldn't have it in the first place."

"Liz, Liz, Liz, always the worrier," her twin said as she grabbed a pile and flipped through it.

It was mostly utility bills, and the name on them was… Steph did a double take. It was the name of the property owner she'd been unsuccessful at getting hold of.

"Hey, look at this. Arkan Belcher. The guy we've been looking for. The owner with the tenants. Could the body—"

"Oh, Steph, your imagination is running wild. Why would the owner have birth certificates that aren't his? Don't you think someone would've reported him missing and looked around the property?"

"You're right on the last part. But, how do we know these certificates are not his? I suppose he could've left the bag behind for whatever the reason," said Liz. "Who cares anyway. We've got grandpa's house, and soon, we'll finish the renovations and have our new home!"

"Wait, are you abandoning the historical search of the property?" asked Stephanie incredulously.

"Noooo. I guess I'm tired too. Let's finish these stacks and call it a night. Hopefully, tomorrow, they'll start in the kitchen, and you and I can finish this living room." Liz waved her hand around.

The twins read more letters without names, sorted through the bills, and flipped through the newspaper clippings mostly of motorcycle ads. As they did so, Steph and Liz took turns taking a picture of each for their scrapbooks.

There was nothing else to peruse. They returned the items to the briefcase, and Stephanie ran her fingers through the outside pockets. There were pens and pencils, an old watch, and a few miscellaneous items she returned to where she found them. There were a few more pockets inside. She unzipped one, and the zipper with its material came away in her hand. She pulled at the pocket to peer inside before sticking her hand in it. She grabbed the small items at the bottom when Liz bent over the table to look.

"Wow, is that ever pretty?"

Stephanie handed the pearl ring and one earring to Liz to look at.

"I wonder where the other earring is and who these belong to?" asked Liz pulling the briefcase toward her.

It was her turn to check the other inside pocket. The hunt wasn't as rewarding. She came away with nothing.

"Okay, let's put this stuff back. I'll call Detective Miller tomorrow and give him this."

"What will you tell him? Are you sure we won't be in trouble?"

"Leave it to me, Liz. I have it figured out." With that, she tossed one coat to her sister and put on the other one. "We can leave one of the lamps on."

Chapter 26

May 6, 2018

Amanda once more brought out the contents of the box. She dug through the pile and extracted the pearl earring, wishing she had its mate. Without thinking, she poked the stem into her ear lobe and twisted the clasp to fasten it.

Her ear lobe burnt a little. She was no longer used to wearing anything in them. Absently, she rubbed around it, loosened it, and shook her head gently, feeling the faint jingling of the gold chain and pearls. The last time she wore the earrings was on her twelfth birthday. They were her mother's when she was a young girl, gifted to her when she was young, and her grandmother held onto them for all these years. Amanda wondered what happened to the mate and the ring.

She was sure she had them in this very box. She was sure she never took them off and left them anywhere. It sickened her that they were gone.

Leaving the earring in her ear, she picked up the papers one by one. The last time she looked at the contents of the box was the day her grandmother came to get her. She had grabbed what she thought was important and shoved them in the container, which she hadn't opened since then.

The overhead light wasn't enough; she turned on the desk lamp. Her birth certificate was the first she looked at; she had forgotten it was there and had to obtain copies for school and other legal matters over the years. This, she had set in safekeeping, "just in case." She folded it and set it aside.

She thought the next one was her mother's or dad's, but when she read it, her mouth formed an O. Stacy's! How on earth did she get that? It had to have been with her dad's papers she'd gathered. She thought of finding Stacy online and sending her the certificate but opted not to. She folded it and was just about to rip it to pieces when a little voice said, *Hold onto it...* She set it in the "to keep" pile.

Next was a copy of her dad's birth certificate. Amanda did a double take. She remembered grabbing it but didn't recall reading it. After all, she was only twelve at the time and did the best she could to gather loose papers before she left the house for good. She stared and silently read the name. Andrew Kevin Bowen. *Andrew Bowen?* Her dad's name was... was Andrew Bairn. Why would this birth certificate say Bowen, not Bairn? Maybe it wasn't his. Just like Stacy's certificate, this, too, was someone else's. If it belonged to her dad, he would've taken it with him, surely.

She set aside the remaining three papers and booted her computer. In the search bar, she typed, Andrew Kevin Bowen. Many results showed up. She amended her search and added May 8, 1962. The first three hits looked promising. She clicked on the top one. There was no image, but it listed an Andrew Bowen as next of kin to a war veteran who died. She didn't recognize any of the names listed, though she wasn't sure she remembered or knew her dad's parents' names.

Drumming her fingers against the glass desk, she thought back on her life and how dysfunctional it had been. She was repeating the pattern with Brad. Thankfully, she hadn't brought any children into the world; she was in no position to offer a life different than hers, growing up. She didn't know what "normal" was.

Returning her gaze to the screen, she clicked on the second link; an old man stared back at her. Definitely not her dad. Moving to the third link, the image was not what she had expected. It was a scan of a newspaper article dated 7/31/1995, pleading with the public to come forth if they had any information regarding a missing child. The detective in charge was A. Bowen. A coincidence of names. Her dad was not a cop.

This wasn't the article she found in her previous search, but the date of that article caught her attention. It was around the time her dad left her. What was not a fluke was the dead man in the basement of the house she lived in back then. Amanda's hand fluttered to her mouth, stifling a gasp. Dreading what was to come next, she was sure it wouldn't be long before the autopsy was completed and the man in the basement was found to be her dad... and they would know he was poisoned... and they would be arresting her any day now.

Heart beating fast, she stacked the papers and returned them to the box. She fingered the trinkets on the desk: a necklace, a bracelet, a doll shoe, Ernie's eye that had fallen off her slipper, and a scrap of paper with Ms. Coop's phone number – this she crumpled and tossed in the bin next to her right foot.

She was running out of time. Soon, her past would come knocking at the door, snatching her up and burying her in its bowels. First, she'd have to deal with Andy. Now, she'd have to deal with killing her father. Amanda wondered how long she'd be in jail. The rest of her life?

Two hours later, near eleven o'clock, she heard Brad move about, breaking the silence that had shrouded the house. She knew he'd be getting ready for bed shortly, and although she was not sleepy, she was exhausted.

Amanda tidied her desk and ripped to shreds what she didn't want anyone to find, including the birth certificates. She wouldn't be saving anything for later. Not anymore. There wouldn't be later.

What she hid under the carpeting in the closet, her journal, and the rest of the items in the space, she would destroy the next day after Brad left for work. She would also send a letter of resignation and be done with that. Time to clean up and straighten out her affairs. This was it.

She made her way to the bedroom. Images of Brad sleeping on the couch again descended on her like a cloud. It didn't matter, she reasoned. Once he discovered her past and her guilt, he'd leave her. She might as well get used to life without him. At the door, she looked at the expanse of the empty bed, turned around, and went back to her office, and locked the door. Time to go through all her paperwork.

She plugged in the shredder and went to work. Any paper that remotely connected her to her past, she shredded. It didn't take long to fill the first plastic bag. Amanda tied it and set it aside. Methodically, she went through drawers and files. She was sure once the police made the connection, she would be put away for a long time.

Next, she tackled the boxes in the closet. Most were filled with decorations and household items she cared very little about. The boxes with her school papers, she shredded. The others with her childhood drawings, not that there were many, she also shredded. There was a sense of satisfaction in ripping apart the past. She wished she could do the same to the memories that haunted her.

It was almost one in the morning. Exhaustion and apprehension sent their tentacles throughout Amanda's body, but she was nearly done. There was only one item left, and Amanda reached for it after pulling the carpet away from the tack strip.

She leaned against the back of a chair and read the first entry. It was such a long time ago. Now, she kept a digital journal locked away in the depths of the online world, secured with a password. She didn't have the heart to shred it; she would, but not at that moment. Setting it aside, she returned the boxes to the closet and closed the door. There was nothing else left to do for the night, what was left of the night. She might as well try to close her eyes.

She clutched the journal to her chest, turned off the light with her other hand, and softly walked to the bedroom. Lifting the end of the mattress, she tucked the journal there. She would destroy it later in the day.

Amanda curled on her side in bed and stared at the shadows playing on the wall until, finally, sleep claimed her.

Chapter 27

May 6, 2018

Brad rubbed the small of his back. His eyes could no longer focus, but he persisted until done with reading and commenting on his students' essays. It was almost eleven, and he hadn't seen Amanda for hours. He contemplated whether he should check on her. Taking the stairs one at a time, he gently tapped on her office door and turned the knob. It was locked. He could hear movement and the buzz of the shredder. Amanda didn't unlock the door. She must've not heard him.

He made it to the shower; he was keyed up. In his boxers, instead of falling into bed, he went downstairs and grabbed a beer, headed to the living room, and surfed social media on his phone.

The last thing he remembered was reading an update on the body found in Stephanie and Liz's basement, entering Stephanie's info in his contacts, and leaning his head back against the pillows. The incessant vibrations of his phone woke him up at 5:45 am the next morning. He was grateful he had set the alarm.

For a few moments, he considered calling in sick, but his need for distraction overruled his fleeting thought. He folded the throw. He didn't recall covering himself, but he had to have at some point. The house was still cool, and he heard the central air system crackle and hiss to life.

Brad looked up the stairs. Their bedroom door stood open while the office door was shut. He wondered if Amanda was still awake. He didn't go up. There were plenty of clothes in the laundry room; both neglected to take upstairs and put away. He got dressed in there.

By 6:45 am, Brad slung his messenger bag with the graded papers on his shoulder, opened the garage door, and hopped on his bike. Without looking back, he pressed the remote control mounted on the handlebars and heard the gears groan as the door came down.

His short ride was invigorating, and he was glad he didn't stay home. Leaving his quandary behind for a short time might have been just what he needed to clear his head and think logically.

Once in the schoolyard, he secured his bike, removed the remote and popped it in his bag, and headed toward the classroom.

"Good morning, Mr. Verchall," Joe, the custodian, greeted him.

"Oh, hey, Joe."

"Getting an early start on the day?"

Brad nodded and kept moving.

"Didn't know anyone would be here at this time. I'll set up the coffee when I get done putting up the flag and unlocking the gates," Joe said to Brad's back.

Still facing forward, Brad raised his hand in a wave and said, "Thanks, Joe. Much appreciated."

Brad unlocked his classroom door and entered to the musty smell that greeted him every Monday morning. He turned on the lights and opened two windows for fresh air, although the breeze was cool.

At his desk, he unloaded what was in his bag into bins marked "Period 1" through "Period 4." While he was lost in the task, a knock made him lift his gaze to the door.

"Mr. Verchall, you heard about the body?" Joe leaned his ancient, hunched frame against the door jamb.

"What body?"

"The one they found in the basement of Old Man Branson's house? You know, the one his granddaughters bought." He waved vaguely behind him.

"I did," Brad said as he finished stacking the papers and turned around to face Joe.

"Sure is a strange one."

"How so?" Brad asked, flicking his wrist to check the time. He had half an hour before the first bell rang.

Joe scratched his stubbly chin and shook his head as if puzzled. "That place had not been lived in since…" He scratched his chin some more. "Oh, many years. A girl and her daddy lived there for a short time."

"Oh?" Although curious about the found body, Brad had a few things left to do before the kids descended on his classroom. He didn't want to be rude to Joe, but he needed to get going with the tasks he lined up for himself.

"Yeah, his girl was here. Don't recall her name, she was a strange one. She kept to herself—"

"Joe, I'm so sorry—"

"She had this weird thing she did with her eye… Oh, I'm keeping you. Never mind, Mr. Verchall. We'll catch up later. Have a nice day, now."

Brad lifted his gaze, but before the words came out, Joe had left. He finished straightening the desks, making sure he had board markers that worked, and few odds and ends. It was time to face the masses. What Joe said about the girl's eye, momentarily set aside.

The first three periods zipped by, most of the time spent on giving feedback on the essays such as errors with frequent occurrences in many papers. By lunchtime, Brad was ready to get off his feet and find food for his growling stomach. When the last student left, he locked the classroom and headed for the cafeteria. Nothing looked appealing, and he didn't want the company of other teachers. He decided to walk the few blocks to the deli.

Joe was in the hallway, and Brad, feeling guilty he ran him off earlier, offered to buy him lunch. "I'm heading to Frank's. Can I get you anything?"

"Martha packed my lunch, but I sure could use a ham and cheese sandwich. Thanks for asking, Mr. Verchall."

"Be back in a few."

The walk was pleasant, and Brad was back in less than twenty minutes. "Here you go, ham and cheese with chips and pickles on the side."

"Thanks, Mr. Verchall."

Both men found a shady spot in the staff courtyard and dug into their meal.

"So, you knew the kid who lived in the Branson house? Did you know her dad, too?" asked Brad.

"Nah. Never met him," said Joe around a mouthful.

"They say the body has been there maybe twenty or more years."

"Well, his kid was nice but strange, I tell ya. I heard through the grapevine he dumped her and left. Not sure who took her, but she stayed here… I mean, in this town and school."

"Interesting. Well, I must be off. The bell is about to ring, and the monsters will be coming in soon."

Brad and Joe exchanged a chuckle. Both knew the other loved the kids. A few steps away from Joe, Brad abruptly stopped, turned, and called, "Joe?"

Joe looked up from where he was still seated. Brad retraced his steps and returned to the table. Something Joe said earlier struck him. "You said the kid was weird and did a funny thing with her eyes?"

"Yeah… she would wink at people. Not sure what that was all about."

Brad shook the thought away. Why it bothered him, he didn't know. Perhaps because of Amanda's familiar tic?

"Okay, thanks, Joe. Have a good rest of the day."

He tucked the fleeting thought away, and the rest of the teaching day went without a hitch. When the students left with the last bell, Brad walked around his classroom, picking up papers and straightening out the desks and chairs, readying the room for the next day.

It suddenly dawned on Brad that the school year was almost at an end. He had no plans for the summer, and the two weeks he and Amanda shared during his time off would be strained unless they sorted the mess they faced. Brad turned and walked out of the classroom; the self-locking door clicked shut behind him. He exchanged small talk with colleagues before one pushed open the exit door. She was ready to go home. Brad trailed the small group.

"Say hi to the missus," Joe said, ready to lock the door behind Brad.

"Thanks, Joe."

"You asked about the kid earlier. You know, she has the same wink as your missus."

The hair stood on the back of Brad's neck, but he said nothing. He nodded to Joe and left the building. Before climbing on his bike, he sent a text to Amanda: *I'll pick up something for dinner on my way home.*

His thoughts turned with the wheels of the bike. He did a quick calculation. That was about the time Amanda would've been in school. *Stop it. As if she's the only one with an eye tic.*

Chapter 28

May 7, 2018

It was nearly ten o'clock by the time Amanda woke up. Groggy and disoriented, she opened her eyes to the sun streaming in from behind the shutters. The dust danced in the rays, and the house was eerily quiet. She pulled herself up and sat at the edge of the bed, surveying the room, wondering how long she had to call this place home.

Amanda shook a pill out of the bottle. There was no glass on the nightstand. She had two choices: swallow it dry or get water. Closing her fingers around it, she stood, stretched, and walked to the bathroom. She cupped her hand and greedily drank from the faucet.

When she straightened her now skinny frame (she had lost weight), her eyes met a reflection she didn't want to see. Quickly, she lowered her gaze and returned to the bedroom for clothes.

After showering and getting dressed, Amanda forced herself to the kitchen and made breakfast. There, she looked around, wondering when the last meal to prepare for herself would be before she was locked up.

Brad was at work, and she had the rest of the day to finish destroying any evidence of her past. On her way to the office, she looked in the laundry room, picked up a basket, and slowly made her way up the stairs with the heavy load. But she didn't put the clothes away. She reasoned what she still needed to do was a priority. The basket landed with a thud on the floor, and her feet carried her back to the office.

There wasn't much left, but what was left, Amanda had to deal with. Once more, she went to work, shredding and destroying all memories of her past. She shed no tears, she experienced no nostalgic moments, and she had no regrets. All she wanted was to erase the evidence of her past existence. She would need none of this where she was going – jail. Dry-eyed, she methodically went through all her boxes and hidden items.

Amanda's next stop was the bedroom, where she hid her journal. Time to destroy that, too, along with all the other scraps she'd tucked under stored items in the closet and her drawers where she was sure Brad would not find them.

Two hours later, she was done. It was time for a shower. She let the hot water fingers dig in her flesh while her mind planned for what was to come. Lost in thought, the water ran cold. She stepped out, dried herself, and put on jeans and a loose T-shirt, her curls tamed by a scrunchie.

She glanced at the time. She still had several hours before Brad got home from work. She picked up her laptop and made it to the kitchen. Her office no longer felt a haven, stripped of its secrets.

Amanda waited for the tics to subside. Despite the medication, anxiety and stress increased the frequency. She popped a pod in the coffee maker and reached for a snack. Standing by the sink, waiting for the coffee to brew, she surveyed her small backyard, then turned around and walked through the downstairs rooms. *Funny,* she thought. *I have no attachment to this place.*

In reality, Amanda didn't develop an emotional attachment to material objects; she never afforded to. The constant changes in her life made her detach from her surroundings. Nothing had been permanent. Now, she wondered if that explained why the possibility of jail and away from Brad didn't bother her much. What bothered her was having to go through a trial, the isolation. But, was that much different than the life she had lived so far?

Coffee done, Amanda heard the chime of the machine and returned to the present. She filled a mug and made her way upstairs. Knowing her time of freedom was limited, she wanted to close doors before someone slammed them in her face. So, first things first. She composed an email to her boss, thanking him for his patience and support, but with regrets, she needed to tender her resignation. She

155

left no room for discussion nor for anyone at the office to change her mind.

Next, it was Brad. The email to him would be difficult, but no matter how hard she had to turn him loose, she had to give him his freedom. Amanda didn't deserve him. He was too nice of a person, and she wanted to spare him the embarrassment of witnessing her arrest and incarceration.

After multiple failed attempts at starting the email, she got up and paced the office. She returned to her desk, no more putting off what needed to be done. But before she made it to her chair, the front doorbell chimed. Amanda walked to the window overlooking the front yard but saw no one. Though Brad had many friends, she had no one. Puzzled as to who that was, she walked to the landing and started her descent but quickly turned around and looked out of the window once more — no police cars.

"Coming," she yelled and headed to the front door.

"Good morning, my dear, I saw your car and…" said Mrs. Krupp, handing Amanda the newspaper.

"Wha… what's that for?"

"Oh, your husband was curious about the case. You know, the one with the unidentified body. There's more in today's paper, and I thought I wou—"

Amanda was ready to slam the door in her neighbor's face but thought better of it and, interrupting Ms. Krupps, said, "Thank you. I'll be sure to give it to him when he gets home."

"Well, I must be going, dear." She turned around and walked the short distance to her home while Amanda watched her.

After Amanda closed the door, she quickly opened the paper and gasped. "Body found has been identified. Police are searching for next of kin." Her heart drummed, sending vibrations through her skull. She scanned the article, not able to read it word for word, looking for details. Details that would finish her off. Sure enough, "…estimated time of death, June 1995…"

Amanda didn't need to count back. How could she forget that day? It was forever imprinted in her memory. The day she killed her father. She slid to the floor, realizing this was the end of her freedom. Her eyes, through unshed tears, scanned the long article for a name, but it wasn't on the page. The article continued on Section C, page three. With shaky hands, she flipped the pages. It wasn't there.

Panicked, Amanda got up and ran to her office, booting the computer before her body was in the chair. Fingers trembling, she clicked on the local paper. It wasn't difficult to find a link to the story. Impatient, she clicked on "find" and typed Andrew Bairn, but nothing came up. Puzzled, she tried again. But how could that be? It was May 29, 1995. Could it have been someone else? A coincidence? Or, was it perhaps a homeless person who came after she moved out?

With a jumble of thoughts racing through her mind, Amanda clicked at the top of the article to read. She didn't dare hope her dad was out there somewhere and that she didn't kill him.

Her cell pinged with an incoming text. She didn't want to remove her eyes from the article; she did anyway. It was Brad, telling her he'd pick up dinner on his way home. Amanda once more glanced at the time. She couldn't believe it was that late. She knew she had half an hour to forty-five minutes before Brad made it home. Returning her gaze to the screen on her computer, she jumped to the rest of the article, but there was no name.

Amanda kept reading. When she finished, and for a fleeting moment, she thought this had nothing to do with her and all the items she destroyed, the papers she shredded… was that for nothing?

Though the article was not about her dad, did he survive? Where was he if was still alive?

No, she decided. She was still not safe.

Chapter 29

May 7, 2018

"Oh, my gosh! Steph? Stephanie, where are you?"

Stephanie rushed into the room. "Are you okay? What's wrong?"

Liz handed the phone to her twin. The local breaking news flashed with the update. Stephanie's eyes rounded. She didn't blink as her pupils scanned the words on the screen. "Wow, our squatter has a name!"

"Don't be heartless."

"Lighten up. He's already dead. But seriously, how did they find out who he is, I wonder?"

"Probably dental or… maybe he has a criminal record. At least now we know."

"I still want to know how he died. I can't believe he has no relatives. How is that even possible?"

Both shook their heads in unison, right hand raking their hair. It was Liz who broke the silence that permeated the house and snapped them out of their thoughts. "Better get back to work, right?"

Stephanie nodded but didn't move from her spot.

"What's the matter, Steph?"

She pointed toward the hallway. "What do we do with that…" She wanted to say stuff, meaning the items she took from the basement that she shouldn't have.

"We should give them to the police."

"Okay."

"We *are* going to give them to the police, right?"

"Yeah."

"What do we say? How do we explain why we have it?"

"Leave it to me. Take my lead on that, okay?"

Stephanie took her phone back from Liz and scrolled through her contacts. "Hi, this is Stephanie Branson."

Liz could only hear her sister's side of the conversation and stood quietly, waiting for what she would tell Detective Miller.

"I… I found, I mean, we found something you may want to see." She paused. "Aha… no…Well, it looks like a briefcase, an old one." Stephanie took a deep breath before answering the next question. "Well, we, I mean, I… yes, I did look through it. I was curious who it belonged to."

Liz's eye rounded. Frantically motioning with her hands for her sister to stop, she mouthed, "No."

Stephanie dismissed her sister's concern with a wave of her hand, continuing her phone conversation. "Yeah, I'm sorry. I didn't know it could be of importance." Another pause. "Yes." She nodded as if the person on the other end could see. "Okay. We'll wait for you." She pressed the end call button.

"What the hell is wrong with you?" demanded Liz.

"Calm down. They're going to know we've been through it. Our fingerprints are all over the stuff, and you can see, none of it is dusty anymore."

Liz shook her head.

"Seriously, it's better this way than having them catch us in a lie."

Liz, not convinced, ran her fingers through her hair, mirroring what Stephanie did at that very moment.

"I guess we can get something done while we wait for Detective Miller." She tapped Liz on the shoulder. "Right?"

"I guess so."

Stephanie brought the briefcase out along with the thermos.

"Where did we find this stuff?" asked Liz.

"No reason to lie about that. In the basement. After they took the body."

Liz arched her eyebrows. "So, the police failed to do their job and didn't see it? Is that what you're going to tell the detective?"

"Sort of. Too late now. It's a done deal. Let's hope for the best."

It was less than thirty minutes when Detective Miller and another police officer knocked on the door.

"Here goes…" said Stephanie.

Liz sucked in a breath and opened the door. "Hi, detective. Come on in."

"Ms. Bronson," greeted the detective as he and an officer stepped into the living room, heading straight to where Stephanie stood, next to the table with the case and thermos. "Where did you say you found these?" He pointed to the objects while removing a pair of latex gloves from his pocket and peering into the case.

Stephanie cleared her throat. "In the basement after your guys left."

"Where exactly in the basement did you find them?" he asked without looking at her.

"Tucked in the corner, under the flooring."

"Perhaps, you can show me?" He straightened and made eye contact with Stephanie.

Stephanie quickly looked to the ground. Liz stood a distance away. She had wrapped her arms protectively around her waist.

"Um. Sure." She glanced at her sister as she led the way.

Liz followed at a distance.

"Right there." Stephanie pointed to the furthest corner of the basement, to a corner tucked away from view.

Detective Miller shook his head. Liz and Stephanie exchanged a glance. He said nothing else and walked back to the house, trailed by the officer and the twins.

"This may be important to the case. I wish you had called and not touched it."

Feeling a bit more emboldened that he was not arresting them for tampering with the evidence, she looked him straight in the eye and said, "How should I know? This is our house. We found other material tucked in the walls and the cabinets. This was no different."

"And, you're sure everything was returned to the bag?"

"Yes, of course," the twins responded.

"Thank you for calling us. Ladies." He turned to leave.

Stephanie closed the door behind the pair. They let out the breath they were holding and clutched each other's shoulders, leaning in for support.

Chapter 30

May 7, 2018

Brad picked up Chinese takeout and cycled home. He hopped off the bike, pressed the remote, and inched toward the garage door. He ducked his head before it rolled up and made his way in. With his foot, he pressed the kickstand and was about to lift the bags of food when he heard his neighbor's voice.

"Yoo-hoo!" she called.

Usually, Brad had a lot of patience for the old woman, but not at that moment. He was tired and hungry and had no idea what awaited him with Amanda. He didn't want to be rude. "Good evening, Mrs. Krupp."

"I brought over the paper earlier and gave it to the missus."

"Thank you." He lifted the bags from the insulated container attached to his bike. He didn't want to ask what that was about.

"I won't keep you then."

Brad opened his arms wide. "I'll catch you later. Got to take the food in before it gets cold."

"Oh, sure thing. I have to get back to Henry before he burns down the house. He's in the kitchen cooking." Mrs. Krupps turned and shuffled home.

Amanda opened the door leading to the garage. "Who were you talking to?"

"Our neighbor," he said, and climbed the two steps into the house.

"She brought the paper over earlier," Amanda said.

"Yeah, that's what she told me. Is it about the dead body they found over at the Branson's?"

"It's on the counter in the kitchen."

Brad raised an eyebrow in surprise. What had changed? Just two or so days ago, his wife didn't want anything to do with the neighbor, let alone the newspaper and the dead body. He set the bags on the counter and reached for the paper. It didn't take long for him to scan the article on the front page. "C section is missing," he said.

"That's the way she gave it to me. I bet you can read it online."

"Did you read it?"

"No. Had other things to do."

"I'll look for it after dinner. Are you hungry?"

"I could stand to eat," she said.

Something about Amanda was different. She didn't appear as stressed as she'd been. Dare he hope for normalcy?

Brad pulled the food out of the bags and popped open the Styrofoam containers. The forks and napkins were at the bottom. Amanda lifted them while Brad was readying the food. In silence, they sat opposite each other and ate. After a few bites, Brad, not wanting to change his wife's good mood, opted for a neutral subject. "When do you go back to work?" he asked, assuming she'd taken a few days off while not feeling well.

For a moment, she didn't answer. Brad watched her face but could read nothing in her blank expression. He waited for her answer, which came after she swallowed. He did notice that she took the bite after he asked the question. Brad wondered if it was a delay tactic.

"I submitted my resignation," she said, shifting her gaze back to her food.

"Wait. What did you just say? Did I hear you right? You quit and didn't think it was important we talk about it *before* you quit?"

"I had to."

"Why?"

"I had a breakdown in San Francisco and botched up a presentation. It was either I quit or get fired."

Brad set his fork down. He truly wanted to be an understanding and supportive husband, but how could he when she didn't bother to communicate with him? Teetering between wanting to snap at his wife and wanting to reign in his anger, he said, "Look, this isn't going to work out. I don't know what's going on, you don't talk, and honestly..." he paused.

"And, you honestly what?" she demanded.

Shaking his head, he said, "I don't know. I really don't. I'm your husband, and it seems the last one to know what's going on."

"It wasn't a big deal."

"Must be a big deal. Big enough to quit your job over."

Amanda set her filled fork back in the container and pushed it away from her. Folding her hands under her chin, she stared at a spot past Brad's shoulder.

"So, are we going to play twenty questions, or are you going to tell me what the hell is going on?" He regretted his harshness but had no choice. His life was unraveling like an old sweater that snagged on a rusted nail. Either he got to the bottom of this madness and figured it out, or the stress would have him committed.

He watched Amanda shrug as if she didn't care. He raised his eyebrows questioningly. "So?"

Amanda pulled her hands away from her chin and opened them in a gesture of supplication. "Well, I fell apart in San Francisco. Maybe it was the stress of traveling, every day on the go — every few days on a flight to somewhere. I don't know. I just couldn't handle it."

"Why didn't you tell me?"

164

"At first, I thought I could handle it on my own. Then there was—"

"Go on," he coaxed.

"There was a text message from Andrew—"

"I already know about that. You said he got in touch to tell you about his dad," Brad said, interrupting her.

"You need to listen. Don't say anything, okay?"

Brad nodded.

"No, that's not what he wanted to tell me. He threatened me."

Brad opened his mouth to say something, but she shook her head to silence him.

"No. That's not why he got hold of me. I don't know what he wants, but I know he'd threatened me, and now, he knows where I live."

Brad watched her face intently. At that point, he didn't know what to believe. He didn't know if he would believe anything, Amanda said. Breaking into his thoughts, she continued, "When I was fourteen, I lived with the Bakers. They were okay, but they had other foster kids. One…" Amanda bit her lip.

He wasn't sure if she was stifling a sob or preparing for more lies.

"There was this… girl… a couple of years older than me. She mercilessly teased me and made fun of my tics. I hated her, but you have to believe me, I didn't hurt her."

Brad stared at her wide-eyed. Who was this person? She was a stranger he didn't know. But, as she'd asked, he said nothing.

"Her name was Ashley. One day, we got into it, and she pushed me. I pushed her back. We were at the top of the stairs. She didn't fall right away. When I went into the room, I shared with her, she was still at the top of the stairs holding onto the railing."

165

Amanda looked up. Brad met her gaze, and once again, he opened his mouth to say something. She silenced him with a wave of her hand.

"I heard her fall, and I walked out. She was at the bottom of the stairs. I don't know if she was alive or not. By the time the ambulance came, my social worker was there, and she gathered my things and took me to another home. You have to believe me. I didn't kill her. I didn't hurt her."

When he continued to be silent, mouth agape, she said, "You do believe me, don't you?"

"Honestly, I don't know what I believe. I don't get why you have said nothing all these years. And, why all of a sudden would Andy get hold of you and send these horrible notes?"

One shoulder went up and down, and she rapidly winked as Brad waited for her answer. Nothing made sense. None of it made sense.

"I don't know. I don't know what to say."

"I think we should call the police," Brad said, reaching for his cell.

Amanda's arm shot out to stop him. "No. No."

"Why not? If you're innocent, and he's threatening you – yeah, me, too – we should call the police."

"I'm afraid of what he'll do if we call the cops."

"*I* am afraid of what he'll do if we don't make the call. This isn't just about you, Amanda."

Silence ensued. Neither spoke. The kitchen got darker as the sun set. Brad stood to turn on the lights. Amanda stood to leave. He was not about to let her do that. There was too much still unsaid. He had reached the end of his patience. This was it. If she wasn't going to come clean, he was done, and whatever had happened in her past, she was on her own.

Taking a deep breath and letting out, he said, "Don't leave. This is not going to work out. Either tell me the truth, or I cannot stand by you like this."

Slowly, Amanda turned to face him. "Why? What do you care?"

"You are my wife. I care. But I cannot care by myself. If you walk out on this conversation, I will call the cops. This is no longer just about you if… if you were telling me the truth."

Brad could see her tics were getting worse. *She has to be stressed,* he thought. He wanted to extend compassion, but he was at the point of breaking. The past few days had taken a toll on him.

Two things jumped at him at once. Lifting his left hand to his ear, he asked, "Did you lose it?"

She mirrored his action. "Oh, that. Yeah. I must've lost its match," she said as she pulled the pearl earring out of her ear, slipped it into her pocket, and sat opposite him.

That was the simple question, mundane, and an ice breaker. The second question Brad wanted to ask could send Amanda off into the land of silence or hostility. He took a chance. Brad wanted to know. Joe's comments rattled around his brain. "What school did you go to?"

"What? Where did that come from?"

"Just answer, please. You never told me anything about where you grew up, hardly anything about your past."

"What difference does it make where I went to school?"

"I guess no difference. But it was something Joe had said."

"Joe?"

"Yeah. You know, Joe, our custodian."

Brad watched her face as he spoke for any telltale sign of change. Her eye twitched. She shrugged. He wondered if it was her that Joe talked about. "So, what school?"

"What did he say?"

"Not much. Just that he remembers a girl at the junior high school… and I thought, maybe it was you."

"It wasn't me. And, he had no business talking about me."

"Whoa. He wasn't talking about *you*. It was just something he said in a conversation that made think—"

"Well, don't. It wasn't me." She stood to leave once more.

"I don't get it. Why so hostile? Why so, secretive? This isn't the Amanda I married. The gentle and sweet wife. What happened to you?"

Amanda turned to face him. "Nothing! If you want to leave me, go ahead. I have nothing else to say to you. You didn't ask me any questions for twelve years. Why, all of a sudden, the interest in my past? Why?"

"I'm not willing to throw away our marriage. But it takes both of us working on it, and right now, it seems the distance is widening. I cannot support you if you can't be truthful with me."

Torn between guilt and anger, Brad stood and slowly made it around the counter to where Amanda sat. He reached for her hand, and she backed away from him.

"Amanda, please. Let's not throw our marriage away. Just tell me what's going on. I want to be here for you."

He watched her wrap her arms around herself. A tear trickled down her cheek. She turned her face away from him. Brad closed the distance and hugged her. "Please trust me. Whatever it is, we'll get through it together."

She was stiff in his arms, and after a few minutes, she said, "You will know everything soon enough." With that, she left the kitchen.

He didn't stop her this time.

Chapter 31

May 8, 2018

Amanda didn't sleep much despite the sleeping pills she took. She couldn't drown out the noises in her head. Another night alone with the moon admonishing her actions and choices; he'd been a witness, he knew.

The morning couldn't come soon enough. But what was she in a rush for? There was nothing left to shred or destroy. The only thing hanging, unresolved, was what happened to her father? If only she could find out, then maybe, just maybe, she would know for sure if she would live free or behind bars. For a fleeting moment, she thought of turning herself in to get it over with.

Amanda hadn't bothered to read emails or text messages since she submitted her resignation. She had no idea if she still had a job or not.

She took her coffee to the office. There had to be a way to find out what happened to her father. Amanda brought out the birth certificates and snapped an image of each with her phone. She reasoned she could quickly delete them later. She fed the papers to the shredder, noticing the two bags off to the side, filled with strips of papers. Since Brad wasn't around to ask questions, she lifted the two bags and carried them to the trashcan outside, making sure her neighbor was not around.

Back at her desk, she was tempted to look through text messages, but opted not to. Why had she not heard from Andy in the past few days? So, she changed her mind and scrolled through the texts. There was nothing from Andy nor her work. Relieved, she stared into space, mind whirring with clashing thoughts. What if it wasn't Andy Baker who sent her the messages?

Once more, she booted the computer, and this time, she searched social media for Andrew Baker. He had a Facebook page. It was his image, though he looked so much older than she remembered him. She perused his posts, what she could because of his privacy settings, and glanced at the photos. He had a family with grown kids. *Then, why is he contacting me now?*

She clicked on "About," and "Family Members." There, his wife's name popped up. She clicked on the others. None were of Matt. *Strange.* It was possible Matt didn't have a social media account; he was a private person, quiet and reserved. She then scanned Andrew's friends' names. One caught her attention, Ashley Baker. *No way.* She quickly clicked on the link. Sure enough, it was Ashley. The same Ashley from so long ago. She had survived the fall.

This became even more confusing to Amanda. Why hadn't she thought of checking social media sooner? It was the damned text message at the airport. She had no reason to give this part of her past a second thought before this moment.

Baker. Ashley Baker. If Ashley survived the fall, she must've married Matt? If so, then there was no way it was this Andrew, Andrew Baker, who had been in contact with her. Then, who? She pulled out her phone and looked at the messages, sure the call came from a private number, but wanted to check anyway. It was a private number.

Amanda returned her gaze to the image on the screen. *Twenty-two years.* Though Ashley had changed, she was just as pretty – perhaps more sophisticated beauty. The page was not restricted, and Amanda spent time looking through it. So, if Ashley survived the fall, why then, hadn't she told on Amanda? Did Amanda dare contact Ashley? She quickly let that idea go. She had more urgent matters to deal with.

Fingers resting on the keyboard lost in a world that wasn't the present, she stared out of the open-curtained window. A blue sky beyond, a few white clouds meandered past, and her mind traveled back in time. She stood and leaned on the sill, scanning the neighborhood below.

It was a day just like this day, bright and sunny, June of 2006 when she married Brad. Though she dated, it wasn't consistent, nor was it with a commitment in mind. He was the only one who didn't pry into her past, didn't prod and coax her to tell him details. Brad accepted what little information she shared. She could say it was a happy day when they exchanged vows in a garden wedding at a friend's house: his friend. She had none.

So, why was he suddenly interested in pursuing knowledge of her past? That wasn't fair, was it? He had accepted her just as she was. She absently closed the curtains and returned to her desk with a sigh. The email she drafted to Brad was still on her computer. Should she send it, end this charade of marriage before he discovered her truth?

Amanda clicked out of the email; the draft was still in its current status of a draft not sent. She would set that aside for the moment.

Amanda got up, stretched, then sat, swiveling her neck from side to side and up and down to loosen the stiffness, a paper caught her eye on the floor next to her left foot. With her right arm, she pushed against the edge of the desk, rolling the chair back a few inches, bent, and retrieved the scrap. It was the paper with numbers from her grandmother so long ago. She flipped it around with her fingers. She should toss it, a useless scrap. But, something deep within stopped her. She picked up the paper from the trashcan and smoothed it out. Then, into the shredder, it went.

Amanda steepled her fingers under her chin, lost in thought once again, wishing she'd not married Brad, wishing she didn't have a criminal past. For the first time, her mind didn't rationalize her behavior. For the first time, she didn't make excuses. She was a criminal, what she did was horrid, and she deserved whatever punishment came her way. And, it was on its way.

Irene came into her blurred vision, and Amanda swiped at an errant tear, then brought her fingers up and looked at them. She was crying. When was the last time she shed tears? Too long ago to remember. Perhaps when her father took her from her auntie's house. Yes, it was that long ago. Why was it now, when her future was coming to an end, that she would feel? Why now?

Then, an abrupt thought entered without knocking, her mother, Irene. How long had it been since she'd seen her? At least four years when she lied to Brad and told him she had to travel for work but instead, made the trip south to see Irene. The visit was no different than others she'd made; there was no love nor had her mother improved.

Though she was never a real mother to Amanda, Irene was still the woman who gave birth to her, and she couldn't help her mental illness. She had to see her one last time before the police came for her. Decision made, she pushed away from the desk, and with purpose in her step, she grabbed her purse and walked to the car. Amanda didn't bother to text Brad. She looked at the time and figured she would be back before he got home.

She didn't need the GPS. Her foot steady on the gas, Amanda drove the long miles to the facility, tapping her fingers nervously on the steering wheel, checking her mirrors every few minutes. Her demons and guilt chased her.

When she made this trip in the past, Amanda's anxiety had her nerves in knots, and her stomach refused to hold food nor drink. This time, however, her anxiety had nothing to do with seeing Irene. This visit would be her last. It was time to say goodbye to her past and, along with it, her future.

The facility loomed on the horizon; no sign of life for miles on end. Surrounded by empty fields, the building with its tall walls and impeccable landscaping was an oasis, except, it wasn't paradise. Hardly any resident noticed their surroundings, each lost in their delusions and illness.

At the far end of the parking lot, Amanda shut off the engine and sat for a few minutes, collecting her thoughts. It was nearly one in the afternoon, and if she made the visit short, she would be back at the house well before Brad returned.

With a purposeful stride, she got out of the car and locked it, making her way to the gate, where she rang the intercom button. Someone asked her name and the purpose of the visit.

"Amanda Verchall. I'm here to visit Irene Dunkirk."

A buzzer sounded, and Amanda pushed the gate open and stepped onto the brick path. She heard the lock click and imagined the metal gates clanking shut in prison, isolating the inmates – the movies had to have portrayed reality.

A uniformed staff greeted her before she arrived at the receptionist's desk. "Good morning. You're Irene's daughter?"

"Yes."

"I'm Michelle. You probably don't remember me. It's been a while.

Amanda said nothing. The face was familiar, but she couldn't get hold of where she knew her from. She was sure not staff from years ago. "Um—"

"I know. It's been too many years. Anyway, nice to see you again. Maybe we can have coffee after your visit and catch up?"

Amanda looked at the phone, not wanting to commit to social visits. "I'd like that, but I'm in a bit of a bind for time today."

"Oh, no worries. I didn't mean today. I'll text you my number." Michelle pulled the phone out of her pocket and looked at Amanda expectantly.

Amanda had no choice but to give her number, and Michelle promptly sent a text, then looked up. "It was nice seeing you again. I've got to run."

With a wave of her hand, she took the few steps to the sliding glass door, but before she entered the lobby, her spine stiffened, and her legs refused to move when she heard Michelle say, "Oh, by the way, did you hear what happened to Ashley?"

Collecting her wits, Amanda slowly turned around. She had no intention of staying in touch with Michelle, but, at that moment, with the dawning of who Michelle was and where she knew her from, she had no choice. Michelle of long ago – Michelle of Ms. Ellie's foster home.

Amanda mouthed, half in a whisper, "What did you say?"

"Oh, I thought… I mean… never mind. We'll chat later."

Amanda closed the distance between them and tried not to sound anxious. "It's okay. I can spare a couple of minutes."

"Well, it was kinda weird. After I left Ms. Ellie, I lived with another foster family for a couple of years… the Bakers. You probably don't know them."

Amanda swallowed. "And?"

"I overheard her talk to the social worker." Michelle stopped in mid-sentence and checked the time on her phone, then said, "Long story, I have to get back to my shift."

Amanda reached for Michelle's arm. "Please, just tell me. You got me curious." Sweat trickled down Amanda's back. Her palms were cold and clammy.

"She lost her baby when she fell down the stairs—"

"She… she was preg…" Amanda didn't finish her sentence. The sight of blood staining Ashley's pants after she kicked her was no longer a distant memory.

Chapter 32

May 8, 2018

The day was too long. It didn't want to end, and Brad's classes were unusually chaotic and noisy. He couldn't get the students to settle down and focus. Most were restless after the long and grueling standardized testing. And, Brad had no patience left.

Usually, he would find academic activities that were fun to distract his students, but this year, he, too, was restless. His home life was anything but stable, and his mind was riddled with questions that had no answers.

Brad looked up at the clock above the door. Seven minutes to release. With a sigh of relief, he gathered items and placed them in his bag. His students must've noticed something amiss; he had never cleaned his desk ahead of the bell. Suddenly, the room fell quiet. The absence of sound made him look up. Several eyes were upon him. Brad scratched his head and gave them a tentative smile. Four minutes to go.

Finally, the shrill sent the kids scampering out the door except for two, who tentatively approached him. "You okay, Mr. V?"

Brad nodded, his ragged face and hair betraying him.

The two walked off, turning twice to check. With a wave and a nod, he dismissed them. "See you guys tomorrow," he said.

For the first time since he began his teaching career, he didn't stay to straighten and organize the classroom. Brad shoved the last of the papers in his briefcase, flipped the lights off, and locked the door behind him.

"Where you off to in a hurry, boss?" Joe intercepted him in the hallway.

"Long day, Joe. Long day."

Joe leaned on his long-handled broom, said nothing, but didn't get out of Brad's way.

"Well, see you tomorrow," Brad said.

Joe shook his head side to side. "Not like you."

"You know how the kids get this time of year."

Once more, Joe shook his head, clearly, not believing Brad. "Say hi to the missus." He turned to walk away.

Brad hesitated for a moment, wanting to leave, but felt bad that his behavior was dismissive toward Joe. His emotional exhaustion won, and his feet carried him out of the door. He was not in a hurry to go home, it didn't feel like one, but he wanted this phase with Amanda to be over with, one way or another. He no longer had the energy nor the fortitude to deal with this discourse.

Outside, the air was fresh, and the sun welcoming. He rounded the corner to where he secured his bike and almost wanted to cry at the sight of a flat tire. Frustrated and angry, he knelt and touched the rubber, fighting the urge to scream. He could leave his bike and deal with it later, but it wouldn't make the problem go away, and he didn't want to walk home.

Like a child with a broken toy, he returned to the building, where Joe was slopping the wet mop back and forth across the floor. At the sound of footsteps, Joe looked up. "Thought you left, boss."

Raking his fingers through his hair, aggravated, Brad said, "My bike has a flat."

Joe placed his mop in the bucket and leaned it against the wall. He set a "Floors are wet" sign in the middle of the hallway, raised one finger, and said, "Be right back. Wait here."

A few minutes later, Joe returned with a tool pouch and an air pump he used for kids' bikes. "Come on, Mr. V, let's get it done."

Obediently, glad for someone else to take charge of his immediate destiny, Brad followed Joe out and stood by, helplessly watching the old man – not that he was helpless. This was something he could've done for himself, but at that moment, too worn out to do so.

"So, what's eating at you?" asked Joe, hunched over the tire, pumping air in it.

"Long day and now this."

"Nah, Mr. V. That's not it. I've known you too long."

Brad squatted next to Joe and reached to feel the tire. "Looks good. Thanks, Joe."

Joe turned and grabbed Brad's arm to steady himself as he got up from his crouched position. Their eyes briefly met. Joe shook his head. "Known you way too long, Mr. V."

Brad stood. In his eyes were a thousand questions that Joe might have seen. On a whim, he asked, "Hungry?"

"Always," replied Joe.

"Okay. I'll be back in a bit."

"Not my break yet, but I suppose I can take an early one."

Brad hopped on his bike and peddled toward his destination, Frank's Deli. He locked his bike by the entrance, grabbed his bag, and headed inside. The place was practically deserted as it was too late for the lunch crowd and too early for dinner.

He reached for his wallet as he gave the order for two sandwiches and drinks, placing his card in the digital payment device.

"Your order will be out in a few," said Michael with a smile.

Brad was too restless to sit. He paced the small waiting area then walked outside, pacing some more. He should go home. He should… but he would take the food and sit with Joe for a while. Maybe it would clear his head, talking to the trusted old soul.

"Well, hello again. We need to stop meeting like this," said Liz with a chuckle, startling Brad.

He turned around, and for a few seconds, Brad stared at the twins, then jolted to the present. "Oh, hey."

Brad wasn't in the mood for socializing, but his intrigue with the house they purchased, and the body uncovered in their basement pushed him forward. "What's new with the case?" he asked.

"Nothing yet. The police won't tell us anything, which makes me mad. After all, it is *our* house!"

"Yeah, I would be frustrated, too."

He watched them exchange a glance, which puzzled him. He raised his eyebrows questioningly – a habit he acquired as a teacher, tuning in to his students' sudden behavior changes.

"Oh," said Stephanie.

Liz nodded.

"Weird. We found a bag in the house that had all kinds of papers and jewelry. Not much—"

Liz interrupted. "We gave it to the police. We don't know if it belongs to the dead guy or someone else."

"Anything interesting in the stuff you found?" he asked.

"Not—"

"Well, we didn't look, but—"

"We sort of checked it out because we didn't know… Anyway, the papers were too hard to read – washed out birth certificates and such. The jewelry was nothing to brag about. There was a ring, a necklace, and one pearl earring," said Stephanie, shaking her head. "Well, anyway. We'd better put in our order. Stop by some time; we'd love to show you the house."

Brad was still processing their find – a pearl earring? Then, he realized they were walking away. "Oh, thanks for the invite," he said to their backs.

Liz wiggled her fingers over her shoulder, waving.

Dumbfounded, Brad got lost in his thoughts and didn't hear Michael calling to him with the bagged order in his hand. *Too many coincidences. Way too many.*

"Mr. V., here's your order," Michael said as he approached Brad.

Startled, Brad took the bag without so much as thanking the young man. In a fog of unsettling thoughts, he walked toward the school. Halfway there, he realized he should've been riding his bike, but continued forward. He'd pick it up later. It was less than a mile from the school.

Shoulders hunched with the weight of what was on his mind, he pushed himself to move one step at a time, troubled with what he didn't know about his wife — rattled by the one pearl earring she had on, flustered by the kid with tics Joe mentioned, and angered by the phone calls and notes. He knew, deep inside, Amanda had lied to him or, at best, was withholding the truth about her past.

Without realizing it, Brad had arrived at the school and was reaching for his keys when Joe said, "Must've been busy at Frank's."

Puzzled, Brad looked at Joe.

Joe pointed to the bag.

"Oh, no. I forgot I rode my bike there and walked back. Guess I'm not used to riding there." He gave a feeble smile.

Joe shook his head. "Whatever is troubling you, son, you need to get help for."

Brad followed Joe to the staff lounge. One teacher was there, checking the mail in his cubby hole. He nodded toward the two men and left with a stack of papers bundled under his arm. "See you tomorrow," he said on his way out.

Joe unwrapped the sandwich that Brad handed him from the bag and took a bite. Brad did the same, but instead of taking a bite, he returned the food to the table before it touched his lips. He wasn't hungry.

179

They sat in silence for a few minutes. Joe, eating, and Brad staring into space. Finally, Joe spoke, bringing Brad back to the room. "Got to get back to work in a few." Pointing at the food, he said, "You haven't touched it."

Brad shook his head, fighting the urge to let the droplets gathering behind his eyelids loose. He looked at the table. "I wish I can tell you, Joe. I don't even know what all is eating me up."

"Start somewhere, even if you're not sure," Joe said, prompting Brad to talk.

"I have a question. Remember the kid you told me about? The one who lived in that house… where they found the body?"

Joe nodded.

"Anyway, you can tell me her name?"

"Not sure I remember it. It's been a long time ago."

"Maybe a name that sounds like it?"

"Why the interest?"

"Well, I'm not sure, but I may know that girl."

Joe arched his eyebrows.

"Can you try? Please?"

Joe rubbed his chin and crumpled the sandwich wrapper. After he took a sip of soda, he said, "Honestly, I don't remember. Maybe you can tell me the name of the girl you know? I might recognize it."

Brad hesitated. He didn't want to mention his wife's name.

"Her name starts with A. Amber, Angela, or something like that. Sorry, I don't remember."

The blood drained from Brad's face, and he felt his palms sweaty and clammy. *Amanda?* his mind screamed but said nothing.

Joe had to get back to work.

"Yep. Time for me to hit the road, too," Brad said as he got up. "Here, keep this for later." He handed the uneaten sandwich to Joe.

"Need a ride to your bike?"

"Oh, no, thanks. It's not far."

When Brad got to the door, he turned around. "Thanks. See you tomorrow." With that, he left.

Chapter 33

May 8, 2018

Shocked by what she heard, Amanda crossed the threshold and entered the building, leaving Michelle with a puzzled look on her face.

With a shaky hand, she signed in and checked her phone twice to jot down the correct date. Somewhere within her, a voice screamed to run, to leave the facility, and keep going without looking back, but her determination to deal with the past won. Straightening her back, she addressed the receptionist. "Is my mother in room 212?"

"Let me check," said Jane, clicking the keyboard. "Looks like…" she peered closer at the screen. "She's still there—"

"Thank you," Amanda said, cutting Jane off and walking toward the double sliding doors.

"Wait."

Amanda turned around, one eyebrow raised.

Tucking a hair strand behind her ear, Jane kept her gaze on the screen and didn't look up

"What is it? What's wrong?" demanded Amanda.

Jane put up her forefinger, indicating for Amanda to wait a moment, then lifted the phone and pressed a number. "Can you come to reception, please?"

"I asked you what is wrong?"

"Please, hang on. My supervisor will be here in a minute."

Before Amanda could object, the sliding glass doors whirred open, and a tall, silver-haired woman in an immaculate suit strode through, arriving behind the desk where Jane pointed to the screen.

"You'd better tell me what is going on, and now. I waited long enough."

Margaret, her name tag read, said, "Mrs. Verchall, why don't you come with me, please. We can talk in private," she said as she pointed behind Amanda to a couple who had just entered the facility.

Jane flipped her hands open, communicating she had no idea what was going on.

Amanda's heart thudded in her chest. Mixed emotions clamored to the surface; guilt blended with anxiety. Surely, if her mom had died, the facility would've notified her, wouldn't they have?

Margaret led the way, Amanda following. At the next hallway to the left, Margaret twirled her keyring and inserted one in the lock, twisting it to the left. Amanda tapped her foot, anger now joining other emotions.

"Please," Margaret ushered Amanda in, walked to a chair by the conference table, rolled it out, and sat.

Amanda stood. "Well?"

"Please, have a seat."

"I'll stand."

Margaret cleared her throat. "There's been a mix-up, but don't worry. It has been sorted out."

"What the hell are you talking about?" Amanda could no longer contain her irritability.

"Mrs. Verchall, your mother was moved to another facility." She held up her hand, silencing Amanda, and continued. "She took a turn for the worst, and her psychotic episodes could no longer be managed here. She's now at Longridge—"

"How dare you move her without notifying me? And… and… she confirmed the room number when I arrived," Amanda said, pointing vaguely towards the reception area.

183

"May I remind you, ma'am, you are not her guardian nor fiduciary. This"—she moved her forefinger between them— "is a courtesy conversation with you."

"Damn, damn, damn."

"No need to be vulgar, Ms. Verchall. I'm trying to help," said Margaret.

Amanda lifted her hand to her mouth, her eye twitched, and her shoulder involuntary shrugged. "I… I… have ti…" then, "Never mind," as she stormed out of the room and out of the facility.

In the car, Amanda Googled Longridge. There was no way she would have time to drive the additional hour south and be back at the house before Brad got in. Frustrated, she turned the ignition on and slammed the gear into drive.

The highway leading to the main freeway was virtually empty. Amanda fished out her phone, and with glances at the screen, she dialed Longridge's number. When the operator answered, Amanda, asked for her mother's room and waited. Her phone automatically connected to the car's hands-free system, and now her fingers tapped the steering wheel impatiently.

A few minutes later, the operator returned to the call, "Mrs. Verchall, I will transfer you now."

A voice she almost didn't recognize came on the line.

"Irene?"

"Yes. Who is this?"

"Amanda."

"Amanda? I don't know an Amanda. Do I?"

Amanda heard someone in the background telling Irene, "It's your daughter."

"Oh," said Irene, her voice stronger as she must've got closer to the handset. "Amanda? Where are you?"

"I will come to see you soon. I'm driving now. No one told me you moved."

"I didn't move. Who did you say you were?"

Amanda let out a gasp. Her mother didn't recognize her. They told her she had the onset of dementia, but she didn't expect this… not this soon. She tried to jog her mother's memory and focus. "Mother, this is Amanda, your daughter."

"Hi, Amanda." There wasn't a hint of recognition in her voice.

Amanda held back the burning questions she wanted to ask her mother. *Who is my father?* was at the top of the list. The rest didn't seem as important at that moment. Returning her attention to the call, she said, "Irene, can you put the nurse on the line?"

She waited, listening to shuffling and muffled voices.

"This is Marge, Irene's nurse."

"Hi. What's happened to her? She was fine the last time I saw her." *Two years ago, or was it three or more? I can't remember.*

"She has her good days. Are you planning to visit?"

"Yeah. I came by today. I mean, I came by the other facility… they didn't tell me they moved her."

After a few moments, Amanda thanked the nurse and pressed the end call button on the steering wheel. *Now what?*

Wondering how much time she had left before she was arrested and metal doors forever slammed behind her, Amanda decided if she was still free, she would drive to see her mother the following day. If not, the mystery of the birth certificate would haunt her for the rest of her days.

Amanda eased up on the gas pedal when she noticed her speed was past the posted limit. She didn't want to rush a confrontation with the police. The time would come soon enough.

When she realized she hadn't received a text from Brad, she was relieved. This meant he was still at school and not on his way home. If he called while she was still on the road, Amanda would tell him not to worry about dinner; she'd pick something up. She doubted he would ask where she was, anyway.

Amanda had another forty-five miles to go. And, another night of dodging questions and sleeping alone, but that was the least of her worries. Her eyes tracked the road and the traffic, making sure she didn't drive fast. Her mind wondered. She could no longer pretend all was okay.

Ashley had lost her baby. Now, Amanda was not only guilty of poisoning and killing her father, she was also guilty of causing a miscarriage. Even though the man in the basement wasn't her dad, she was sure her dad died because of what she put in his coffee.

But, why hadn't Ashley told on her?

She replayed that fateful day while her foot stayed steady on the gas pedal. Somehow, the images were now fuzzy. Amanda remembered the argument, which was more of a fight, then what happened? They were at the top of the stairs, pushing and shoving each other. Was her mind playing tricks on her now? As hard as she tried to bring back the moment before Ashley tumbled down the stairs, the image shifted. One minute, she saw arms shoving Ashley, and the next, she had turned her back when she heard the thudding of Ashley's body going down.

Her dad was among the flashes of lights and faces, which came rushing at her as if in a sci-fi tunnel. Disoriented, she slammed on the brakes, or did she?

The glass shattered, and a metallic taste filled her mouth. Familiar yet strange sounds and voices came and went. Searing pain shot up her leg and the left side of her body. Amanda tried to flicker her eyes open, but the intensity of the light was more than she could stand. Her mouth wanted to move but couldn't form words.

In the distance, she heard someone say, "That's it. Look at me."

She couldn't. She didn't want to. They were there to arrest her, and as much as she wanted the nightmare to be over, how could she face a future in prison? Amanda retreated into the darkness.

Chapter 34

May 8, 2018

Before he started his trek to Frank's Deli, Brad sent a text message to Amanda, letting her know he was on his way. He didn't receive a response, which puzzled him. Even throughout their difficulties, she responded quickly to his texts. He waited until he got to his bike before sending another message. Once again, there was no response.

Brad unlocked his bike, secured his bag, and peddled home. Using the remote control, he let himself in through the garage and walked into the kitchen. The house was eerily quiet. He wasn't surprised there wasn't a pot on the stove; neither had bothered to cook or, for that matter, grocery shop for several days.

Instead of calling her name, Brad climbed the stairs. Her office door was slightly open, with no light nor sound inside. He poked his head in, and as he suspected, she wasn't there. Brad checked the bedroom; quiet, nothing disturbed. For a moment, panic set in, and he rushed to the closet, slamming the doors open so hard it almost broke the glass. Her clothes were there. He took two long strides to her dresser and yanked the drawers one by one, but her underwear and other clothing were there. "Amanda!" he yelled as he walked out of the bedroom and to the landing.

"Amanda!" This time louder.

He pulled his phone out of his pocket in case he missed the text notification.

Nothing.

Brad fired off one more text. *Where are you?*

He went downstairs and back to the garage. Her car was gone. Only his bike next to his blue Prius stood in silence. He hadn't even noticed the black car wasn't there.

188

Where could she have gone? She had no friends nor family that he knew of. He'd wait. Her belongings were still there. She'd come back.

His stomach rattled the silence with a growl. Brad ignored it. He was not hungry and couldn't face food. He walked back to the stairs, contemplating if he should resume the search through Amanda's office since he had no idea where she was and when she would come back. Berating himself for thinking of doing so, he stopped short and sat on the bottom step, firing off another text message.

"Where is she?" he asked, but the walls had no answer.

Fifteen minutes passed, then half an hour. The next time Brad looked at his phone, it was 9:30, and the house was shrouded in darkness and silence. He hadn't bothered to turn on lights. Reluctantly, he got off the couch, flicked on a switch, then headed to the kitchen. A massive headache was descending on him, and he had to eat.

Brad opened the refrigerator and stared at its skimpy contents. A salad would do, he decided. There was a box of crackers on the counter, and he took them along, perching on the high barstool. He forced a few forkfuls down and washed them with water from a glass already there.

Contemplating what he should do, he finished his bowl and drank the last of the stale water. Should he call the police and report her missing? Should he... Wait, could she have gone back to work? Wouldn't she have told him?

Frustrated, Brad slammed the counter with his fist then raked his fingers through his hair. Tears choked him again, but he swallowed them. He didn't want to feel sorry for himself, but enough was enough. He reached for his phone and checked his messages — nothing from Amanda. His next move was to call the police and report her missing. Brad would not allow himself to believe she left him. Not like that. Not without telling him she would.

Guilt and grief flooded him. He mourned the loss of the past twelve years of marriage, and he felt guilty for allowing his mind to

189

wander into dark areas, calling into question his wife's innocence. If only she had talked to him. Why did she have to lie and not tell the truth? Then, just as quickly, he flipped his thoughts to feeling badly for thinking that.

Brad thought of his students, their innocence, and what hardships some faced. He needed to be more understanding. He didn't know what Amanda's past held, but he reminded himself she was a child then, a victim of her circumstances, as all children are.

But she was no longer a child.

He pounded the wall with his fists, hung his head, and let the tears flow. He would be patient. Maybe he was at fault. He didn't create safety for her to confide in him. What could she have done as a child to be so bad? Brad reasoned it was a childhood issue because she passed background checks to land the job she did. It had to be something in her long-ago past, and whatever it was, he would be understanding and help her get through it. *Just please come home. We can work it out together. I promise.*

With tears still streaming, he walked to the bathroom and washed his face. *Get hold of yourself,* he admonished himself and walked back to the living room, where he flicked the television on and waited. Whatever was on the screen, he didn't see it, his mind conjuring scenarios too frightening to consider. Then, the thoughts streamed in: the pearl earring, the girl with the tics Joe told him about, the note, the phone calls… they couldn't all be a coincidence.

A knock on the door jarred him back to his empty reality. Slowly he got up and looked through the window, knowing it wasn't Amanda; she had a key. Anxiety and panic crept in, and he wanted to run to the door, but his feet wouldn't let him. Another knock followed by the doorbell made him move forward. He opened the door.

"Brad Verchall?" asked one of the two officers at his doorstep.

Brad nodded, eyes wide, too scared to ask the question, "Amanda?"

"Can we come in?"

Brad looked on in confusion, then moved aside to let the two officers inside. His senses flooded in as he watched them stand in the hallway, waiting for him to usher them to where they could sit. "Some… something happened to Amanda?" The words rushed out.

"Your wife has been in an accident. She was taken to Kindred Hospital—"

"Is she… is she… What happened?"

"We don't have the details. The accident took place on Highway 83, outside of Denver. It appears to be a single-vehicle accident."

"Highway 83?" repeated Brad, dumbly.

"As I said, she has been taken to Kindred Hospital. They are treating her there. Do you have someone who can drive you?" one asked.

Brad shook his head. "I'm okay. I'm okay," he said as he gathered his keys from the side table and opened the garage door, aiming for his car, at the same time, Googling the hospital address and phone number.

Their job done, the two officers left, closing the front door behind them. Before they were in their patrol car, the garage door flew open, and Brad reversed out of the driveway, spinning his wheels as he slammed his gear in drive and raced down the street. He didn't get far. Blue and red lights behind him signaled him to stop. Brad stopped and lowered his window and waited as the officer got out of his car and approached.

"We don't need another one in the hospital, and we don't need you to hurt or kill anyone," said one of the officers pointing his index finger at Brad. "Now, either find someone to drive you or call a cab. You're in no shape to drive," he said, extending his hand for Brad to give him the keys.

"It's okay. I'll call a cab," Brad said, pocketing his keys.

The two officers waited as Brad pressed the cab app on his phone. He turned the screen to show them; a ride was on its way and would arrive within three minutes. They didn't leave. Brad didn't blame them. He would get back in his car and rip through the streets.

He pressed the call icon and selected the hospital's number he stored a few minutes earlier when he downloaded the map for directions. The receptionist switched him to the emergency room, but the nurse who answered the call gave him no information, citing patient privacy.

At least she is alive. He resolved if Amanda came home okay, he would do all in his power to assure her of his love and let her know he would stand by her no matter what she did in her childhood years.

Brad paced and looked at his phone. Finally, Mike and his cab were close by from what the app showed. "Thanks. You can leave. The cab is almost here."

The officer nodded but didn't move. The second one walked to the car and got in the driver's seat, leaning over his shoulder, lips moving, but Brad didn't hear what he said.

A gray car pulled up the curb. "Brad Verchall?"

"Yes," he said as he climbed in the rear seat, and Mike, the driver, put the gear in drive.

"Kindred Hospital?" Mike verified.

"Yes. Please hurry."

Mike attempted small talk but was met with silence. He finally stopped and turned the radio louder; fast drumbeats. Brad found himself gritting and grinding his teeth. "Look, do you mind turning the radio down?"

Mike obliged without a word.

Nearly an hour later, the cab pulled up to the hospital entrance. Mike said, "Good luck, man. Hope all turns out okay."

Brad got out without a word. He would thank the driver with a tip from the app if he remembered.

There was no one in the lobby. He stepped up to the receptionist and asked for, "Amanda Verchall."

Without looking up, the receptionist tapped on the computer keys, but before she gave him any information, she said, "I need your ID, please."

Brad extracted his driver's license from his wallet and handed it to "Maisie."

Maisie looked up. "ER is just past the bank of elevators when you turn left by the gift shop." She pointed to the direction she mentioned.

Before she could finish, Brad flew through the lobby, down the empty corridor, and to a double door marked, "EMERGENCY ROOM – Authorized personnel only." He pushed at the door, but it was locked. Another sign gave instructions. Following what it said, he lifted a handset near the entrance, and when asked for his name, he gave it.

"Please, wait one minute. Doctor Belding is on the way out to speak with you."

"I want to see my wife," he demanded.

"You will, sir, as soon as the doctor—"

"I don't want to wait. I want to see my wife."

Before the nurse answered, the double doors swished open and woman in green garb, mask hanging askew at her chin, walked out. "Mr. Verchall?"

His heart sank, and he trembled.

"I'm Doctor Belding. I've been taking care of your wife. Please follow me."

She didn't wait for Brad; he had to hurry his steps to catch up.

A few doors away, she ushered him into a dimly lit room lined with couches and deep-seat chairs. The doctor walked to the coffee machine, put in a pod, and placed a cup under the spout. While doing so, she said, "Amanda was involved in a car accident. She was brought in by ambulance about two hours ago." She gestured with the coffee cup, offering him a drink. He shook his head, and she continued. "She's in pretty rough shape, but she should recover well. There is no internal bleeding that we can detect. She did break two ribs, but her lungs are okay. She has multiple cuts from the glass and most probably will be sore for a while—"

"I want to see her."

"I'm admitting her for observation, and once her room is ready, she will be transported to the fourth floor, trauma wing. You can stay until they move her."

Brad was almost to the door before the doctor finished her sentence.

They moved quietly through the hallways until they arrived at ER. The smells, the noise, and the frantic rush of footsteps assaulted his senses, and he found himself on the verge of collapse, overwhelmed by a mixture of relief and dread.

Doctor Belding moved aside a curtain, revealing a bandaged person on a bed, hooked up to IVs and machines beeping and pinging. With small steps, he approached the side of the bed and collapsed in sobs that wracked him to the core. He collected himself when a hand landed on his shoulder, forcing him to look up into gentle brown eyes — a nurse.

Brad nodded and wiped away tears with the back of his hand. "I'll be okay," he said. Pointing at Amanda, he asked, "Is she awake?"

The nurse shook his head. "She will be soon. She's sedated for now."

Amanda's eyes were swollen shut, dark purple rings circling them. He almost didn't recognize her. "Amanda?" he whispered.

The nurse rolled in a chair. "Here, may be a while before they move her upstairs."

He didn't wait for a response and closed the privacy curtain on his way out.

Brad held Amanda's hand, laid his head on the bed, and let the tears flow.

Chapter 35

May 9, 2018

Her head throbbed, and her mouth was parched. Disoriented, Amanda tried to open her eyes, but she couldn't. Strange noises surrounded her; she wondered where she was. Was she in jail?

The dull ache throughout her body didn't allow her to slip back into the blissful oblivion she came out of. Burning sensations scattered on her face, head, and arms, why? She lifted a hand to feel the area, but her arm was like a leaded weight, heavy and immovable. A moan escaped her lips.

Somewhere in her fog, she heard voices; one sounded like Brad. Amanda struggled to ask, "Where am I?" The words came out garbled.

"She's waking up," an unfamiliar voice said.

"Amanda, talk to me. What happened?" Brad said.

Amanda looked at him.

"It's okay. You're going to be fine. I'm here for you," he amended.

Amanda succeeded in peering through a narrow slit between her eyelids, at least one eye. She couldn't see much. She lay on her back, head elevated. What she could see were stark white walls and bright lights. She forced her eyelids to open a bit more. Across from her was a whiteboard, but the writing was out of focus. She turned her head to look around and immediately regretted it; the searing pain was beyond what she could tolerate.

"Easy there," the voice said as gentle hands helped her resituate her head on the pillow. "On the scale from one to ten, rate the pain."

100, screamed her mind. Another moan escaped.

"Please, give her something for the pain," begged Brad.

"Not time yet. We need her to wake up."

Amanda listened to the conversation as if she were elsewhere, eavesdropping. None of what she felt was real except the pain. She forced her thoughts to go back and bring up images of where she was before this place.

"Mrs. Verchall, Amanda. My name is Bennie. I'll be your nurse today. If you need anything, the call button is near your right hand. Your doctor will be in to see you soon."

"Thank you, Bennie," said Brad.

Wait! Nurse? I'm in the hospital, but why? Slowly, Amanda's mind woke up. She was in the car. She was driving to… where? How long had she been asleep?

Amanda lifted her fingers, though she aimed to lift her arm.

Brad must've noticed. "Do you want something?" he asked.

"No," she croaked, testing her vocal cords. She moved her hand again, this time a few inches from the bed. Her shoulder hurt, and she released it back to the bed.

"Amanda, I'm here. I won't leave you no matter what," Brad said. "Please, tell me what you need. Are you hurting? You want water?"

"Yes," came her throaty response. "Whe… where am I?"

"Kindred Hospital. You'll be okay."

"Wha… why?"

"You were in an accident on Highway 83. They don't know what happened, but no other car was involved. The doctor said you'll be fine—"

"B-Bra—"

"Yes? I'm here. I'm not going anywhere."

When Amanda said nothing else, Brad continued. "You hit a tree, and the windshield shattered. That's why you have cuts, and they had to sew some of them up. But, you'll be okay," he repeated the assurance.

Amanda closed her eyes. The memory flooded in. The faces came at her, yelling accusations. Her mind screamed, *I didn't want to kill my dad… I didn't mean to hurt Ashley… I don't hate you, Mom.*

"I did it. It was my fault."

"What?" asked Brad, confused. "The accident wasn't your fault. You probably blacked out."

"No."

"You're not making sense. Probably the medication."

The footsteps and chatter in the hallway came closer. Amanda cracked open her eyes to see white coats approaching. She closed them again, listening to their words.

"Good morning, Amanda," said one.

Amanda heard the scraping of a chair against the tile and felt Brad's movement. She didn't dare turn to look. The pain was too much. She lay still, her eyes open to slits.

"I'm Doctor McAnglo. I have excellent news for you. You can go home today."

Brad raked his fingers through his hair, a habit he had acquired when stressed and anxious.

"We will send you home with instructions. I'll also call in a prescription for pain medication. Take it as directed." He turned to Brad. "She needs to rest for the next few days and no heavy lifting for six weeks. Do you have a family doctor?"

Brad nodded and reached for his wallet.

Doctor McAnglo, standing at the foot of the bed, scanned the name on the card and jotted something on his clipboard.

"We'll get you up and make sure you're good to go. Do you have any questions?"

"No," was all Amanda could manage.

How was she supposed to move with this much pain? Would they arrest her anyway? Broken ribs and torn skin? She wished all of this was over.

Amanda opened her eyes a little wider and looked to the side, following Brad's movement. Why was he there? There was no way she would allow him to take care of her. She needed to let him go. *I don't deserve him.*

A tear escaped, but she couldn't wipe it away. It tasted salty as it made its way down to pool in the corner of her mouth. Brad's back was to her, and she hoped he wouldn't notice. But he turned around and walked closer to the bed.

"Are you in pain?"

She was in pain, physically and emotionally. She said, "I'm okay."

By the afternoon, Amanda was out of bed, cleaned up, and in a wheelchair – ready to go home. Brad took a cab home earlier, picked up fresh clothes for Amanda — hers were ruined— and drove back to the hospital.

The drive home was agony. Amanda hurt all over and cringed at every dip and bump, but the pain paled compared to the emotional anguish she suffered. She kept her gaze straight ahead, and her mind focused on what she needed to do next. First, she would send the email to Brad. She would set him free. No matter what he said, no matter how understanding he was, she would let him go, and she would face her future alone.

"Amanda? What happened?" His voice broke into her thoughts.

She said nothing.

"I want to be there for you, no matter what. I will stand by you. I love you."

A tear escaped.

In her peripheral, she caught him glancing her way every so often. He would know soon enough what she had done. *He thinks he loves me. He thinks he will stand by me. He won't when he learns the truth.*

"Amanda, I love you," he repeated.

"Stop," she said. "You have no idea what I've done. You won't say that when you learn the truth."

"No matter what it is, you must believe I'm here for you. I know what I said was not right. I should've never questioned you."

More tears flowed. "Then, stop asking what happened."

"I mean, what happened – the accident…"

"I don't know. I must've blacked out or something."

They drove in silence the rest of the way. Brad pulled in the driveway and shut off the engine. Amanda sat quietly, unsure how she would get up and out of the car.

Brad came around and opened her door, extending his hand for her to grab. After a moment's hesitation, she accepted the offer, and with much difficulty and pain, slowly, she stood, leaning on her husband as they made their way up the few steps to the front door.

With one arm supporting Amanda, Brad flipped the keys around with his other hand, inserted the house key in the lock, and turned it. He pushed the door open, and a card fluttered to the ground. Amanda's eyes followed its path.

"I'll pick it up after I settle you in," he said, pointing at the card.

Amanda made her way to the couch, the closest place where she could sit and, if lucky, lie down. Once seated, she watched Brad leave the living room, and she assumed he was going to retrieve the business card.

At the door, he turned around, "Can I get you anything?"

"No." Then, "Thanks."

A few minutes passed. Amanda closed her eyes, leaning against the back of the couch, propped up by pillows. Brad's return to the living room made her open them again. She waited for him to say who the card was from. She was no longer apprehensive nor worried. She would welcome her fate, just to be done with this agony.

"I guess they want to talk to you about what happened."

Her heart involuntarily constricted, then let go, beating so fast it nearly choked her. Her swollen eyes widened in shock, but she said nothing. That was it. Her past came knocking on her door. It was right there with them.

"I'll call the officer to let him know you're home if they want to talk to you."

"Wait," she said, determined to tell him the truth before he heard it from the police.

She watched his eyebrows arch questioningly.

"You might as well—"

The doorbell interrupted her. Frustrated and relieved all at once, she closed her eyes against the exertion and pain. Just when she finally dared to tell him about Ashley and what she did to her father, someone had to stop her – maybe she needed to keep her mouth shut.

"Hold on," he said as he went to answer the door.

Amanda heard the voices drifting from the entrance, fifteen or so feet away. She heard Brad say, "Come in, officer. She's in the living room."

"Thank you. This won't take long."

"She's in a lot of pain. Two broken ribs and multiple cuts that are stitched."

"It won't take long," the officer repeated as he appeared in the doorway. He nodded at Amanda. "Ma'am."

Amanda didn't respond.

"Can I ask you a few questions?"

"Yes," came her weak reply.

To her shock and surprise, the questions had to do with the accident, and nothing to do with Ashley or her dad. Relief flooded her. At least for a while, she was spared.

She carefully worded her answers. She remembered nothing about the accident nor why she was driving on that road. Amanda avoided looking at the officer when she spoke. She didn't want to see the doubt in his eyes. What she told him was a lie. She had become good at telling stories that were not true.

Her mind drifted to the accident. The overwhelming guilt of what she had done, suddenly, was right there for her to deal with. For all these years, she had justified her actions and made believe it was all long ago and forgotten. It wasn't. It was her present and would be her future. She no longer could escape it. The images… the accusations… was her conscience finally awakening? She wanted to end the nightmare.

"Mrs. Verchall?"

Back to the living room. Back to the present, she returned. This time, she met his eyes as he leaned forward, sitting opposite her.

He knew. He knew the truth. His eyes told her so.

"Mrs. Verchall," he said once more.

Amanda's lips parted, but the words refused to leave her tongue.

Brad interrupted. "Can you please come back another time? You can see she's not in a good shape," he said, pointing to Amanda.

"I'm almost done. Just one last thing. If you remember anything at all"—he handed her his card— "give me a call, please."

Brad grabbed the card. "Thank you," he said.

The officer left, and Brad returned to the living room after she heard the front door close, and the click of the lock. "So, what was it you wanted to say?"

"Nothing."

Chapter 36

May 12, 2018

Brad had to remind himself to be patient. Amanda's accident was recent, and she was still recovering, though he wondered what it was she wanted to tell him. Dare he hope she would finally confide in him and trust him with her secrets and her past? But he had no choice. He would not push her.

It had been four days since the accident, and Brad had called in sick the past three days. He would go back to work on Monday. It was nearing the end of the school year, and there was much to do. Although Amanda was not fond of their next-door neighbor, he would call on Mrs. Krupp to check up on his wife if needed. Watching Amanda shuffle and move about, he doubted he would have to call in sick or have his neighbor come by; she seemed to be managing on her own.

Torn between the promise he made to himself to be understanding and patient and the doubts that kept nibbling away, Brad kept himself busy so he wouldn't have time to think. "Be back in a few," he told Amanda.

She didn't look up or ask where he was going.

"I'm going grocery shopping. Can you think of anything we need?" It was a rhetorical question; the refrigerator was empty, and so were most of the cabinets. It was his way to let her know where he was going, and he hoped she would engage. She didn't.

He rode his bike. There wouldn't be time to work out. The store was a mile away. Though this wasn't enough exercise for him, he thought it to be better than nothing at all.

Once in the store, he filled his basket and headed to the checkout when he realized the container on the back of his bike wouldn't hold his purchase. Brad didn't want to refund the items. They needed all he bought. He double-checked to be sure his bike was secure and called for a cab ride. What was he thinking? His preoccupation with his current situation distracted him from even the most basic things.

"Hi," he said when he entered the hallway and saw Amanda still in the same position on the couch.

No response. She did lift her head and meet his gaze.

"I guess I'll put the groceries away. I have to go back for my bike…"

When Amanda said nothing, he carried the bags he had set by the front door into the kitchen and put the food away.

"Hungry?" he yelled to Amanda.

Brad heard her say something, but not what was said. He walked to the living room. "Was that a yes?"

"I said, I'm not hungry."

He felt a pang of hurt. She may not feel well, but why was she so dismissive? Before he could catch himself, he said, "Look, I understand you're not feeling well… but damn it, you need to stop!"

He watched her lift her eyebrows questioningly. Brad had never snapped at his wife before. It even surprised him. "I'm sorry. I didn't mean to snap at you. But honestly, this has gone on long enough. I'm trying, and you're not even meeting me anywhere." He turned to leave.

"I'm sorry, too." It was almost a whisper, and he stopped in his tracks.

Leaning against the doorframe with his arm extended, head resting on it, he said, "I want us to work out. I can't help you if you don't talk to me."

"I'm sorry."

He slowly turned to face her. "What are you sorry about?" He approached Amanda and knelt before her, his hands on her knees, his eyes imploring.

He watched her eyes well; one tear escaped. He reached to wipe it with his thumb. Amanda jerked her head and winced. Brad retracted his hand, placing it on her knee once again. Part of him wanted to get up and run to save what was left of his sanity and emotions; the other insisted on staying to see this through. "Please, talk to me," he begged.

She said nothing as the tears rolled down one by one, then caught in a stream.

"Whatever it is, we can get through it together. Whatever happened in the past, we can learn to live with it."

"Not that easy."

"Maybe not, but I promise to stand by you."

"You can't promise that. So, don't."

"I'm giving you my word. You must believe me."

"You won't stay. You won't love me. Not when you know the truth."

"How bad can it be?" He regretted asking that. The word "murderer" loomed in front of him. "I mean, no matter how bad… we will get a lawyer—"

"Stop! I told you, you can't promise anything. You don't know. Why don't you just leave? You won't stay anyway when you find out."

Her words were sharp-edged. They sliced through Brad's thin emotions. Brad reached for a Band-Aid, applying it to the wound. *She's hurt. She doesn't mean this. It's the pain and the shock talking,* he thought.

Brad refused to leave, even when she pulled away from him. "I'm not going anywhere. You'd better get used to that."

She finally looked at him.

Hope crept to the surface.

"What difference would it make anyway?" she asked and averted her gaze.

He lifted himself from the floor and sat beside her. "Talk to me, Amanda. Please."

Chapter 37

May 12, 2018

Across town, Liz and Stephanie settled into their new home. The only thing left to do was landscaping.

"How much money do we have left?" asked Liz.

"Probably enough to finish the landscaping. Why don't you check the account?"

Liz nodded. "Later," she said.

"Don't you think it's odd we haven't heard back from Miller?"

Liz laid the new living room curtains on the back of a chair and looked at her sister. "I don't get it, either. With all the technology, DNA, and what have you, you'd think by now they know who the guy is and—"

A knock on the door interrupted Liz, mid-sentence. She exchanged a glance with her twin. "Oh, must be the landscaper to give us an estimate," Liz took a few steps toward the front door.

"Wait," said Stephanie. "Let's not commit to any work until we're sure we have the funds."

Liz opened the door, and a woman in her mid to late twenties asked, "Ms. Branson?

She didn't look like a landscaper. The woman was nicely dressed, flats on her feet, a microphone in her hand, and behind her, a scraggly looking guy with a camera. Liz turned to look at her sister.

"Who's at the door, Liz?" she asked as she approached the entrance.

"I'm Delores from KRLF. Can I ask you a few questions?

Stunned, Liz stammered, "What? Why?"

"They identified the body, and I just have a few questions."

Stephanie grabbed Liz by the shoulder and practically shoved her inside, slamming the door in Delores's face. "The nerve!"

A few more knocks followed, and Delores pleaded to interview the twins. It would be exclusive, she said. It would only take a few minutes.

"Help me," Stephanie said as she reached for the blinds and closed the one in the window facing the street. Liz did the same.

"Why?" asked Liz.

"Why what?"

They both stopped and stared at each other, then said in unison, "The body!"

After a breath, Stephanie said, "They know who it is."

The realization that Delores had the information when the detective had promised to tell them incensed Stephanie. She picked up her phone from the side table and pressed Detective Miller's number. "Detective Miller," she said into the phone to whoever answered the call.

There was an edge to Stephanie's tone, and Liz signaled for her to bring it down a notch, mouthing, "Cool it."

"Well, tell him he'd better call me right away. It is urgent."

A beat of silence, then, "Stephanie. Stephanie Branson." She pushed "end call," tossed the phone on the couch, and paced, all the while rubbing her chin. "The nerve," she once more said.

"Steph."

She looked up.

"Why do they want to interview us? We had nothing to do with the dead body. I don't like it."

209

"I don't know. We don't need this…"—she pointed toward the front of the house. "this intrusion. That's just not right."

"Do you suppose what was in the briefcase helped them identify the body and find his relatives?" asked Liz.

Stephanie shook her head. "I just don't know."

"We're not in trouble, are we?"

"I don't think so."

"What if—"

"Don't even think it, Liz. Even if what was in the case helped, they still had to do an autopsy and run a DNA test. It wouldn't have mattered if they got the items sooner."

"If you say so."

"What did we do with the inventory list they gave us?"

"I think it is in the filing cabinet." Liz pointed to the cabinet in the corner. "Want me to pull it out?"

"No. I think I remember the items. The only puzzling part, besides the birth certificates, was the one pearl earring. Strange, a guy would keep an earring. One earring."

"Maybe it wasn't his. Remember? They said he had a twelve-year-old daughter who lived with him. Maybe it was hers."

"Do you ever wonder what happened to her?"

"If she stayed in town, they will find her. But, I doubt it. Probably, she was taken in by someone."

"I wonder what her name was," said Liz.

"What difference does it make?"

"Oh, no difference. I feel so badly for the kid."

"If she's still around, she isn't a kid anymore."

"Yeah."

"What do you say we head to the store? I don't think I want to go out to eat again now that we have our kitchen finished."

Liz nodded.

Keys in hand, Stephanie headed for the kitchen door to make sure it was locked when she spotted a van parked at the end of her driveway. Camera crews and reporters dotted the sidewalk. "Shit!" she said and stomped back to the living room.

Liz's eyebrows shot up.

Stephanie pointed toward the front of the house. "Take a look. Just don't open the blinds."

Stephanie pressed Miller's number again. She was livid.

A knock on the door made her look up. Liz flipped her hands upward as though asking, "What do we do now?"

"Go away!" Stephanie yelled. "Or I'll call the cops."

Another knock.

Stephanie yanked the door open, ready to verbally assault the intruders. Detective Miller stood on the porch, raised his hands indicating no harm, and said, "Whoa."

The door banged against the wall when Stephanie slammed it open. "You'd better get rid of them." She pointed at the press.

"A unit is on the way. We can keep them off your property but can't keep them off public streets."

"I don't care what you can or can't do. This is an invasion of my, our, privacy." She tapped her chest.

"Who's the dead man?" asked Liz, which made the detective make a half turn to face her.

Neither twin invited the detective and his partner to sit.

211

"So?" said Stephanie.

"We identified the body, but that's all I can tell you for now."

Stephanie crossed her arms over her chest and tapped her foot, waiting for him to say more. When he didn't, she said, "And?"

"We have the right to know, especially with the press outside our door," Liz said.

"I can only tell you the autopsy revealed the victim died from a blunt force to the head—"

"You mean he was killed? Here?" Liz shivered.

"What's his name?" asked Stephanie.

"I can't tell you his name yet. Not yet. We've launched an investigation. When it's completed, the information will become public."

"What do we do about them?" asked Liz.

"I can't stop them from asking questions. If they trespass, our officer will handle it. You don't have to answer their questions. The captain will be holding a press conference this afternoon. Hopefully, they'll get their information and leave you alone."

"We need to get to the store," said Stephanie.

"I'll walk you out. Our officer will make sure you can get in and out of your driveway."

Neither twin was happy with the current situation, and as they left their home, the news reporters rained a barrage of questions on them.

"What did the police tell you?"

"Did you know the man?"

"Can we film the basement?"

212

Stephanie turned to Liz as they left the driveway. "Why the sudden interest in this case?"

Liz shrugged. "They must know something the police have not told us."

"Maybe."

"I just wish they'd go elsewhere!" Stephanie blew out a breath, exasperated.

"I think we should go out to eat after shopping. I don't want to go back and deal with this."

"Good idea. Frank's again?"

"Sure."

Chapter 38

May 12, 2018
Amanda finally made eye contact with Brad. "I wrote you an email. Everything is in it."

"I didn't—"

"I didn't send it. Not yet."

Brad waited, expectantly. When she said nothing, he implored, "Tell me."

Amanda's gaze shifted to the muted television that had been on for hours. "I'll let you read it."

As she said that, her focus landed on the ticker below the image. "…police identified the body found in a local home…"

She gasped and felt Brad's weight shift, his fingers heavier on her leg. He reached for the remote and turned up the volume, momentarily distracted from the email.

Her heart beats hastened. She wanted to hear the interview on television and at the same time, wanted to cover her ears. "Turn it off!" she demanded.

"Okay! Okay!" Brad said, his eyes still glued to the screen.

What's the use? "Sorry…" she said as her eyes read the words crawling at the bottom of the screen. "Wait. Turn it up."

Amanda saw the confusion etched on Brad's face. She shifted a mere few inches away from him. "That can't be. No." Her mumbling barely audible. Then louder, "They don't know what they're talking about."

Brad raked his fingers through his hair. "What are *you* talking about?"

She didn't respond; eyes still glued to the news conference.

"Do you know the guy?"

Amanda turned to look at Brad. An involuntary chuckle escaped. She almost confessed to killing her father, and the man in the basement was killed by a blunt force to the head. She had narrowly escaped. Relief flooded her, and a sudden elation permeated her countenance. She didn't care to register the bewilderment on Brad's face. "I think I'm hungry."

"Wha-what about the email… what you wanted to tell me."

"Never mind that. I changed my mind."

"You can't do that, Amanda." He appeared to be searching for words. "First, you tell me…"

She shrugged.

"You can't just dump this whole thing as if nothing had happened. I can't… can't—"

"Live with me? I told you, you can leave if that's what you want."

He shook his head. "That's not what I meant."

"Maybe, I'll send you the email after all." *After I change the content, that is.*

"Okay." He didn't sound placated nor convinced.

Amanda fumbled for her phone and watched Brad in her peripheral, backing away from her. He stood, slowly turned around, and left the room.

Her eyes bulged when she realized she had already sent the email. When did she do that?

More images trickled in. Just before the accident, that wasn't an accident. She had clicked send. She wasn't supposed to be here to deal with the aftermath. She was supposed to be dead.

Two things happened at once. The doorbell rang, and Brad returned to the living room, cellphone in hand, screen facing Amanda. "Yo-You ki—"

She said nothing.

Someone rang the doorbell again. Brad swallowed; Amanda watched the muscles in his neck, then his jaw working into a grip or grind as he moved to answer the door.

Amanda recognized the voice. It was the officer who interviewed her. This time, she didn't tense, nor was she worried. Whatever was there to deal with, she was ready.

"Ma'am." The officer dipped his head slightly.

Brad backed up a few steps.

Neither she nor Brad invited him to sit. The officer placed one hand over the other and stood, feet slightly apart as he addressed her.

With him was a female officer this time. She moved closer to the couch and sat a foot away from Amanda, hands in her lap. "We'd like you to tell us what happened on May 8."

"I don't remember. I already told you what I know."

"I don't understand," Brad said. "She already told you she doesn't remember."

"Sir, if you wouldn't mind—"

"I'm not going anywhere. Do we need a lawyer?"

The two officers exchanged a glance, and Amanda said, "I don't need a lawyer." Turning to the officers, she asked, "What do you want to know?"

"There were no skid marks…"

Had Amanda looked toward her husband, she would've seen the realization bloom on his face as he heard the words. She didn't. She only felt the rush of air as he closed the distance between them and kneeled in front of her, tears streaming down his face as sobs wracked him.

"Amanda?" he said. "Is it true?"

Silence.

"Ma'am…"

Amanda didn't respond. She knew the ramifications of her silence. She would be taken in for a psychological evaluation and may be locked up for a few days, and she still had things to do. "I think I blacked out. I think I had a headache and blacked out. I don't remember."

This left the officers no choice but to retreat. They had no reason to take her in, not for this. Once the officers left, and Brad closed the door and locked it, he returned to the living room. Beads of sweat glistened on his temples though it wasn't hot.

"I-I," he started, faltered, then said, "Where does this leave us, Amanda?"

Silence.

"I read your email. Did you—Did you really do it?

Silence.

"So—so—the note, is true?"

Silence.

"Is that why… the accident?" He waved his arms around.

Amanda watched him. His face told the agony he was in as he absorbed the information and processed it.

"I can't. I need time to process this." He shook his head, grabbed his keys, and slammed the door to the garage.

A few moments later, Amanda heard the garage door gears grind, and imagined him on his bike, peddling away.

What was I thinking? How could I be so stupid?

If Ashley didn't die and had said nothing about the fall to anyone, then why would Andrew Baker send the message? The only other Andrew she knew was her father. But, why would he send this message? None of this made sense.

Gingerly, she dragged her broken body up the stairs. There was nothing left to delete or destroy except her memories. Determined to unravel what was cluttering her mind, she turned on the computer and waited for it to load applications. A sudden thought crossed her mind... Michelle. She retrieved her cell from her pocket and pressed the number.

The text was short, but she had to make the connection to find out what had happened with Ashley and Andrew. She typed: *Hey... sorry about the other day. I was distracted... well, with my mother and all.*

Amanda waited. Fifteen minutes passed, then thirty. She wanted to pace, but her body would not allow her to. She turned her attention to the computer screen. Licking her dry lips, she opened the Facebook app and went straight to Ashley Baker's page. Condolences flooded the timeline.

Who died?

Methodically, she read through the forty-nine posts. The original post was vague. It wasn't until the thirty-second response someone, Bethany something or another, said, "So sorry for your loss, Ashley. Andrew was special to me."

Wait! What?

Amanda scrolled back to the original post and checked the date and time. May 7th, 2018 – 10:38 pm. She reread it, then scrolled through other posts hoping to find out what had happened. When she didn't see anything else, she clicked on Andrew Baker's page. There, she read more condolences, but nothing about how he died.

Michelle still had not responded. Amanda clicked on the Google search bar and typed Andrew Baker's death. She was rewarded with multiple links and news stories. She squinted at the screen not believing her eyes as she read, "Andrew Baker—"

A ping from her cellphone alerted her to an incoming text message. She swiped her opening screen and clicked on the icon.

Michelle: *Hey. Got it. np.*

Amanda: *Got a minute to chat?*

Michelle: *LOL that all I got.*

Amanda: *Can I call you?*

Michelle: *Let me call you when I clock out in an hour.*

Amanda had no choice. *Ok.*

Another text message came in from Angeline, the secretary from her work. *Heard about your accident. Sorry. When are you coming back to work?*

She ignored Angeline's text and returned her gaze to the computer. The hour would seem like an eternity waiting to talk to Michelle, and she had no idea where Brad was and when he would return. Maybe, just maybe, she would line up a good story to tell him, repudiating what the email contained. She shook her head and winced. What difference would it make? She wanted him out of her life, didn't she? Better she broke it off than he rejected her. Wasn't it what he just did, couldn't handle what he asked for, and left?

From what Amanda read, Andrew died of "natural causes," but what happened?

Maybe, just maybe it was him who sent the threats, and if so, good he was dead. Is that why there were no more texts or messages? Amanda hoped so.

An hour and a half later, there was still no message from Michelle and Brad had not returned. For a few moments, she wondered where he had gone to and what he was doing, but she shrugged her shoulders. *I don't care.*

She was tempted to call Michelle but didn't want to appear anxious. She spent the next twenty minutes searching online for more information about Andrew, relieved it must not have been her father, contacting her, though the idea was ludicrous… why would he call her "murderer?" He wouldn't have known she put anything in his coffee.

The cellphone rang, jarring her out of her thoughts. She pressed the green icon "answer call" and steadied her breathing. "Hey," she said.

After a few minutes of mundane chatting, she inhaled deeply and said, "You said something about Ashley losing her baby…"

Michelle filled her in on the events of that day as if Amanda was never at the scene.

Amanda gasped at the new information coming her way and tried to be casual in her response. "Oh? I thought Matt was her boyfriend." After a short pause, she said, "I thought she married him?"

To Michelle's question, she responded, "No, you're right. I didn't know. I was guessing." She quickly recovered.

Amanda wanted to end the call. She learned all she wanted to about Ashley, Matt, and Andrew. There was nothing more to keep her on the phone but didn't want to appear rude. "Hey, thank you so much for calling. My husband just got home—"

She ended the call after Michelle told her she understood and hoped they would grab lunch or coffee soon. Amanda had no intention of doing either. What Michelle had told her was enough to know she was safe. It had to have been Andrew Baker who was sending the threatening messages. She formulated a story, she would tell Brad, when, if, he came home.

At 4:30 pm, Brad was still not home. Amanda considered sending him a text message but chose not to. Though food and cooking were the last things on her mind, she shut the computer and carefully made her way to the kitchen.

Brad had stocked the refrigerator, and the cabinets were full. Amanda held her chest as she winced against the pain, and with her other hand, she pulled out the items needed to make spaghetti. She would show Brad, what? She wasn't a murderer... by cooking a meal?

Her mind flitted as she worked to prepare the dinner. First, she wanted to come clean and free her soul. Now that the situation had changed, she had second thoughts. Why bring up the past if it was dead and gone?

That left the outcome of the body in her old house. There was no way it was her father. Wouldn't they have come after her by now for DNA if it was?

Amanda would not deal with it for now; she would cross that bridge when she got to it. Not much she could do about it at that point. She berated herself for her stupidity – she shouldn't have sent the email to Brad. At least, she was smart enough not to mention her dad. For that, she was grateful.

Chapter 39

May 12, 2018

Brad pedaled furiously until his calf muscles cramped. He had no destination in mind except to get as far away from his home as he could manage. He did. At a park on the outskirts of his town, Brad got off his bike, welcoming the pain in his muscles to distract him from his thoughts, at least for a few moments.

He leaned over, hands on knees, and vomited; the bile as sour as his mood. From his bag, he pulled out a water bottle, took a few sips, and splashed his face before collapsing at the foot of a cypress tree.

Brad let the tears he had held for so long flow, lamenting what has become of his orderly life… what he thought was an orderly life. He didn't want to believe the note, he didn't want to believe Amanda was capable of hurting another human, but there he was. The email an admission of her past… of murder.

He pulled out his cell with one hand, dried his tears with the back of the other, and stared at the email. It was short. It said what he asked for. It said what he dreaded.

I can't talk about this. I know after you read it, you will leave. I don't blame you. I know Andrew, and I know why he sent the messages. Yes, there was more than one. I guess you won't understand, and probably, I have no excuse, though I was a kid…

The email wasn't detailed. It told of the fight and Ashley's fall that wasn't an accident. Brad shook his head. Even if she was a kid… he couldn't bring himself to think his wife had pushed someone to her death. He picked up a blade of grass, then another. His action became more violent with each subsequent pull.

"Whoa, there. What did that do to you?" a familiar voice asked.

Brad tossed the grass in his grip and looked up. He was in no mood to be social with anyone.

"I guess your day is as good as ours," said Stephanie.

He lowered his gaze to his feet.

"Can we join you?" asked Liz, sitting across from him, taking his choice away.

The three sat in silence. Liz reached in a bag and took out sandwiches. She offered Brad a half. "I can't eat the whole thing."

He shook his head, still staring at his shoes.

"So, we heard what happened to Amanda. Is that why you're bummed?" asked Stephanie.

"Yeah, we're sorry to hear the news. How's she doing?"

"Fine," said Brad. *For a murderer.*

"I guess she must be better. Otherwise, you wouldn't be here, right?" said Liz.

There was no way the twins wouldn't have noticed tear streaks on his face. He wanted to dump his anguish on someone, but he didn't know these women. A deep sigh escaped his lips, causing the twins to meet his gaze when he finally looked at them.

"That bad, huh?" Liz said.

A one-shoulder shrug was the answer.

"Well, let's see. How about if we dump on you first?" Stephanie said.

"Sure," accompanied another shrug.

"The police identified the man in our basement," Liz said.

This brought Brad back to the park. "Who is it?" he asked.

"Here's the thing," Stephanie said around a mouthful of sandwich. "They won't tell us an—"

Liz interrupted. "And, the press is crowding our home, making it difficult to think. That's why…" she gestured around her, indicating why they were not at home.

Brad reached for the sandwich Liz had left close to him.

"It's ham, swiss, and arugula," she offered.

"Thanks."

He took a bite and looked at them, expecting more information and watched the two exchange a subtle glance. Stephanie nodded.

After looking around her to make sure no one was within earshot, Liz said, "This is weird. We found a case, and it had birth certificates and other papers. There was also a box with pieces of jewelry."

He was grateful for the momentary distraction, but still not in the mood to socialize, and although he was at one point interested in the events at twins' house, that was before… before the nightmare, he stumbled into. Liz's voice jolted him to attention.

"…and one pearl earring."

"What did you say?" asked Brad, with all that had happened, he'd forgotten this bit of information she mentioned earlier.

Liz repeated, listing all the items they found and was quick to say, "Of course, we gave it all to Detective Miller."

"Ca-can you tell me about the earring?"

Brad could see the bewilderment in her eyes as she glanced toward her twin then said, "Um, sure. It was about this big." She made a quarter-inch space between her index and thumb. "Of course, a round pearl hanging from… oh, about an inch chain, and it had a stud."

When Brad said nothing, Stephanie said, "It was just a regular pearl earring, nothing special about it except it had no match."

"Oh," said Brad, now worried he may have made them curious as to why he was interested in the earring. "So, there were a few jewelry items and papers, too? That's interesting. What did the papers say?"

As Liz and Stephanie jabbered on, interrupting and completing each other's thoughts and sentences, Brad had a sinking feeling. Amanda's reaction to the local news may not have been a coincidence, especially when he added Joe's comments about a girl who was "different."

"Thank you for the sandwich and your company," he said, rising from the ground. "I think I'd better get home before it gets too late."

"Yeah, nice to see you again. You know, you and your wife are welcome to stop by. We'd love to show off what we've done to the house—"

"But, of course, after the press madness dies down." Stephanie finished for Liz.

He hopped on his bike, turned around and thanked the twins once more before he peddled away. Brad had no intention of going home. There were a lot of loose pieces that didn't fit. He looked at the time. 4:17 pm. It was still early.

Brad checked his phone and turned the volume up. Just as he suspected, there were no missed messages or calls from Amanda. He was now on a mission to uncover what his wife was hiding. Off to Joe's house, he cycled, intending to pull and push Joe's memory to tell him more about the twelve-year-old who lived with her dad at the twins' house all those years ago.

He was no longer afraid of the truth of his wife's past. How much worse could it be than pushing another kid down a flight of stairs to her death? What else was Amanda capable of?

A thought struck him, and his heart raced and not from the furious peddling. What should he do? Should he go to the police with the email? He peddled faster toward Joe's house. *I'll do the right thing.*

Chapter 40

May 12, 2018

5:15 pm, sauce bubbling on the stove, noodles cooked, and the only thing left was a salad to prepare. Perspiration from fighting pain beaded on her forehead and trickled down to her cheeks. She swiped at them with a paper towel. Refusing to take pain killers, she endured the agony of her pain, perhaps penance.

Amanda picked up her phone to send a text to Brad, her fingers fighting to form the right words. After multiple attempts and deletes, she sent a simple text: *I can explain.*

She didn't expect an answer. Amanda wasn't even sure why she bothered to contact him and explain anything. Why would she care? Her marriage was over, or maybe, it never was in the first place. Her gaze traveled through the kitchen window and landed on the small yard. A bird fluttered in the birdbath. She inched closer to the sink to look. When did they put that in?

The next things to catch her attention were the rose bushes by the fence. Amanda inched her way to the door and opened it, then slowly made it down the one-step and onto the cement slab where an umbrella and two chairs stood. She surveyed her surroundings and couldn't recall the last time she had stepped foot outside.

Leaning on the door frame, she lifted one foot and then the other and returned to the kitchen, turned down the burner to low, and walked to the front door. She unlocked it and stepped outside as if seeing the neighborhood for the first time. As painful as it was to maneuver, she made it to the end of the driveway and looked up at the house. Was this really her home?

Her thoughts drifted to when they bought it a few months after they were married, almost twelve years ago. It was surreal to her, and as hard as she tried, she couldn't bring up the feelings of those first months.

Amanda shaded her eyes against the bright evening sun, watching it dip behind the distant mountains. She hugged herself against the chill that covered her in goosebumps; it wasn't cold. It was reality seeping under her skin.

As she turned around to go back into the house, the curtains waved in the upper window of her neighbor's house. Before Mrs. Krupp had the chance to open the window and call out, Amanda held her ribs and hurried up the front steps. In the distance, she heard a click, a creak, then "Amanda, yoo-hoo!"

Amanda ignored the call, walked in, and locked the door behind her, her muddled thoughts trailing close at her heels.

In the hallway, she looked around; the walls were bare. She took a few steps to the living room. Only one painting hung on the opposite side from where she stood. A painting she and Brad bought from an open market soon after they moved in. The splashes of burnt orange, browns, cream, and white were supposed to represent poplar trees in the fall; they didn't. What they created was an unsettling, chaotic scene in a lunatic's mind – she never said a word to Brad about how she felt about the painting. Why didn't she?

Only two photos stood idly on a shelf beneath the TV on the wall: one of Brad's family and the other taken at their wedding. She shuffled closer and picked up the first image, staring at his mother, father, and siblings. Amanda ran her fingers over their faces; there was no mistaking they were related. His mother, Rosalie, was kind to her. She even helped with a modest wedding. Though Amanda wasn't rude, she also wasn't friendly and had not kept in touch with them over the years. She left that to her husband.

She accompanied Brad when he visited his family for holidays or special occasions. The rest of the time, he visited when she was out of town, which was often. This brought Amanda's thoughts to the job she left behind. A job that allowed her to bury herself in work and travel to a point the past years whizzed by, and she had no time to reflect, effectively diminishing the importance of the past.

A deep sigh escaped her lips as she shifted her gaze to the wedding picture, suddenly realizing their anniversary was coming up, but quickly dismissed it – there wouldn't be any celebration, not that there ever was one beyond their first year together. After that, Amanda had ensured she was out of town for the date and didn't have to deal with it.

Her insides twisted. For the first time in her life, emotions she didn't know she had assaulted her, and she found tears had escaped and ran down her cheeks. Absently, she walked to the kitchen, where the smell of the sauce called her. She lifted the lid, and thankfully, it had not burned. She twisted the knob to off, her feet took her upstairs, and she hung on the railing as she ascended.

At the door to their bedroom, she paused for a moment, then went inside, not sure why she was there. Her tics intensified as her stress increased, causing her to grit her teeth from the pain radiating from the broken ribs. Amanda ignored the physical agony and opened the top drawer of her dresser. The last of the things she held onto, she brought out and dumped on the bed. Methodically, she tore papers and tossed the other items in the trashcan, not bothering to cover them. The pearl earring, she cupped protectively in her hand, then slipped in her pocket. She would throw it away later.

The only thing left from her past was the little box in the office closet, which she would take care of as soon as she healed — if her life didn't end up belonging to the system again — this time, the prison system.

Satisfied, she retraced her steps to the kitchen, turning on lights as she entered — 6:30 pm and no sign of Brad and no message from him.

With nothing to do, she returned to the living room, turning on the TV, flipping the channels in an endless loop. She couldn't focus. Was it guilt she was feeling? She had never felt this way before. Her chest constricted, and more tears blurred her vision as they slipped down her cheeks. What was wrong with her that she had shoved her horrible past behind and pretended it wasn't hers?

228

Her mother's face flitted in and out, superimposing itself on the TV screen. A mother too ill to care for her child. Her fifth birthday, thirty-one years ago, flashed before her – the cake that wasn't, the scary mother who wasn't her mother, and the strangers who came and took her away.

Amanda understood. She understood it wasn't her mother's fault she abandoned her. She was mentally ill, right? But, why had she not visited her mother more often, checked on her to be sure she was okay?

The grandmother, who, along with Auntie Emma, were the only people in the world who cared about her and truly loved her. Why had she not returned Auntie Emma's calls and texts over the years?

Amanda understood. She understood Auntie Emma was a kind friend who had no choice but to give her up to her dad. A heavy, blue feeling descended on her. As if only realizing it at that moment for the first time, she was wrong not let Emma know how much she appreciated all she had done for her. Too late now. Too late.

Among the tears, there was a moment of clarity. She would do what she promised to: to come clean, to confess, to take her punishment, and hopefully, she would, at some date in the future, be free. Free to live. Free to feel. Brad did not deserve this. He did not deserve half a life and half a wife.

Even if Andrew was dead, even if Ashley had kept the secret of what had happened, Amanda still knew, deep down inside, she knew the truth.

With trembling fingers, she reached for her phone and dialed. "Hi, Michelle, it's Amanda."

She got the number she needed, thanked Michelle, and pressed the keypad. The phone rang twice, and a vaguely familiar voice answered. Amanda cleared her throat. "This… this is Amanda."

"Amanda? Amanda from the Baker's?

"Yes. That Amanda."

"How did you get my number. Don't you ever dare call here again."

Sensing Ashley would hang up on her, she quickly said, "No, please don't hang up. I'm calling to tell you how very sorry I am for what happened to you."

Ashley didn't hang up. The exchange left Amanda more puzzled than settled.

"What do you want?" Ashley asked.

"I'm really sorry about what happened. It's been eating away at me for all these years."

"What are you talking about? My miscarriage? Why would it eat away at you?"

Amanda searched for the words, confused at Ashley's response. "We fought that day, and you fell down the stairs while we… I…"

A roar of laughter echoed through the phone. "You've got to be kidding. Are you still as stupid as you were then?" Ashley said.

When Amanda said nothing as a flood of anger and old emotions of rejection and abuse flooded into her awareness, she bit her trembling lip.

"Wait. Wait one damned minute. Do you think it was your fault? Is that what has been bothering you?"

"I—"

"Damn, girl. You had nothing to do with it. Don't you remember?"

"I thought I did."

"We pushed and shoved each other. Then, the front door opened, and you ran to the room."

Amanda tried to put herself in that moment, but all she saw was their entangled hands and Ashley at the foot of the stairs. She shook her head. "Um," was all she managed.

"I had lost a lot of blood and was getting dizzy. Andrew came in, and before I could get hold of the railing, I must've blacked out and fell."

Lip trembling, Amanda said in an almost whisper, "I didn't hurt you and your baby?"

Another roar of laughter. "Oh, hell no. You had nothing to do with it. What made you think that?"

"I… I kicked you when you… then… then there was a text message from Andrew and a note calling me a murderer. I thought… I thought…"

A laugh echoed in Amanda's ear. She was even more confused.

"Well," Ashley said. "The irony. So, tell me, did you think all these years that you killed me or my baby?"

Amanda was lost for words. Her mind worked hard to play the movie of that day. Only snatches came into focus. But, as Ashley continued to explain, she had a natural miscarriage, didn't tell anyone, and had lost enough blood to faint, Amanda's focus dialed in. Relieved and confused, she grappled with the information coming at her – incongruous with the reality she had lived with for all these years; these were not the images logged into her brain.

Ashley's voice made her blink. "Andrew never got over losing our baby. Yeah, he blamed you. I didn't correct his perception. I hated you. But… you've nothing to worry about. Andrew died a few days ago… cancer."

"I see."

"Really, Amanda. You need to put this behind you. While we're at it, I'm not interested in rekindling the past. That part of my life is long gone. So, have a good life. Don't call me again."

Amanda didn't have a chance to respond. The line went dead.

She sat on the couch and stared into the flickering TV screen. Her shoulders sagged. So, after all these years, she hadn't pushed

Ashley? What else had she imagined she did? What about her father? Was that also her imagination?

She shook her head in response to the question. *That* was real. She did put poison in her dad's coffee. Not much. But, she did.

Chapter 41

May 12, 2018

Joe was pruning his roses when Brad arrived. He looked up, a startled expression on his face. When Brad got off his bike, Joe set his shears on the ground by his feet.

Brad said nothing and shuffled his feet.

"What's on your mind, Mr. V.? Not like you to pop in here."

It wasn't the first time Brad had visited Joe. He stopped by from time to time to chat or help Joe with the yard work. Something Brad missed since he moved out of his parents' house, and his home had no land to speak of. "Do you have a minute?"

"Sure, Mr. V. Why don't you come and sit on the porch with me, and I'll make us a lemonade?"

"Don't trouble yourself."

Joe waved a dismissive hand. "No trouble at all. Already made, just need to pour it."

Brad sat on an oversized wicker chair, looking at the flowering garden, not seeing. His mind boggled with questions and stories it conjured.

Joe broke into his thoughts. "Here you go, ice-cold," he said, handing a sweating glass to Brad.

"Thanks."

"So…"

"Trust me on this, and don't ask questions, okay? I have my reasons for wanting to know… for now, at least, trust me?"

"Sure, Mr. V."

Brad took a sip of the lemonade. It wasn't as sweet as he thought it would be, and he fought a grimace making its way to his face. He set the glass on the floor between his legs and met Joe's gaze. "Try to remember what the girl's name was."

"What girl?"

"The girl who used to live in the house where they found the body?"

"Why you want to know?" Joe quickly threw his hands up in surrender to the promise he made.

"I need to know. If I can, I'll tell you more."

"Gee, Mr. V., I can't remember her name. That was too long ago. Kids come and go, you know."

"Can you tell me anything about her. What she looked like, her hair, her eyes, anything you can remember," Brad pleaded. He didn't mean to sound as desperate as he felt. But he couldn't help it.

Joe rubbed his chin and swiped the wet glass across his forehead. He appeared to be deep in thought. Almost as if he was no longer in the present.

Brad waited patiently, hoping Joe would remember something, anything. He had a hunch; it was more than a hunch. He wanted to know to verify who the girl was.

"She had curly hair, long, past her shoulders." He stopped to point with his index finger to where he thought the hair reached on his body. "Her eyes were chocolate brown, such sadness. I don't think I saw her smile once."

Brad didn't interrupt. It appeared Joe was pulling the rope, lifting a bucket of memories from the well. He shook his head slowly as if he was responding to an unsaid question. "Well, Mr. V., I don't know why you ask, but she was different. Kept to herself."

Brad nodded, encouraging Joe to keep talking.

"The poor thing. You know? When I think about it, I think it was the weird thing she used to do."

Joe took a sip of his lemonade. Brad watched him, anxious to hear what he didn't want to hear.

"She used to wink at the kids, and they would make fun of her. Then, she shrugged her shoulder as if she didn't care."

Brad let out the breath he held. "Are you sure you can't remember her name?" he asked Joe.

Joe shook his head. "Afraid not."

"Do you know where she went?"

Joe said, "She stayed here after her dad left. I think her auntie or grandma took her in, but not for long." He rubbed his chin and looked at the sky. "There were rumors, you know, but I never paid them no mind."

"Oh?"

"Mr. V., I wish I could remember. If the Mrs. was still here, she would tell you word for word what happened." Joe's eyes glistened with longing.

"Thanks, man."

"I know you said not to ask. But, Mr. V., this is kinda unusual… your questions about a kid you don't know."

"I promise. I will tell you what I can as soon as I can. Thanks again."

Brad stood to leave. With a heavy heart, he hopped on his bike and peddled. So, he was right. His hunch was right. But, why wouldn't Amanda share that part of her life with him? She was only a kid… how awful it had to have been for her growing up like that. Then, the reality of the email came into view.

But, what does the email have to do with that house?

235

Halfway home, he hesitated. He wanted to confront Amanda, but part of him wished never to step foot in that place again. Brad stopped peddling when he got to the small park less than half a mile from his house. He got off his bike and sat on a bench facing a small pond where ducks swam lazily in circles.

Pulling his cell out of his pocket, he realized he had turned it off earlier when he was with the twins. He pressed the button on the side, and the phone came to life — several missed messages. His fingers hovered over the envelope, and his index pressed it — one was from his mother, two from friends, and one from Amanda. Curiosity got hold of him, and he pressed the one from his wife. His mouth fell open. *The nerve! What's there to explain after you told me you killed someone?* Then, the emotional tug-of-war began again. *She was a kid, hear what she has to say,* his inner voice coaxed.

But, she killed someone. She's a murderer. My wife is a murderer.

A kid, Brad. A twelve-year-old kid. Think of your students, Brad.

His empathy won. He rode his bike home.

Chapter 42

May 12, 2018

Amanda heard the garage door open, then grind to a stop. Her resolve to tell him the truth of her past wavered. She would decide how much to say when the time came.

Frozen in her spot at the kitchen sink, she waited for the inside door to close, listening to Brad's footsteps. Her heart hammered relentlessly in her chest, beating against her broken ribs and bruised conscience. A short hesitation, an interruption in footfalls, had her imagine Brad setting down his keys on the hallway table, raking his fingers through his hair, and resuming his pace to the kitchen.

She said nothing when he appeared in the doorway. She wanted to say hi or something to extend as a peace offering, hoping he would listen. She didn't but reconsidered. "Dinner…" she waved to the stove. "You want me to heat it?"

"You said you can explain."

"Yeah."

"Well, start explaining."

Amanda didn't like the edge in his voice. He had already judged her and made up his mind. Why should she bother? What difference would it make?

"I—I spoke to Ashley today."

"What did you just say?"

She lifted her hand to silence him. "I called her. She is alive. I didn't kill her."

"But, your email," Brad said as he took two steps toward Amanda.

"I spoke to her," she repeated.

"What kind of a game are you playing?" He took another step forward.

"Can you please not come any closer?"

Brad retreated one step and leaned on the counter in an apparent attempt at holding onto something in case what she said assaulted his senses. She knew him too well.

"Can we sit down? I need to sit down." She clutched at her ribs and inched her way to one of the high stools.

Brad remained where he was. Rooted. Anchoring himself to the counter. Part of her felt sorry for him… only a part of her.

"I went to see my mother, the day of the accident."

"You what?"

She raised her hand once more to silence him. Amanda couldn't read what was in his eyes, so she looked down at her feet before she continued. "My mother. I didn't get to see her. They moved her without telling me… to another place. Anyway, I met up with someone I knew from school who told me Ashley was alive."

Amanda told him what had happened and her call to Ashley earlier that day. She omitted the part of how her accident happened. He didn't need to know how desperate she was to end it all. How tired she was running from her past. She also didn't say a word about her dad nor included any events outside of Ashley. When she was done, a deadly silence descended on the kitchen.

Brad said nothing.

She finally lifted her gaze to meet his expression: jaw slack, eyes rounded. She watched him as he collected his thoughts and returned his face to neutral.

"You see, all these years, I thought I had killed her. I did not." Remorse crept in, and for the first time, it wasn't only the fear of being caught and punished she felt, but real remorse, real guilt that she had perhaps contributed to the agony of another human being, even if that person, Ashley, was her tormentor.

Brad remained silent. His eyes vacant.

"I don't blame you if you don't believe me."

"What else?"

"What else, what?" she asked.

"I know nothing about you. Twelve years, Amanda. Twelve years, and I know nothing about you. Why?"

She shifted her gaze. It landed on a stack of neglected mail. A blue enveloped peeked out, staring at her, daring her. Amanda lifted herself and reached for the pile, pulling it toward her and leaned her elbow on it as if resting.

"We've been through this. Why, all of a sudden, your interest in my past?"

"Let's see, maybe because you told me you pushed a kid to her death and now recanted? Maybe because…"

Amanda held her breath.

"…because, you were the kid at that house?"

Slowly, she let the air out of her lungs, careful not to look nor sound anxious. "I've no idea what you're talking about. What house?"

Brad slammed his fist on the counter, startling Amanda. "The damn house where they found the body! *That* house!"

"N-n-no!" She shook her head.

"No, what? Do you deny that was you?"

Amanda opened her mouth to speak, but Brad cut her off. "Don't even bother to lie. I'm done. Do you understand? I'm done with your lies," he said as Amanda watched him get up and pace, raking his fingers through his hair until it stood in different directions.

She wondered how much he knew, where he found the information to connect her to that house. Her promise to come clean and tell him the truth was quickly replaced with self-preservation. Amanda didn't trust him with the truth. His reaction so far told her as much. He would turn her in. She would be in jail.

"I don't understand," she said, mustering as much innocence in her expression and tone as she could.

"*Stop*!!! Just stop." The last part was said in almost a whisper.

Brad returned to his seat and covered his face with his hands swiping them down. "I know the truth," he said, still in almost a whisper.

Amanda stood and backed up, leaning against the sink. She eyed the door. Could she make it past him and out of the house before he caught her? She remembered her car. A car she no longer had. *His keys. I can get to his keys if I can make it out of the kitchen.* Her eyes darted, measuring the distance, assessing how she could escape.

Brad stood, facing her, blocking her path. "Amanda, I know the truth. I promised to help you and stand by you, but you haven't trusted me. What am I supposed to do now?"

"Even if that girl was me, why would you care? My past is mine and mine alone. Get out of my way," Amanda said as she tried to get past him.

Brad held her by the wrists. "Look, I don't know what happened in that house. I don't know who that dead guy is. I don't know if you had anything to do with it… all I know is my head is about to burst," he said as she struggled against his grip.

She winced from the pain. "*Let me go!*"

"No. I'm not. Not until you tell me the truth."

"Why? What difference does it make?"

He let go of her arms but still blocked the doorway. "I don't know what difference anything makes. I just know none of this is normal. None of the past twelve years are normal. I don't get why you won't trust me with. I just don't get it."

Amanda wrapped her arms around her chest and turned her back to Brad. Something in her chest fluttered. Something in her heart gave way. Once more, in less than a few hours, tears streamed down her cheeks.

Brad took a few steps and rested his hands on her shoulders, leaned in, forehead to the back of her head. "I'm confused. I don't want us to end, but…"

She stifled a sniffle. He turned her around, wiping an errant tear.

Amanda moved her head to the side, away from him.

"This is crazy. Please, talk to me. Please."

He escorted her to her seat, pulled his closer, and sat, holding her hands in his. Amanda didn't pull away. Another first for her. She struggled against unfamiliar feelings. Maybe, the end was near. Maybe, this nightmare would be over soon.

When she said nothing, Brad stood, walked to the stove and turned it on. "I have an idea. How about we eat, then talk. This time openly and honestly and see where this will take us."

Amanda felt her head nod, ever so slightly. She was ready. She looked at the door one last time, giving up the idea of running. There was nowhere for her to run to. She would stay and face her past, letting the future take her to wherever it wants.

"Just tell me one thing," she said.

He turned to face her.

"How did you find out?"

Chapter 43

May 12, 2018

After a dinner they picked at, Brad guided Amanda to the living room. She sat on the corner of the couch, and when he approached to sit next to her, she motioned to the opposite end. He did. Sat as far from her as he could.

The room lit only by the glare from the muted TV; they sat in silence until he could stand it no more. He leaned, resting his elbows on his thighs, face cupped in the palm of his hands. "I ran into Liz and Stephanie at the park. We got to talking." He toed a button that had fallen on the carpet. "They said they found a bag."

"A bag?"

"Yeah. I guess it had jewelry and birth certificates."

He looked up and watched Amanda's eyes widen. Brad didn't wait for her reaction. He continued, "Amanda, it had the match to your pearl earring."

"Wh-where is it?"

"With the police."

He watched her reach into her pocket, the fabric bouncing from her fingers, reaching or searching for something, but she didn't pull anything out.

"Was that your earring?" he asked, trying to keep the judgment and accusation out of his voice.

An ever-so-slight nod and her eyes flitted to the images bouncing on the screen.

"What happened?" he asked.

Silence.

"Amanda," he said, a bit more forcefully than he intended. "What happened? I know it was bad for you. You were a kid. An innocent kid. They said your dad just up and left one day."

"Who told you all this?"

"Does it really matter?"

She shook her head.

"So, what happened?"

When she didn't say anything, he followed her gaze to the TV. Flashes of lights brilliantly illuminated a house. Reporters scampered to be the first to push their mic into two women's faces. Brad recognized them. "Yeah, Liz and Stephanie told me the press has been hounding them. This is awful."

Amanda blinked twice. Afraid that whatever was going on would alter the course of the topic he wanted to focus on, he reached for the remote. "Here, let me turn it off. I'll turn the lights on."

She held tight to the remote, not removing her gaze from the screen.

"So, tell me about what happened," he repeated.

Slowly, Amanda dropped the remote in her lap and turned to face Brad. He watched Amanda shrink back into the sofa, pillows cocooning her. Her mouth opened and closed twice as if struggling to push the words out. He waited. Said nothing. Waited.

Amanda broke the long silence. He could see desperation, loneliness, desolation in her vacant eyes. Once she started to talk, she didn't stop. She never once made eye contact with him.

Brad struggled to stay focused, to restrain his brain from wandering and wondering. How could a child have gone through that much without support, without family? He couldn't imagine it. His point of reference was a loving, caring family who would never have abandoned him, never would they have watched as he suffered alone.

He snapped to attention. "Sorry, what did you just say?"

She turned her gaze to him as if mocking him. "I guess nothing important. I knew I shouldn't have said anything."

"No, please, wait. Please. I can't believe what you've gone through and why no one was there to help you…"

Amanda gave him a sidelong look, shook her head, and clammed up.

"Amanda?"

He watched a tear trickle down her cheek. Brad wanted so much to reach and wipe it away, hold her, and assure her he would be there for her no matter what happened. He took a chance, even though she might reject him yet again, and inched his way toward her and watched. She didn't shrink from him.

Brad got braver and sat close to her, forcing Amanda to turn around and face him. "You have to believe me. I love you. I'm here."

Maybe she believed him; he hoped she did. Amanda lowered her head and leaned into Brad. Carefully, so as not disturb her injuries, he ever-so-gently pulled her to him.

"I only missed the last part. The part about your dad leaving," he said, stroking her curls.

"It's nothing. Not important. He left me and gave me to my grandmother."

"So, you are her. The little girl who lived in that house."

A slight nod.

"You told me what happened afterward, your grandmother, the foster homes… you started to tell me about when your dad left. I wasn't ignoring you. I didn't tune out because I wasn't interested. Please believe me. I can't fathom how a kid, you, endured this pa—"

She pulled away. "You need to stop. I don't want you to feel sorry for me. Just stop."

"I-I-I didn't mean. I mean, I couldn't have survived it. I know I couldn't have."

Somehow, the moment was lost. It was his fault for interrupting her, for tuning out. Guilt wormed its way into his soul, along with a niggling need to know what happened to her father. Was the man in the basement of the house her dad? Was she connected to his death?

Brad shook his head. He wouldn't allow himself to go down that road.

Suddenly, the lateness of the hour and emotionally stressful day caught up with him. He wasn't sure he would be able to shut his thoughts off, but his body was screaming for rest. He reached for her hand. "It's been a long day. Let's rest. Tomorrow is another day."

He stood. She remained seated.

"Come to bed. Come to bed with me."

He took a step, but she didn't stand. Brad waited and watched her as she reluctantly leaned on the arm of the couch and lifted herself. One step at a time, they made their way to the bedroom.

Ten minutes later, after taking a shower, Brad lay in the dark, waiting for Amanda to finish getting ready for bed. He felt the bed dip as she lowered herself to the edge as if contemplating if she should stay. Brad reached for her and, with a gentle touch, coaxed her to lay beside him. She was as stiff as a board.

"Let's put all this aside for tonight," he said.

He felt her shift, not sure if she was in pain or wanted to put more distance between them.

"I'm confused, but I'm also angry that you went through such a tou—"

"Don't. You don't know everything," she said in almost a whisper.

"Whatever it is, we will get through it together."

245

"That's not possible."

Brad wanted to assure her, to reassure her he would see her through whatever it is, but he bit his tongue as the night silence descended on the room. He was exhausted, and it didn't take long for him to fall fast asleep. He didn't even move from his position, didn't hear Amanda get up an hour later, and leave the room.

Six hours later, he woke, feeling as if he was drugged. Brad wanted to go back to sleep, but the empty bed next to him said otherwise. He assumed she had slept and was up early. He flipped the covers to the side and swung his legs to the floor. Steadying himself, he stood and went to the bathroom. The water he splashed on his face was a welcoming coolness.

He checked the time, 8:35 am and wondered if he should get dressed or go downstairs in his shorts. Brad opted for the latter, and after he opened the curtains to let the sun in, he made his way to the door leading to the upstairs hallway and froze.

The dresser drawers were open, the sliding door to the closet, too. He checked the drawers; there were a few items in each. He wasn't sure if they were always that way but found it odd they were not closed. That was not how remembered them from the previous night. It was dark, he reasoned, and he may not have noticed.

The closet, though, didn't look right. Brad took a few steps and peered in. Several hangers had nothing on them. This was not usual. He quickly surveyed the room, and a sinking feeling overtook him. She wouldn't have left, would she? He dismissed the notion as ludicrous. So much had happened in the past two weeks, he probably had not noticed the changes to his surroundings.

More confident, Brad went downstairs. The house was eerily quiet. He checked the kitchen; it stood empty bathed in light. The coffee pot felt cool to the touch, and the indicator light was off. *She must've been up for hours,* he thought.

Brad popped a pod in the coffee maker, placed a mug in the holder, and waited the few moments it took it to brew a cup. The first sip invigorated him. He swallowed, enjoying the flavor as it tickled his senses awake.

Moments later, sure Amanda was in the living room as he saw the TV glare dancing on the walls, he made his way there. Amanda wasn't there. A dread worked its way up and down his spine. Setting his cup on the nearest surface, he raced through the house, calling her name. Up and down the stairs, he checked every room, but she wasn't there.

He ran to the garage and opened the access door from the hallway. The garage door was fully open, and there was an empty spot where his car usually sat. There had to be an explanation for her absence. Maybe she went to the store? But she wasn't supposed to drive yet.

Brad cursed himself for leaving his phone upstairs and took the stairs two at a time to fetch it. It wasn't on the nightstand. Frantically, he dismantled the bedding, then looked under it. He was sure he had left it on next to the bed, in its usual spot… then he remembered and retraced his steps to the top of the dresser, where he had set it after checking the time earlier. Relieved, he flipped it on and looked for a text message from Amanda, but he had none.

His fingers fumbled with the digital keyboard when he sent her a text. He waited, checking the phone every few minutes, even though he had turned the volume and notification on high. When nearly half an hour went by with no response, his knees went weak with worry. Where could she have gone?

He grabbed his sneakers and sat on the bed to put them when he realized he was not dressed. Brad didn't want to waste time showering. He grabbed the nearest T-shirt and put it on, then slipped his feet in his shoes, quickly tying them, and dashed down the stairs to his bike.

When he was about to mount, he stopped, shook his head, and went back into the house. Where was he thinking of going? On a bike, at that. He had no option but to wait to hear from her.

Baffled at the possibility she may have up and gone after he thought they made progress connecting and talking, he went into the living room and sipped his now lukewarm coffee, blankly staring at the TV.

His head swam, anger mixed with dread flooded him. Brad rechecked his phone, but no word from Amanda. He typed the twelfth message to her, asking where she was and if she was okay.

The pacing didn't help. Talking himself out of worry and dread didn't make a difference. Why? Why would she leave?

He reached in the creases of his memory, unfolding each to look within, to what she said about her dad before he zoned out. He kicked himself for not paying attention. A few words fluttered from his subconscious... what did they mean? Did it have something to do with her dad? Did she say she killed him?

"No!!!" he yelled to stop his whirring thoughts. No way would she have done anything like that. But what if it was in self-defense? Did he hurt her?

Brad swiped his hands down his face before he went back to pacing and raking his fingers through his hair. He sent a desperate text, pleading with her to come back.

He sat at the edge of the couch, legs spread apart, head hanging low, arms resting on his thighs with one hand holding the cellphone.

A few minutes passed, and then a few more. He lifted his gaze to the TV where images danced, and people came into view and left – he stared blankly. The chirp from the phone jerking him back from wherever his mind went. It wasn't Amanda. He debated whether he should answer, not in the mood to chat with anyone, but it was Joe. So, he did.

"Hey, Joe."

"Just wanted to check up on you, Mr. V. Everything okay?"

"Yeah, I'm fine. Thanks for checking in."

"Okay, Mr. V."

"Thanks again, Joe. I appreciate it."

"No problem. I guess now they know who the guy is—"

"What did you say?" interrupted Brad.

"Haven't you been watching the news? They ID'd the guy."

Brad reached for the remote control and fumbled with the buttons, trying to turn up the volume and change the channel to the news.

"Mr. V.?"

"Um, yeah. Okay. Thanks for calling."

He pushed "end call" without waiting for what Joe had to say. His eyes were glued to the television – someone in a uniform stood at a podium with tens of mics thrust toward him.

Eyes and ears focused on the TV, Brad was afraid to blink or swallow. The name the caption mentioned was not familiar – nothing like Amanda's father's name. At least that he knew.

He fired off one more text: *Amanda, please call me. I have news.*

Chapter 44

May 13, 2018
Shame and guilt. These two unfamiliar emotions ate away at Amanda as she sped south. All her life, it was fear of being discovered and punished; now, this.

Fighting tears, she drove, her mind punishing her worse than facing incarceration for what she had done. Even though Ashley said it wasn't Amanda's fault, she clearly remembered their fight, the nasty words they exchanged, the pushing and shoving, and the fall. It was her fault, no matter what Ashley said. Then, there was her dad, who she poisoned. That was no accident. She did it, and now, he was dead. She killed him. How would she ever forgive herself?

Realizing the speedometer pegged at ninety-five miles per hour, she lifted her foot off the gas. "Not yet… it isn't time yet."

Amanda had one more thing to do before she would find peace. As she neared the facility where her mother lived, she found herself calm. The sweaty palms had dried, her mind was gently grinding, it would all be soon over. No more agony. No more running away.

At the reception desk, she set the flowers she bought earlier on the counter and signed in. The woman behind the desk smiled pleasantly but said the bare minimum, and only what was required. "You can go through that door" —she pointed to a sliding glass door— "when you hear the buzzer. Have a pleasant visit." With that, she turned her attention to the computer screen, and Amanda walked to the door.

She had it all planned out. What she would say and ask.

After a long walk down endless hallways, she found the courtyard where her mother sat under the shade of an elm tree, two other patients nearby.

"Hi, Mom," she said as she got closer. "I got these for you." She handed the flowers to her mother.

Irene looked at them as if she'd never seen anything like it before and didn't know what to do with them.

"Here, I'll find a vase," Amanda said as she retrieved the bouquet and found a glass of water nearby. "Aren't they pretty? Roses used to be your favorite."

There was a slight nod from Irene.

Amanda was hopeful. Perhaps she caught her mother in a lucid moment. She plowed ahead. "Mom?" The word tickled her lips with an unfamiliar taste.

Irene's gaze remained fixed on the roses since she first followed Amanda's movements. She didn't respond. Maybe she, too, found the sound of the word unfamiliar.

"Look at me, please. I have something to say."

Slowly, Irene moved her eyes, but not her face, toward Amanda.

"I'm sorry." The words tumbled out.

Her mother turned her face to gaze into her daughter's eyes as if not comprehending.

"You see, I never understood why you left me. I hated you for not baking my cake; for leaving me…" Amanda swallowed unshed tears. "But now, I understand it wasn't your fault."

Irene said nothing.

"Anyway, the past is behind us. I just wanted to say I'm sorry for not visiting… sorry for not…" She looked into the distance, not sure how else to say what she felt.

Irene stretched her gnarly fingers to pat Amanda's hand.

"You are here! You do understand," Amanda said. "Will you ever forgive me?"

A tear escaped down Irene's cheek. She nodded and, once again, patted Amanda's hand.

They sat in silence for a few minutes. Irene didn't say a word.

"I have a question. Do you think you can answer it?" Amanda asked.

Irene nodded.

"Is Andrew Bairn my father?"

"Wha-why do you ask?" Irene said in a feeble voice, almost a whisper.

"Please, just tell me."

"I love roses. I remember when I was a kid…" Irene reminisced.

"Is Andrew Bairn my father?" Amanda repeated.

"We used to go to this field. Do you remember? I used to take you there when you were little. The field behind Agnes's house. Oh, the ros—"

"Please, stop. Answer me! Is Andrew Bairn my father?"

Irene traveled to where her mind took her. She was no longer in the present. No longer responsive to Amanda's pleas.

Amanda tried several times, but Irene was gone. Her eyes were vacant, and her words made no sense. She finally stood, looked at her mother, and whispered, "Goodbye."

She was now sure the man she poisoned was not her father. She killed a man who didn't want to raise someone else's child. How could she blame him for leaving? Her guilt ate away at her.

Confused and no longer sure of what to do, she sat in the car for an hour. Her tics became worse with the stress of the truth that descended upon her, and she reached for her medication.

Amanda was tempted to turn on her phone and check for messages. No doubt, there would be a few from Brad. *Poor Brad.* It wasn't his fault; he ended up in this horrid situation with a criminal wife. What did she think would happen when she agreed to marry him without divulging her past? Did she think she would forever conceal it?

She wondered how he found out about the house where the body was found. Who told him? Who would've known it was her… the girl whose father dumped her and left? She laughed aloud. She now doubted he was her father, and her mother's reaction confirmed it.

Her mind wandered to the two years at 282 Magpie Lane. It now all made sense why Andrew wasn't a father to her, why she didn't look anything like him, and why he had enough of the responsibility of a girl who wasn't his, and her guilt surfaced for what she had done.

As her thoughts circulated, they landed at the school she attended. Then, the realization came. The only person who would've known about her would be Joe, the custodian who now worked with Brad. A distant memory crept in when she first met Brad, and he took her to a school staff party where she saw Joe after all the years that had passed. He didn't appear to recognize her, but she avoided him anyway until they met up by accident at the buffet. Her apprehension of being discovered caused stressed, which in turn caused the tics to intensify. She recalled how he looked at her for a long time but didn't say anything. Could her tics have caused him to remember the girl who was bullied and taunted?

It had to be him who told Brad, she thought.

Amanda didn't know nor would she know, Joe didn't make the connection. It was a coincidence that brought the realization to Brad.

Though the thoughts whirred, not once did she wonder who her biological father was. It wouldn't matter anyway. Either her mother didn't know, or her mind wouldn't let her remember. It didn't matter; it would all be over soon. But she had one last thing to take care of: Brad. She had to let him off the hook, to free him from any misgivings he had, and to apologize for dragging him into her messed up life.

Afterward, this time, she wouldn't make any mistakes; she would end it as she failed to do a few days ago.

Her fingers felt for the phone in her purse and pulled it out. She sucked in a breath and turned it on. There were at least two dozen calls and texts. Amanda didn't bother to read any of them. She went to her email to type what she couldn't say aloud. She clicked on the app, and her fingers didn't hesitate.

I'm so sorry. I should not have dragged you into my miserable life. I didn't want to tell you about my past, not because I was embarrassed, but because I didn't want pity from you. I don't deserve pity. Though I believed I was the cause of Ashley's fall and it turned out I wasn't, I am still responsible. I could've not fought with her, but I did.

This wasn't the worst of my actions. I killed my father. The man in the basement is my father. I poisoned him. I killed him. I killed Andrew Bairn.

Amanda paused for a minute, wanting to erase what she typed, but she didn't. She had made up her mind, this time, no lies. This time the whole truth. This time, to set him free from her. She didn't deserve someone like Brad. He was too kind, too gentle.

It won't be long before they find out he was poisoned and come for me. I don't want you anywhere near this mess. You are free now. Free from me. Free from the past. I left my wedding rings in the drawer by your side of the bed. I hope what I've done will not come back to hurt you. You are a great teacher, and you don't deserve what I put you through.

Please don't come looking for me. By the time you read this, I will be forever gone.

Without delay, she pressed send.

Now, she was ready for her final journey. No one would miss her.

She turned on the ignition, and before she slipped the gear from park to drive, a thought struck her. She grabbed her purse, turned off the car, and got out. Amanda made her way to the receptionist and asked for the manager. When Thom Buckley came to meet her, she handed him a check that cleared out her personal savings account. The check was made to Irene Dunkirk. "Please, deposit this in her account to use for anything she needs."

"Thank you, Mrs. Verchall. I will see that it's taken care of."

Amanda nodded and left the facility for the last time. That was it — nothing more to do.

She hesitated for a brief moment to take in the scenery, the pond in the distance, the water fountain lazily splashing water, and the array of greenery and flowers surrounding the facility. Her mom was in the right place. Brad would be okay, too. He'd be better off without her.

With sure steps, she returned to her car, sat in the driver's seat, and turned on the ignition once more. She fastened her seatbelt, mocking herself at the irony, but she didn't want to get stopped before she had accomplished her mission.

Slowly, she drove through the parking lot and onto the main highway, aiming for the spot where she was sure it was a point of no return. She had passed by that spot many times on her way to visit her mother at the previous facility.

Those who left the highway never…

Almost two hours to go, and it would be over. No more running, no more shame, no more guilt.

Chapter 45

May 13, 2018

"Nooooo! No, Amanda, *no!*" Brad yelled as he frantically dialed 9-1-1 after he read the email.

"Please… this is Brad Verchall… it's my wife… she's—she's—"

The emergency operator spoke calmly, aiming to extract information from Brad. It took a moment to convince him to take a deep breath and answer her questions. Brad was almost incoherent and couldn't focus, but managed to give his car description and license number.

The dispatch operator told Brad she's sending an officer to speak with him, but Brad cut her off. "No! Send him to look for my wife."

She reassured him that would be taken care of, and she had already dispatched the car information.

While still on the phone with the operator, the doorbell rang, and the dispatcher told Brad it was one of her officers and to open the door.

He did as instructed, automated.

Two officers stood outside the door; Brad recognized one of them. She was the one who had interviewed Amanda a few days before.

"Good evening, Mr. Verchall. Can we come in?" she said.

Brad stood aside, the phone still to his ear. His mouth opened and closed, but no words spilled out.

"It's okay. You can hang up now," said the second officer while the other spoke in her lapel mic.

"Let's sit down," the first one said as she guided Brad to the living room.

"Please, find her," Brad begged.

"We have units looking for your car. Why don't you start from the beginning? Tell us what happened."

"I think she's going to kill herself." Brad struggled to say the words.

"What makes you think that?"

Without hesitation, he handed his phone to the officer to read the email. While her mouth silently formed the words and her eyes shifted from left to right and back again, Brad said, "She doesn't know. She didn't read my text messages. She thinks… Oh, God." He put his face in his hands and wept.

"This is unreal," said Liz.

Stephanie shook her head as they listened to the police spokesman, wrapping up reading a prepared statement and was ready to take questions from the press.

"So, our guest is… was Emery Kevin, who didn't live here, but was a friend of the renter." Stephanie was bewildered by the events.

"Yeah, and the police seem to think he ended up in an argument with… what did they say the other guy's name was? Oh, right, Andrew. So, he and Andrew had an argument, a fight, or whatever?" said Liz.

"Seems so."

"So, Andrew took off, leaving his daughter and a dead man behind. What a nice guy."

"I wonder if his daughter knows," said Stephanie.

"I hope she didn't see what her dad did. This is so awful. I can't imagine what trauma the girl faced or faces. Let's hope she doesn't know. Poor thing."

Liz fluffed the pillows around her, and Stephanie leaned back from her position, perched at the edge of the couch.

"Looks like they're going to take press questions. I'm sure glad they are no longer camped here. I hope they don't come back!" Liz said exasperated.

"Me, too… shh… they're starting." Stephanie put her finger to her lips.

The news reporters shouted over each other. "Why do they let them do that?" asked Liz.

It didn't take long to bring order as one by one; the reporters asked their questions.

"How did you identify the body?"

"Are you going to charge Andrew Bowen with murder?"

"What are you doing to find Andrew Bowen?"

"Where is his daughter?"

"Does his daughter have anything to do with the murder?"

The captain answered their question as best he could, citing, "It is still under investigation. We will share when we have more information."

He then ended the conference with, "Ladies and gentlemen, thank you for coming. That'll be all for now," he said as he turned away from the mics, although the reporters didn't stop firing questions.

Liz and Stephanie exchanged a glance.

"I guess that's all for now," said Stephanie, reaching for the remote control to turn off the TV, but she held it in her hand, instead. "Hey, what did you think about this Brad guy? Don't you think his reaction was a bit weird?"

"Yeah. His reaction to the ring and stuff we found was weird," said Liz.

"Well, anyway. How about we—" Stephanie halted, pointing at the TV with the remote she still held in her hand.

Liz turned her attention to the screen; her mouth fell open.

An all-points bulletin for a dark blue Prius, listing its license plate number, appeared in a ticker at the bottom of the screen. "What now?" asked Liz.

Glued to the TV, the twins heard the announcer say the police were looking for this car, its occupant was in danger, though not a danger to others. They described the woman as thirty-six, five-foot-six, shoulder-length curly black hair, and a medium complexion.

"No way!" said Liz.

"You think it is—"

"Nah, can't be."

Stephanie waited for a few minutes to see if they would repeat the name, and when they didn't, she pressed the off button. "Enough of drama for one day," she said, rising to stand.

"What do you want to do?" asked Liz.

"Hmm. How about we work on the scrapbook for a while and maybe take a walk before summer sets in."

The twins spent the next two hours working on the scrapbooks, in their newly remodeled home. They had finally finished renovations, the kitchen completed, and the ancient house brought back to life through hours of hard work. Their great grandpa would be proud of what they did had he still been around.

Chapter 47

May 13, 2018

An hour left to go of the longest two hours Amanda had ever been through. She was now anxious for the end of the trip. Though an hour wasn't long, it was an eternity for her. She kept the car at the assigned speed limit, not wanting to attract any attention to herself.

The car shrouded in silence, Amanda was left to her thoughts. They were no longer jumbled nor muddled. Her head was clear, and the images playing in her mind were pleasant. A handful of memories that she had not turned off. Aunt Emma's garden and kitchen. She imagined herself covered in dirt, bathed by the sun as they dug and planted, and when the fruit ripened, picking it and popping it in her mouth as she savored the sweetness or tartness that made her pucker.

She wiped at the imaginary drool at the corner of her mouth and smiled. Thirty more exits. It wouldn't be long now.

Amanda smiled a genuine, from-the-bottom-of-her-heart smile. She recited the "I'm sorry" for all who she had wronged and hurt and gave a special, "I'm sorry, Andrew. I didn't want you to die."

In a haze of almost euphoria, she approached her exit, turned on the blinker, and swerved the steering wheel to the right. It was a long exit, and her focus was now on the carrot dangling less than fifteen miles away. Still daylight, and the sun had not set, she didn't see the blinking blue and red lights behind her until she reached the stop sign at the end of the exit.

"Damn. Damn. Damn." She was not speeding, had followed all traffic laws. What did the cop want with her?

She would comply. They had no reason to stop her. It wouldn't take long.

Amanda pulled to the shoulder and stopped the car. She watched the trooper exit his car and approach her, his hand on his holster. He motioned for her to roll down her window. She did.

"Ma'am," he said in a deep and gravelly voice.

She shrugged, and her eye twitched. The trooper didn't react. Perhaps he thought she was flirting with him. She almost laughed aloud. Then, reality hit her. She quickly pulled out her wallet and extracted her driver's license handing it to him. He took it.

"Ma'am, I need you to step out of your car."

"But why? What did I do?" Amanda stopped herself before she said anything else that might prolong the traffic stop.

Panic set in. She was too close to her freedom — just fifteen more minutes.

"Is this your car?"

"Yes. I mean, no. I mean, it is my husband's," she said as she realized she was not driving her car. "But it's my car, too."

Another trooper car pulled to the right of the first one, further over on the shoulder. A patrolman exited and came around to the passenger side of the Prius. Amanda bit her lip as he opened the passenger door, then the glove compartment and pulled out the registration. He read it, looked up, and nodded at the first trooper.

"Ma'am, I'm going to ask you to sit in the patrol car," he said as he guided her toward it.

She couldn't fight his grip. She wouldn't run. Amanda couldn't. Her ribs still hurt, and she was in no shape to get away. "I—I don't understand. Why are you doing this?"

"It's for your protection," he said as he gently guided her head inside the car, and she sat on the unforgiving hard plastic seat.

He closed the door, a door without inside handles. She was trapped. Her plans ruined.

The two officers exchanged words that Amanda could not hear, only the deep rumble of their voices. Both walked to the Prius, and looked inside it, under the seats, in the trunk, and the only thing in one of the officer's hands was her purse and cell when he emerged.

Amanda shook with rage and frustration. Her tears flowed down her cheeks, with salty pools in the corners of her mouth when reality sunk in. They know. Brad must have called them and reported his car stolen. She beat on the window with her fists and screamed for them to let her out... they had no right to detain her. She screamed louder when her ribs ached from the movement and agitation until one officer came back — the one with her purse.

He poked his head in. "Ma'am, if you don't settle down, I'm going to have to cuff you."

She didn't.

The second officer opened the rear door, and the first opened the one closest to her, and with one quick move, they cuffed her hands behind her as she screamed in agony and despair.

"Let me go!" She kicked the back of the driver seat – a crazed woman.

"Ma'am. Ma'am." The second time, louder.

Her head snapped up, and she looked around as if trying to figure out where she was. "Please," she whimpered. "Let me go. Please."

"Ma'am, when you're ready to listen, I will talk to you."

Amanda's tics grew worse. With her hands behind her back, the jerking motion caused a searing pain in her chest. Her ribs screamed louder than she did. "I—I—need my medi—cation."

The trooper extracted the pill bottle from Amanda's purse and read the directions. "Says here you take this at bedtime." He made a show of looking at his wristwatch. "Nope, not time yet."

Her tear-streaked face, wild unruly curls, and sunken cheekbones gave Amanda a maniacal appearance, but she quieted down. Her only hope of being let go was to cooperate. They had no right to stand in her way.

The trooper's eyes were on her, but there was no anger or judgment.

"Please," she whispered.

"Are you ready to listen?" he asked.

She gave a slight nod.

"We got an APB describing the Prius and license number. Tell me they are wrong. You weren't gonna harm yourself."

Amanda averted her gaze. Beyond the green pastures in the distance, she imagined the spot she aimed for and cursed herself for being careless, for sending the email to Brad, for taking the time to go back into the facility to drop the check. Those precious few minutes were all she needed to end the misery called life.

"Well, ma'am, we have orders to take you in."

Amanda saw sympathy in his soft blue eyes.

"Can you please uncuff me? It hurts."

He called out to the other trooper, and together, they uncuffed her hands from behind and latched the cuffs to the metal bars in the car next to her. "Ma'am. If you quit struggling, they would hurt less."

With that, the two troopers walked to the back of the vehicle, and a few minutes later, the one parked to the right, reversed after he looked through his driver's side window and nodded toward her. She heard the tires crunch the gravel, and the sound of his engine faded.

"Where are you taking me?" she asked the trooper who returned to his vehicle, got in, and fastened his seatbelt.

"Ma'am, to Denver Health."

Amanda's heart sank. She didn't deserve to live. Though arrest and jail would be a punishment for what she did, she desired to die.

The long hour drive dragged on. Once at the facility, the trooper handcuffed her hands together, this time in front of her with a threat that if she didn't cooperate, he would cuff them behind her back. By then, she was docile and had surrendered to her unexpected fate.

Anger rose, bubbling to her throat, aimed at Brad, momentarily forgetting it was her email who had triggered the situation she was in. She didn't care if her anger was misplaced. She didn't care if Brad would hate her when this was all said and done. She hated herself.

As she shuffled to the entrance and beyond, several staff members came to meet them. The trooper remained by her side, hanging on her arm until they secured her in a room with two chairs and a table anchored to the floor and wall, where they left her and locked the door behind them.

Wait. Something's wrong. Why didn't they arrest me? her mind prodded.

Finding it odd, she was not under arrest for the murder of her father; she wondered if they, perhaps, weren't able to find the poison in his system because it was so long ago. She chided herself. That was not possible with the modern forensics and technology available. But why? Why was she not in jail? Maybe after they released her from the mental hospital? Was that even possible?

Before she could figure it out, there was a gentle knock, almost too soft to be heard, and a tall man, her age or close to it, clad in jeans and a T-shirt that hugged his torso, entered, a laptop under his left arm.

"Amanda?" he asked.

She didn't blink. Amanda stared at him. He didn't look like a doctor or a nurse.

"I'm Lucas Djorn."

When she didn't respond, he asked, "May I sit?"

Three consecutive shrugs from her left shoulder signaled she didn't care. He sat. Amanda knew they were tics, but this man couldn't have known from his reaction. She quickly looked down as her eye twitched.

When she lifted her gaze, Lucas smiled at her. "I'm an intake psychiatrist, Amanda. Do you know what that is?"

Incensed he was treating her like an imbecile, she rolled her eyes. She had never done that before, with anyone.

"I would like to have the handcuffs removed…"

She shrugged.

Lucas rose to his feet, opened the door, and called out. A few moments later, the same trooper stepped in and unlocked the cuffs. He backstepped until he reached the door while exchanging glances with Lucas as if to ask him, "Are you sure this is safe?"

With his hand on the door handle, he said, "Ma'am. I hope you feel better real soon."

He didn't wait for a reply, left, and the door made a soft click as he closed it behind him.

Amanda watched as Lucas returned his attention to her. The next two hours went by slow and fast with minimal interruptions by other staff. After resisting for the best part of the first hour, she relented and answered his questions.

Exhausted, she begged to be done.

"Almost," Lucas said. "Are you taking any medication?"

Amanda nodded.

Lucas raised his eyebrows questioningly.

"Clonidine and something else… new medication."

"Okay. We'll get your records from your doctor and go from there. Sleeplessness?"

"Tics... Tourette's Syndrome." By then, Amanda was calm and rational.

"Okay."

"Can I leave?" She didn't ask if she could go home. She no longer had one.

"I'm afraid not. We will keep you for the seventy-two-hour hold, mandatory for all suicide attempts."

"But... I... didn—"

Lucas raised his hand to stop her. "Amanda, we'll talk about all this tomorrow. Let's see if your room is ready."

"Are the police still here? Are they arresting me?"

A puzzled look passed on his face. "No, why would they do that?"

"I killed my father," her words didn't even hesitate at her lips.

"I have no information to that effect." He looked at her as if assessing her sanity.

"I killed my father," she repeated.

"We can talk about that tomorrow."

Amanda banged her fist on the table. "Are you deaf? I just told you, I killed my father... at least, I think he was my father."

Lucas sat and placed the laptop back on the table. "What makes you think so?"

A manic laugh escaped. "You want the whole confession? Okay. I poisoned him back in 1995. He died. He's the body they found in the basement of the house on Magpie. You don't believe me? Check it out."

She watched Lucas as he struggled with what to say next. She knew she caught him off-guard. *Good,* she thought. *They think with their degrees, they are smart and know everything.*

267

"I did hear about the case, but there was no mention of—"

"Yeah? Dr. Know-it-all? Listen, and listen good. I killed my father. His name was Andrew Bairn. I poisoned him. He is dead. Now, you can have them arrest me. Go ahead."

"I think you're mistaken. I listened to the press conference this afternoon. That's not what—" he abruptly stopped himself in mid-thought and reversed direction. "Okay, Amanda. I believe you. I'll report it if you want me to."

She knew for sure he was placating her. He didn't believe her. She didn't care. To hell with all of them.

Three shrugs had him stand again. "We'll get your medication order filled to control the tics and help you sleep." He didn't wait for her to say reply. "Someone will be in very soon to take you to your room."

Amanda watched his muscles ripple as he made his way to the door, exited, leaving her to her chaotic thoughts, but she was too tired to allow them to run in her head. She crossed her arms on the table and cradled her head.

Chapter 48

May 13, 2018

Brad listened to the caller with mixed emotions. They found Amanda, and she was taken to Denver Health. Relief and sadness racked him. At least, she was safe, for now. He thanked the officer as he pressed the taxi app. It was getting late, nearly 8 pm, and darkness blanketed the house and its surroundings.

He locked the front door and turned when a slight movement caught in his peripheral. Mrs. Krupp opened her window and gave him a sad wave. "I'm sorry about your wife. Saw it on the TV."

Brad nodded and made his way to the sidewalk. His app showed the cab a minute away, and just as he stepped out of his gate, the silver car in the app pulled up. He opened the back door, sat, and reached for his seatbelt.

The driver verified the address and pulled away from the curb. Nothing was said the entire trip. Brad was grateful for the time to think. As they approached Denver Health, Brad exited as his phone pinged with incoming messages. His apprehension at seeing Amanda had him rooted to the spot where he stood. He checked the first message, a delay tactic, he knew.

Stephanie: *We saw the news. Hope Amanda will be okay.*

Brad scrolled to the next one from a colleague with a similar message. He ignored that one, too. Just as he told his feet to move, his phone rang, and he pressed answer. "Hi, Joe."

Joe expressed concern and wished Amanda a speedy recovery. "Yeah, it was her. I had this feeling when I first met her years ago but dismissed it. Glad she's okay. The poor thing, all this, and now they're arresting her dad for murder, can you believe it?"

Brad wanted to end the call. He realized he was in no mood for idle chatting. "Joe, I'm at the hospital. I've got to go."

"Sure thing Mr. V. Give my regards to the missus. Tell her to get better soon."

Brad thanked Joe and ended the call as he made his way to the entrance. The double sliding glass door parted to let him into a sterile hallway that led to another glass sliding door. There he paused, pressed a button, and spoke into the intercom. A moment later, he was buzzed in.

There was a small group huddled in the corner, a tearful woman consoled by who appeared to be her family. Brad's eyes scanned the sitting area for a receptionist's desk. There was none. An older man sat by a door, leaning on his cane. He pointed to the opposite wall where another door stood next to it, a window with wires running through the glass. He approached.

A young man looked up and pressed a button to speak into a two-way intercom. "Can I help you?"

"I'm here to see my wife. Amanda Verchall." The words a mixed taste of unfamiliar feelings.

The man maneuvered his mouse, staring at the screen. "I'm sorry. I can't let you in. They have not finished processing her… There's a note. Hang on a sec."

He picked up the phone. Brad couldn't hear what was said. A moment later, the man returned to the intercom. "Doctor Djorn will be out to speak with you in fifteen minutes. Please, have a seat."

Brad walked to the opposite end of the waiting room from the older man. He had enough on his plate. He didn't want to listen to anyone else's story. The fifteen minutes turned to half an hour, and just when he was about to walk up to the window, a door opened, and someone approached him. "Mr. Verchall?"

"Brad, please."

"Lucas." He extended his hand for a shake. "Let's go somewhere more private."

Lucas motioned for Brad to follow him through a door, into a hallway, and to a small conference room.

Once seated, Lucas said, "You called 9-1-1." It wasn't a question.

Brad nodded.

"To help Amanda, I need to ask you some questions. Is that okay?"

"Yes, I want her to get better."

Torn and unsure of what the future held for him, he opted to answer the questions honestly. But before he did, he asked, "How long will she be here?"

"For now, the mandated seventy-two-hours. We will take it a day at a time."

Brad didn't argue.

At one point, he said, "She thinks she killed her father. I think that's why she wanted to end her life."

Lucas encouraged Brad to go on.

"She thinks she poisoned him. She didn't get my texts, or maybe, she didn't read them." Brad paused for a moment, raking his fingers through his hair.

"Go on," said Lucas.

"She didn't. The man in the basement wasn't her father. He was not poisoned. Someone killed him... something about blunt force trauma."

"Why would she think she killed her father? This does not make sense."

"She said... she said she put poison in his coffee. They found the thermos and analyzed the contents. It was dish soap residue. There was no poison."

271

"When did that happen?"

"When she was twelve. Back in 1995. Here's the kicker: they're arresting her dad for the murder of his friend, the man in the basement."

"And, Amanda doesn't know any of this?"

"I don't think so." Brad pulled out his phone and showed Lucas the messages. None were read. "I don't think she listened to the news either. The radio in my car doesn't work."

Brad lowered his gaze to his clasped hands after he turned the phone upside down on the table. "So, she didn't have to…" He couldn't bring himself to say, commit suicide.

Chapter 49

June 3, 2018

Sunshine flooded the rec room. Amanda closed her eyes and lifted her face to feel the cool breeze through the open window and the sun kissing her face. A novel's cover closed on her lap, one finger a placeholder between the pages.

Her thoughts drifted, capturing the events of the past month, a month that felt like eons. The cocktail of medication the doctor prescribed made her feel calm. The psychiatrist hinted at reducing it, but she didn't care. For once, she could look back and not panic. Amanda liked the feeling of nonchalance. Maybe, she'd ask for a stronger dose.

She opened her eyes and stared at a bird fluttering in a puddle of water left by the sprinklers. It seemed to be carefree. She no longer wished she was. She deserved to be locked up. The world deserved to be safe from her. True, Amanda finally accepted she didn't kill Ashley's baby, it was a freak accident, and Ashley was in the process of a miscarriage well before Amanda kicked her… well before she fell down the stairs. Also, true, she didn't kill her father. Even if he drank the coffee, the dishwashing soap she put in would not have killed him, but he didn't drink it, which was good.

This realization didn't console Amanda. She intended to harm both, and that was all that mattered. Add to that her mother's insanity, and her father was a murderer – yes, the DNA confirmed Andrew was her biological father – no way would Amanda allow herself to be free among innocent people. She was prone to hurting others; she knew it.

"Amanda?" Grace, one of the nurses, broke into her wandering thoughts.

Amanda shifted her gaze from the open window and stared at Grace.

"You have a visitor," Grace said brightly.

Amanda remained silent.

"It's that handsome husband of yours. He's been here every day. Today, he has…" Grace quickly covered her mouth, creating a barricade for the escaped words.

Silence.

"Won't you consider seeing him, Amanda?"

Silence.

"You know what Lucas said. You really should try…" Grace insisted. When Amanda said nothing, Grace said, "Well, too late. He's on his way."

Amanda opened her mouth to say, "No," but a flurry of activity in the hallway stopped her. Her eyes fluttered toward the sounds, and she froze. Several staff members, Brad and Joe, walked behind a nurse pushing a trolley with a cake, a pitcher of lemonade, cups, plates, and utensils rattling as one wheel wobbled on the tile floor. Her eyes rounded, and her mouth followed suit. She wanted to scream, to tell them all to go to hell, but the look on Brad's face, his hands clutching a bouquet of daisies, silenced her.

She was trapped with nowhere to go.

"Happy birthday to you…" chimed the mismatched voices as other patients joined in, too.

Amanda searched for an escape route. There was none. Only one entrance in and out of the room. She remained rooted, glaring at the entourage. She didn't notice until Margaret, her therapist, laid a gentle hand on her shoulder. Then, she leaned in to whisper, "We spoke of today, and you agreed, remember?"

She nodded.

"I'm here. Take a breath and count to four. That's the girl. Now, release it to the count of five."

She did as told.

The group approached, and the nurse placed the trolley in front of Amanda. Brad maintained his position, still clutching the daisies. She lifted her gaze and met his. Timidly, he approached and handed her the flowers. "Happy birthday," he said quietly.

Amanda gripped the novel tightly and brought it to her chest. A nurse reached for the bouquet. "Here, let me put these in water for you."

Brad retracted his steps and stood next to Joe, who took a step forward, then another. "Hi, Mrs. V.," he said in his deep, gravelly voice.

"You knew…" It wasn't a question; it was a statement.

Joe smiled, reached in his pocket, and pulled out his hand, a chain lazily dangled from his fingers. Amanda stared in disbelief. Slowly, she opened her hand toward Joe, and he dropped the chain and locket into her waiting palm.

Amanda stared at the object in her hand, mesmerized. She lifted her gaze to meet Joe's, a question in her eyes.

In a low voice, almost a whisper, Joe said, "You dropped this sometime after your dad left. I kept it, but didn't remember your name until," he paused and scratched his chin, "until recently when it all came back."

She wrapped her fingers around the chain and locket. It was a trinket, but a trinket that brought memories crashing in the present. That moment, thirty-one years ago when Auntie Emma took her in after the disaster that her mother created. The birthday that never was. The cake that didn't get baked, the countless years she was abandoned.

Auntie Emma had given her the chain and locket. Inside was a picture of her beaming mother, Irene, with a drooling toddler on her lap. Amanda had forgotten about it after she thought it was long lost.

"Thank you," she muttered.

"Mrs. V., get well soon," Joe said as he touched her knee and joined the rest.

"Who's ready for cake and ice cream?" someone asked, handing out filled plates.

Brad approached again with a plate in hand. "Happy birthday."

Amanda didn't reach for the plate. Brad set it on a table near her. She looked away. Then turned her gaze to the slice with a fuzzy orange design, and curiosity led her eyes to the cake on the trolley. She gasped. Who did this? How did they know? That was the cake her mother was going to make for her. "No," she whimpered.

It only took seconds for Margaret to materialize. "You've made tremendous progress, Amanda. The past is just that, the past."

"But... but..." she stammered, pointing at the cake.

A familiar voice from long ago said shakily, "It is about time you get your Ernie and Bert cake." The silver-haired woman shuffled closer, tears tracking the wrinkled face.

"Au... Auntie Emma?"

In real life, not all stories end with, "They lived happily ever after." Some just end, leaving unfinished business and hanging emotions. Amanda's would be one such story. Intensive and extensive therapy helped remove the layers of buried and unresolved memories, but she had never forgiven herself, no matter how much the facts told her otherwise.

After her birthday, she filed for divorce, not because she didn't love Brad, in her own way, but because Amanda didn't love him enough, or perhaps, she still had a long way to learn to love herself before she could learn to love another. She was convinced he deserved better, and the damage she caused their relationship could not be repaired.

Brad did not want to accept her decision. However, he had no choice but to sign the papers. He would not force her into a marriage she didn't want.

Surprisingly, he became good friends with Liz and Stephanie, who kept telling him, "If you love someone, set them free. If they come back, they're yours. If they don't, they never were."

As Brad packed the house to get it ready to list for sale, he wondered how long it took for them to "come back." How long would he have to wait for Amanda to come back if she was going to do so? Only time would tell.

For now, she moved in with Auntie Emma. For now, she would continue with therapy and medication.

It is all too often we judge others by outward appearance or action. We should take the time to learn their truth, to understand what lies beneath the surface — the struggles they endure.

If you enjoyed "Shattered," check out:

"Missing: Never Forgotten"

and "Fatal Family Affair"

Please, take a moment to leave a review. I would greatly appreciate it.

I would love to connect with you. You can find me on Facebook: Author Leila Kirkconnell

Made in the USA
Coppell, TX
05 April 2020